P. H. PERRINE

Percenters and the Amber Pendant

This novel is entirely a work of fiction. The names, characters and incidents portrayed in it are the work of the author's imagination. Any resemblance to actual persons, living or dead, events or localities is entirely coincidental.

First edition

ISBN: 978-1-7345013-4-6

Editing by Tim Marquitz
Cover art by David Provolo

This book was professionally typeset on Reedsy.
Find out more at reedsy.com

For Akshay and Riley.

The husband of my dreams
and my best friend.
My life unapologetically grows
happier everyday because of you.

No one should be forced to accept a
Scheme of cooperation
That places their lives
Under the control of others.

P. H. PERRINE

Chapter 1

I try not to remember it, but it's always with me. The blood. The horror. The dead-cold feeling that no one is here to rescue me. The realization that I'm fighting a war no one else is even aware is happening.

I'm lying in the mud. Snowflakes drift down from the sky like wet feathers and cover my face. I am cold...so cold. A loud snarl to my right shakes my core, and I suddenly notice a pack of mangy dogs closing in on me. Gruesome, with visible wounds oozing infection. And skeletal, obviously hungry. Ravenous for meat, any meat...my meat!

They bare their rotten fangs and growl at me with ferocious delight, eager to devour. My eyes blur, and all I can focus on are barbed-wire tufts of fur closing in. The beasts are preparing for a feast unlike any they have had before.

I hear a woman's voice screaming, "Where am I? Why is this happening? Help, please!"

My eyes are watching the dogs get closer while scanning for whoever belonged to that painfully agonizing voice. I hear the voice screaming a second time.

"Help me...PLEASE, HELP ME!"

A blur of blood-soaked fur pushes past my face, knocking me back several feet. I see only teeth reaching for my flesh. Another beast rushes me and clamps down on my arm. It's tearing through my sleeve. Gnawing into my skin, drawing deep red blood. I hear the screams again, louder this time. But different.

She sounded more fearful than before. I look down just as the beast's teeth release my arm. There is so much blood. Fresh crimson covering the old. Looking sideways, I watch as it trickles down onto the muddy ground. I hear the cry again, louder than the times before but fading in its intensity.

It's me. I've been screaming uncontrollably to an audience of no one. I am shocked by the realization that I'm on the Ground. Confused how I came to be here but awakened by the need to survive one more night. My mission, over. I failed. It was all for nothing. A waste. A stupid, stupid waste of lives.

Out of nowhere, a giant cat, no, a Puma, lunges at the beast, salivating for another bite of my arm, snapping it in half instantly and flinging the creature to the side like an old rag. Right in front of my eyes, right before I pass out, I see vicious beast after beast launching into the air as they match my screams.

The world falls away from my weakened sight as the fearful beasts whimper and slink off into the forest of dead tangled trees and vines. Their feast lost. My life saved.

I begin to drift in and out of consciousness, but I am too horrified to force open my eyes. I feel a false sense of security in the darkness my eyelids provide. Too afraid to see what's actually happening around me.

I open my eyes just as the Puma transforms into a boy right in front of me. He's completely naked and has a muscular physique similar to the infamous statue of David. Now I know I must be dreaming.

Forgetting about the massive gash extending from my elbow to my wrist, I shake my head and look back up at the boy who is now close enough to touch me. I try to blink the blood out of my vision to see him more clearly. He looks similar to Alexander, except his hair is different, jet-black, and disheveled, giving him a wild, animal-like appearance. But then again, he was just a giant cat. I can't help but feel I know him.

Crouching down, he spoke to me.

"You're safe, for now," he tells me, offering his hand. "Get up! Hurry! We don't have much time."

Still a bit confused and slightly delusional, the only thing I could muster as a response was, "But you're naked!" I immediately blush and look away like a little schoolgirl, an instinctual response that I didn't know existed.

2

"Wow! Your observation skills are off the charts, Jena" he replies with blunt sarcasm. "No wonder they picked you."

I shake off his comment and struggle to stand. I try desperately to ignore his nudity, but in my sixteen years of life he's the first boy, besides my brother, Alexander, I have ever seen naked, and I can't seem to stop myself from staring at every square inch of him.

His abs are so defined they look like they were etched out of stone. I watch his wide chest heave up and down as he takes each breath. My eyes follow the blue vein running across his peck to his left bicep, bulging with his every movement. I rapidly blink to ensure that what I am seeing in front of me is actually there. Before making eye contact again, I notice his tree trunk legs strong enough to jump fifteen feet in the air.

My body is racked with pain. My hair covers my face, matted with wet leaves and mud. He smiles and extends his other hand and reluctantly pulls me to my feet. I limp horribly.

My bones and muscles are aching. He half-drags me, half-supporting me with his arm around my waist and somehow, together, we head into the cover of trees and darkness. At some point I blacked out and woke up to sharp shooting pain ripping down my arm beneath the cover of some type of homemade wrap. I remember everything now. This, unfortunately, is not a dream.

Chapter 2

Most mornings at the de Fenace' estate in San Sun begin with a gentle greeting from Buzz, the house's communications system. My brother, Alexander, and I named Buzz when we first began to speak. We always thought it was funny how Buzz mimicked the rudimentary sounds of an alarm clock. Buzz is not only the brains of the estate, but also serves as a personal assistant to the entire de Fenace' family.

Buzz keeps our family connected to the entire Sovereign Sky: San Sun in the West, Crystal Sky in the East and Grand View in the Center. Our estate lies directly in the middle of San Sun, a bejeweled city that is comprised of gleaming glass and steel beam structures. San Sun, like her sister cities in the Sovereign Skies, hover over skyscrapers from earlier civilizations that are now immersed in layers of poisonous and toxic air remaining from The Oze. The ground is completely uninhabitable.

When I was four, I once asked father how it was possible that our city could float, and he says, "It's an engineering marvel, to be sure. When The Oze first started, Percenters used their combined powers to build massive magnets with unique molecular structures that reverse the effects of gravity, pushing us away from the ground. If we weren't anchored to the skyscrapers, we'd probably float into outer space," as he geared up to tickle me to make me scream uncontrollably. That was the first time I realize how powerful Percenters could be.

The Middlers, those who are born with Percenter blood but without powers, are forced to live in the top floors of the old skyscrapers where the air quality is barely suitable to sustain life and toxic enough to cause illness or in some cases, even death. When a sixteen-year-old takes the Percenters exam and fails, they are cast out of the Percenter society to the Ground for not having any superhuman powers.

A Percenter, of the same bloodline only, can vouch for the recently declared Barren teenager to be granted Middler status. Destined to live the rest of their life as that Percenter family's house staff.

Middlers are transported to work in the Sky Cities during the day and are required to leave nightly. Spending even just one night in a Sky City is punishable by Grounding, being sent to live on the Ground. A sentence synonymous with death.

Blanketed by the remaining Oze gases, Middlers have no way to escape once they are back in their tower. The closer the Middlers live to the ground, the greater the risks to survival. Those lower floors are usually reserved for Middlers with the lowest percentage of elixir DNA. Even Middlers exercise a caste system.

My father once tried to explain the living conditions of the Middlers to me, and I never asked about them again. His answer was in one ear and out the other. I simply took San Sun and our way of life for granted. I guess all who grow up in the Sky Cities do. At least until we turn sixteen.

In the Sky Cities, the Percenter's manipulation of energy and weather keeps our city's climate sunny and mild all year. We are protected from all external environmental elements that would make living in the sky impossible. It really is a utopia compared to the devastation below.

San Sun, the capital of the Sovereign Sky Cities, has most of the wealth and power. It is also where the annual exams are held. Most Percenter families live in extravagant homes while some, like ours, live in palatial estates with every convenience one could imagine.

Chapter 3

I throw off the covers, get out of bed and grab my robe. Today I will have to be the biggest liar of all. This is not who I am normally, but who I must be…starting today. No matter how terrified I am and, believe me when I tell you that I am terrified, this is what I must do. I don't want to think about last night…not too much anyway. Not yet.

I want to cherish my last few moments as a true Percenter. As a member of an elite society that, until last night, I believed was nothing less than heroic. How naïve I have been all these years. How naïve everyone has been.

The marble floor is smooth and cold on my toes, indifferent to my feelings. I step over to my bedroom's panoramic window and press the "view external" button. Our home is designed so we can view scenes from the Ground before The Oze. Most of the time, I prefer to look at beaches or even mountains. Today, I will be grasping to cherish every last moment of my life in the sky and choose to look out a clear window, no artificial scene.

San Sun's skyline is draped in misty clouds, downy soft and ethereal, wreathing through the trees and statuesque gardens. Silvery leaves on the trees shimmer in the bright white of the sun and nearly blind me. I briefly shadow my eyes with my hands and squint so I can keep admiring San Sun. Far beyond the mist, there is a blue so deep and multifaceted that it sparkles like sapphires. I wonder if those below can see it and find myself mumbling sarcastically, "No, you dummy, of course they can't!"

I can't believe I've taken all of this, all of San Sun, the jewel of the Sovereign Sky, for granted my entire life. I'm soon going to be living a life that very few Percenters are even aware exists. A world far from the luxury of the sky and shrouded in the remaining toxins of The Oze.

My only chance of survival once I'm on the Ground will be to find a Barren pod. But I have no idea how I'm supposed to even do that. A slight smile appears on my face, and I say, "I will soon find out!"

In the perfectly manicured green lawn outside my window, I see Sebastian, our chocolate Abyssinian, one of the few remaining cats. He's trying to stalk a couple of blackbirds as they pick at a scavenged carcass of some kind. I laugh out loud watching Sebastian flip in midair and miss. He's not much of a hunter.

"Jena, are you up?" Alexander yells from the hallway.

"Yes, c'mon in."

Alexander opens the door and waltzes into my room, handsome in his bed clothes, a simple turquoise robe made of the finest silk and bare feet of course. He's smiling, showcasing his dimples and brilliant white teeth. I hate to admit it, but he is as handsome as any storybook prince. He carries himself as someone who has never been spoken to harshly in his life. He is utterly adorable. I love him for his simple mind and honest innocence.

"Jena! Today's the day! Can you believe it?"

"No, Alex, I can't believe it." I use a ton of sarcasm to hide my true fear as I look at my hands, and notice my thumbs twiddling nervously.

"Then you realize that today is the first day of our exams and our first step towards Freelinn Prep!"

"And, again, why do we have to go to Freelinn?" I ask playfully, already knowing his answer.

"Jena! Seriously? OK, one more time. It's the top school for Percenters with the most advanced powers. And...how do you think Dad would feel if we didn't get in? He'd be so disappointed!"

He takes a short breath and continues with the excitement of someone half his age, "Oh, Jena...we are gonna have the most advanced powers, I just know it!" He grabs my hand and waltzes me around the room.

I laugh, momentarily forgetting last night's conversation with my mom and dad. Forgetting that for the first time in my life, I am hiding something from my twin brother and all I want to do is tell him, but I can't.

"Well, if they choose Percenters based on cockiness, then I have no doubt you'll be selected." I roll my eyes at Alexander in a way that always pushes his buttons.

Alexander lets go of my hand, grabs a pillow from my bed, and throws it at me. I dodge and start laughing. He always knows how to have a good time. The boy without a worry in life, that's Alexander.

"I'm NOT cocky," says Alexander, pushing his brown hair-flecked-with-gold highlights off his forehead. "I'm just confident. There's a difference. A big difference." He winks at me as he admires himself in the wall mirror. "I can just hear the announcer now: 'Monsieur Alexander de Fenace', at sixteen years of age you are the most handsome young man in all the Sovereign Skies! You are our champion and have successfully surpassed all others before you!'"

"Oh, puh-leeeese!" I put my hands to my throat and act like I'm gagging from being choked. "You wish!" I pick up the closest pillow and throw it back at him.

I pause thinking about the true meaning, the hidden meaning of the exams slogan: May you surpass all others before you. Thankfully, my wandering mind is interrupted.

"I'm only saying what all the girls say!" Alexander continues.

"By girls, do you mean Raquel Hawthorn?" I look sideways at him with a teasing smirk.

I've known he's had a crush on Raquel ever since we were introduced to her years ago at a family function. All the children in the Sky Cities are homeschooled until we reach sixteen, and it is only then that we go to school with our peers at one of the preparatory schools. Even though we haven't studied together, we are all away of who each other is. The Percenters' society is small and gossipy. Nothing goes unnoticed in the Sky Cities, or so I thought.

Alexander blushes. "Well—"

Buzz appears on the mirror just as Alexander takes a second look at himself and interrupts us. "Good morning Mistress Jenavieve and Monsieur Alexander. It's 7:00 a.m. and by my calculations, if you eat breakfast now you will have ample time to dress for the exam's reception. Shall I have Chef Rose prepare you something and send it to your rooms or will you be eating with your mother in the breakfast nook?"

"I'll be right down," I say.

"Me, too," Alexander affirms. "I'll have my usual—eggs, pancakes and extra crispy bacon. Make sure it's extra crispy!" He rubs his stomach and winks at himself in the mirror, again. "This doesn't just happen overnight, Sis. It's hard work to look this good!"

"And what about you, Mistress Jenavieve?" Buzz asks after he compliments Alex "Looking good, Monsieur Alexander"

"I'm not very hungry," I reply. "A vanilla protein blend will do."

"As you wish," Buzz says before he disappears.

Alexander and I push and pull each other as we fight to be the first to the kitchen. He tripped on the hallway rug giving me a few seconds head start. He easily catches up to me on the stairs jumping clear over my head and beating me to the final step before pushing the door open to the kitchen.

"Mistress Jenavieve," says Buzz, interrupting my heavy breathing, "what powers do you hope to uncover in the exams?"

"Well, Buzz, as you know, each Percenter has an important role which will be given to us by the chancellors after our powers are identified." I recite this like I'm in front of a group reading from a brochure. I take a sip of my protein blend and continue, "No residents are idle without a purpose or mission and our powers determine the type of work we do that separates us from the rest of humanity."

"You will do well," Buzz states. "You are ready. You were born into the de Fenace' family, a Hundred-Percenter bloodline." Buzz tries to have conversations like a normal person, but as usual, he sounds so matter of fact you can't help but chuckle when he attempts emotional support, it's comical.

Instead of laughing at Buzz, as I normally would, I feel sad. I will miss Buzz. But I muster a smile at his voice anyway. "Thank you for the encouragement, Buzz." I wonder to myself, *Does he know what's going to happen?*

"And what about you, Monsieur Alexander?" When we turned ten,

Alexander asked Buzz to call him monsieur and me mistress. Although it was intended to be funny for our birthday, it ultimately stuck.

"Buzz, I honestly don't know, but I can't wait to find out!" I watch my brother begin eating his second stack of pancakes. I simply don't understand how he can fit so much food into his flat six-pack stomach.

"Your anomalous skills of art, writing, and music will undoubtedly contribute to awakening your powers," continues Buzz. "I think you will have extraordinary power Monsieur Alexander." I wonder how much empathy was coded into our mainframe because Buzz seems remarkably human... sometimes.

Rose, our Chef, stepped into the kitchen just as Buzz completed his sentence. She wipes her hands on her apron. "Can I make you some more pancakes, Alexander?" She shares a delightful smile that can only make you return the same.

"I think this is all I need," Alexander says, grinning at her. "Thank you, though."

"What about you, Jenavieve? Can I tempt you with something sweet for your big day? I just finished baking your favorite donuts!" she says as she pulls out a basket of apple fritters, each appearing to be the size of my face.

"No, I'm good, but thank you, Rose. Next time!" My smile turns into a frown as I realize there won't be a next time.

Rose is secretly married to Dan, our Head Butler. It's a secret because Middlers aren't allowed by the Percenter government to engage in romantic relationships, let alone be married and have families of their own. Without any powers, Middlers are not allowed to reproduce because they add no value to the Percenters Society.

If they accidentally got pregnant, Middlers are forced to the Ground, never to be heard from again. Mom and Dad helped officiate Rose and Dan's secret wedding in our living room a couple years ago. They enjoy bending the rules when it helps bring happiness into someone's life. They don't believe the government should control people's love for each other.

I've always been proud of my parents, but how they treat Chef Rose and Butler Dan is something that has left a lasting impression, and I will never forget. My parents have proven to me that love trumps hate, every time. Alexander might believe in love, too, someday, just not yet. He's a typical sixteen-year-old boy with a different crush every other week. I admire that about him.

"Good morning, my darlings!" Mother bounds through the door and joins us in the kitchen. She is a breath of fresh air. "You feeding these children enough for their big day, Rose?"

"Yes, ma'am," says Rose with a grin of pride. "Alexander has a big appetite as usual, so I'm trying to feed the beast inside!" She exchanges a subtle wink and gentle smirk with Alexander.

Having no children of her own, Rose has loved us like a mother since we were born. She was my mother's chef growing up and has been with the de Fenace' family since she failed her exams thirty-four years ago. Her graying hair is cut short to look nondescript. Almost as plain as her uniform. From a distance, she looks the same as all other San Sun Middlers, regardless of gender.

"I hope his prep school can keep up with his appetite," Mom says, laughing. She and Alexander have the same wide smile and dimples.

"Mornin', Mom," says Alexander as he stuffs the last few pieces of bacon into his mouth.

"Hey, Mom." I look up from my nearly completed blend. My mother, Lady Annabel de Fenace', is one of the most stunningly beautiful women in all of the Sovereign Sky Cities. I can only hope to be so beautiful one day. Her skin is like porcelain, and her blue eyes are the color of a cloudless winter sky.

Every morning, she wears her lavender silk nightgown beneath a white robe studded with delicately attached crystals. The sunlight filtering through the window makes her golden hair shimmer as if she has a halo. She walks over and caresses Alexander's face with both her hands. She is the embodiment of what an angel should look like.

"My darling Alexander," she says as a single tear trickles down her left cheek and a nervous smile grows across her face, "before you meet the day with all its glory, I want you to know that you are my everything. You will always be...my everything! You and your sister–both–of course."

Mother turns to me, gesturing her sentiments while placing her hand gently on my right cheek.

"And no matter what happens today–or the next–you will always be my precious, darling, son. You know this, right?"

"Mom, stop. You're embarrassing me!" Looking at Rose, he continues, "I'm not a baby anymore. I'm about to take the exams for goodness sakes and you'll finally have to see that I am a man, not a boy!"

We all laugh uncontrollably. At first, Alexander joins us but we continue to out laugh him.

"Wait a second!" Alexander exclaims.

"And, Jena..." Mom turns to me. "I know you will do very well today." She comes close enough to hug my neck. She whispers in my ear, "We're counting on you, sweetheart. Stay strong and be brave."

"Oh, she'll pass with flying colors," says Alex. "You can trust that we will not disappoint you and Father. No way! No how! We are the..." Alexander raises both hands in the air, keeping a tight grip on his fork and knife, as if celebrating a major win, "de Fenace' twins!"

For a brief moment, an invisible cloud shadows Mother's face. Neither Alexander nor Chef Rose notice it. I blink a couple times and it fades from my vision. I chalk it up to stress and forget about it as Alexander continues talking.

"As for me," continues Alexander, "this is just an exercise in futility to see how many powers I actually have." He is fully confident of his abilities, and all he's really worried about is how many beautiful girls he'll get to impress.

"Honestly, as long as Jena and I go to Freelinn, she'll be fine. I'll look out for her mom, you know. She'd be helpless without me!" He gives me a look, and I scrunch my nose at him. "Jena will do well, and probably, with her luck, surpass–all–others–before–her!"

I punch him in the shoulder. "You are so stupid sometimes!"

"You'll both do great," says Mom. "I'm confidant things will unfold as they should."

I stir what remains of my blend and take a final sip. The cold drink tastes good on my throat. Thoughts of the exams begin to creep into my mind. I take a prolonged fake last sip to cover up the fact that my eyes suddenly start to water up with tears. I worry that I'll start awkwardly crying, which is very unlike me.

Mother frowns. "Jena, are you okay?"

I nod, and she nods back at me understandingly.

"Just a brain-freeze," I say to deflect any observing eyes from Rose or Alexander.

"You're going to be perfect," she says to me. I know there is so much more meaning than what she is actually saying.

"Well, honestly, I can't wait!" says Alexander, stuffing another huge bite of pancake and something else he could fit on his fork into his mouth.

"He's excited about his pending freedom and dare I say…meeting all of the young ladies…and I mean all of them," I grin and say mockingly to Mother.

"Well, he is a handsome devil." Mom laughs. With her hand, she ruffles the hair on top of his head. We all know that underneath Alexander's cockiness, he is a kind, caring and generous young man. A little naïve, yes. The girls will undoubtedly eat him alive regardless of which school he attends.

After breakfast, Alexander and I headed back up to our rooms to dress for the day. The morning is moving so fast already. I'm starting to get cold feet and begin to wonder why I promised my parents I'd go through with this whole plan. I feel powerless in so many ways.

Ben, one of our Middlers, meets us in the upstairs hallway.

"You guys excited?" Ben asks, holding a stack of freshly washed towels. His dark hair, once long and luxuriously thick, has been cut short, close to his scalp, like that worn by all Middlers. He wears beige cotton drawstring pants and a matching beige shirt, the approved Middler uniform in San Sun. Middlers in Grand View wear powder blue and Crystal Sky, white.

"Hi, Ben," I say. "Yes, we're excited," I lied. Well, I guess I didn't completely lie, Alexander is thrilled.

"We'll let you know what it's like after it's all over." Alexander pats Ben on the back. I shoot him a 'Really, did you just say that?' look. Thankfully, it worked.

"Of course…you've been through this so…you mostly…already know." Alexander stumbles over his words as he catches himself.

Graciously Ben didn't pay it much attention. "From what I've heard, they change the exams each year, so you might experience something totally different than I did last year," Ben says. "But I know both of you will do well. So, good luck!"

If Ben only knew how right he was. This exam will be unlike any before it.

I look at Alexander and know what he's thinking. Ben is only a year older than we are, and technically, he's our cousin, on our mother's side. When he didn't pass his exams, when we all learned he had no powers–he started working for our family as a Middler.

Ben's parents immediately disowned him once his scores were made public, so my parents rescued him. My parents couldn't bear the thought of Ben becoming a Barren, which is what would have happened. If my parents hadn't stepped up, he would have been cast out to the Ground within minutes of his name being announced.

Failing the exams was considered a black mark on his family lineage–and in many ways, ours, because we are blood related. It's very embarrassing for any Percenter family to have a child without powers, but it doesn't happen that frequently, less than a handful of candidates each year.

Ben now lives as a Middler in the skyscraper directly below our estate. It's degrading. Humiliating, really. Our family doesn't feel the same way about the caste system the Percenters' have enforced, but we have to follow it or at least give the illusion that we are following Sky law. I just feel so sorry for him–now more than ever.

I wish I had time to talk with him privately to let him know how I felt, but I don't. It's my fault really, never taking the time to understand what it must be like for him. Or even for Rose and our other Middlers. It's just never crossed my mind. I always assumed they were just happy and content with their lot in life because they were spared from being sent to the Ground. Grateful really. And I guess that was true for some, but not the majority.

Ben and Alexander grew up playing together. Ben is still Alex's closest friend, but I have noticed he treats Ben differently since he became a Middler.

Not poorly, just…different. They hang out together more than Alex and I do, but Ben isn't allowed to venture beyond the walls of our estate. He is only allowed to leave our property to return to his place in the skyscraper below us, which I haven't seen and probably never will.

I don't really understand why San Sun Middlers live below us, but I never bothered to ask about that either. Before last night, I guess I had never questioned anything about San Sun or it's people. I was as naïve as Alexander and probably everyone else in the Sovereign Sky.

My mother has always been so gentle with Ben. From the moment he started working for us she welcomed him with open arms and continues to treat him like her nephew, nothing less. His own mother and father barely look at him when they visit, which isn't often anymore. In fact, they prefer he stay out of sight as much as possible when they do visit. He probably does, too, if you think about it.

They were willing to let him be sent to the Ground, basically sending him to his death. It's disgusting if you stop and think about it for a bit. They treat their daughter, Jezebel, like she can do no wrong. For her sake, I hope she passes the exams or she's at risk of being shunned just like Ben. Jezee, as her parents call her, couldn't handle that kind of rejection and my parents probably wouldn't be able to save her with all the eyes on them now. She's always been a little bit of a pretentious nightmare anyways, not like Ben at all, but that still wouldn't justify the Ground.

I watch Ben and Alexander talking about the exams some more. I know the exams will uncover our true powers and determine which prep school each candidate attends, but they also establish our paths forever in the Sovereign Sky communities. At least, that's what will happen for every candidate other than me.

My parents have always sheltered Alexander from this reality to keep his innocence alive and to keep his heart open to those around him. They've always wanted Alexander to believe he is in control of his own destiny, but now I know he isn't. None of us are, not really, anyway.

For some reason, my parents have always treated me like I was a lot older than Alexander, although the reality is that he's less than three minutes younger. "You are an old soul," Mom always says. "Alexander is newer, younger and more innocent. He is very special, and we need you to protect your brother." I've heard this for years and until last night, I never really understood what I was protecting him from. Perhaps that's why they waited until last night to have 'the *talk* with me. The talk that changed my destiny forever.

"Well, good luck!" Ben says to both me and Alex, interrupting my thoughts, again. "I honestly hope it turns out better for you than it did for me." His eyes immediately glisten over with tears, but before we see him cry, he turns and walks swiftly down the hallway continuing his duties as a devoted de Fenace' Middler. No longer just a cousin or a friend, but a Middler until he dies. Ben has no idea that it's going to turn out way worse for me than it did for him.

My mind starts to run about all of the horrors revealed to me now. I am still in shock from last night. For the first time in my life, I am thinking about all those who live below the Sky Cities. And for the first time in my life, I am positive that I will fear them. Not the other way around. But I also know that I am the only one who can help them and that my Parents are depending on me to succeed.

In San Sun, we are surrounded by wealth and power merely because of the blood running through our veins. Because of our parent's powers. Because they were born a Percenter with power. Just as their parents and their parents before them. Without their blood in our veins, Alexander and I would be disposable like any other Barren.

Chapter 4

It's all a lie. This so-called Sky City society. Last night I learned the ugly truth: Many of the Percenters' are ruthless, cold blooded murderers. But of course, they think they're being honorable by keeping our society *pure*, whatever that means.

The thought of this makes me sick to my stomach. It's unsettling to say the least. I wonder why my parents chose last night to completely destroy my reality. I thought we lived in a peaceful, beautiful world. I didn't realize there was such a dark, seedy underbelly to the Percenter way of life. I just wished they waited three days. I am only three days away from completing the exams and becoming a true Percenter. But now, I can't even imagine what that would mean.

I, along with nearly every citizen in the sky, have been sheltered from the harsh truths that maintain our Percenter society. My parents shattered every illusion I had last night. For now, I must act like every other sixteen-year-old entering the exams. As Father asked of me, I must hide in plain site until the moment is right.

"What Moment? How am I supposed to know when *the* moment happens?' I thought.

I'm just not sure how to function now that this…this world seems so diabolical to me. I now know that things need to change, but I can't imagine that I am the one to be the catalyst for that change. I'm not even sure I understand what or how I'm supposed to be fighting for change anyway.

I start to feel overwhelmed with anxiety as I ponder whether or not I'll be able to wear the mask that is required of me. I'm not very confident that I can live up to my parent's expectations.

"Fuck this! I'm not a warrior. How can they think it's fair to ask so much of a me?" I murmur to myself out loud.

All I should be concerned about is which prep school I'm getting into and what Percenters' powers I can activate. Oh, and which cute boy is going to take me to my first formal dance. That's all Alexander thinks about, powers and his first kiss.

I know because that's all I was thinking about, too. Not the genocide of the human race. I'm starting to obsess on the new found chaos. I close my eyes and clench my fists to push the details of the next few days out of my mind. I have to learn how to protect my thoughts, bottle them up inside, or risk being discovered. My parents called it cloaking.

"Time to go!" Alexander pops his head into my room.

Father is standing at the front door, waiting patiently for us. He's wearing his signature dark navy-blue suit with white pinstripes, tailored to fit his body perfectly. Father is thin yet statuesque. His salt and pepper hair gives him a distinguishing look typical of older gentleman in San Sun. But he always stands out from the crowd.

Normally, his eyes are the color of a stormy sea but over the years I've noticed they change with his moods. When he is angry, they go black as night, and when he is happy, they are as bright yellow as the summer sun. Today, they are ever changing with cascading pantones of both blue and black.

When Father sees us, his face lights up with a familiar grin. "You look beautiful, darling Jenavieve. And Alexander, I couldn't be prouder of you, Son." He is such a loving, yet strong, father. I can almost feel his pain as much as he fears of mine. If only Alexander would pick up on this, I wouldn't be alone. It makes so much more sense for us to stick together.

In sixteen years, we have never been apart for more than a couple hours. He's my best friend. Plus, he's much stronger than I am, both physically and emotionally. Although I'm sure he'd say the same about me being the stronger one. I'm going to need him. I've *always* needed him.

Alexander and I are both dressed in our finest. He's wearing a navy suit similar to Dad's, minus the pinstripes, and I'm in a long strapless ivory gown that hugs my waist and falls in soft layers as it trails the floor. The grand reception for the exams is the biggest social event of the year. It's the epitome of Percenter pomp and circumstance. Anyone who is anyone wouldn't be caught dead missing it.

Mom joins us, wearing a bright white cashmere gown and diamond-studded heels. Her sleek jacket wraps tightly around her body, perfectly showing off her hourglass figure. She's jaw-dropping beautiful, as usual. I briefly allow myself to daydream that someday I will be as beautiful as she is right now.

Of course, Mom would scold me if I said anything like that out loud. She frequently tells me that I am even more beautiful than she could ever be. I have the same golden-blonde hair and sky-blue eyes–the same thin yet curvy body. But I haven't grown into my beauty yet–not the way my mother has. And after today, it's not going to matter what I look like, but how powerful I become.

"Don't you just look dapper as ever, Abraham," Mother says as she leans in to kiss him. I notice the same twinkle in her eyes that she has always had for my Father.

"Oh, darling! You look absolutely breathtaking," he says. "I am truly the luckiest man in San Sun. No, the Sovereign Skies!" He takes her hand and kisses it multiple times, slowly up her forearm. I wonder if I will ever be in love as much as my parents are right at this very moment.

"Thank you, Abe. You always know exactly what to say...and do! And don't forget...I'm the lucky one, Mister de Fenace'!"

"Well, we have two bright, beautiful children to be proud of." He smiles at Alexander and then me, locking his soft eyes.

"Thanks, Dad," I tell him with a half-smile on my face. Nothing can replace a daughter's admiration for her father, regardless of the circumstances.

"Well, you have at least one." Alexander winks at Father and punches me in the shoulder.

Buzz pipes in, "Lady Annabelle and de Fenace' family, your chauffeur has arrived."

"Thanks! Bye, Buzz," says Alexander. "Don't wait up!"

Buzz makes a bubbly noise in an attempt to giggle. It makes everyone laugh, including me. My stomach clenches tight from an immediate onset of nerves and my laugh is short lived.

Before I walk out the door, I noticed Ben lingering at the top of the marble staircase that leads from the foyer to the upper floors. He's hiding behind a column but is watching intently. He's probably wishing he could have a second chance with the exams…a second chance to be a Percenter. One of us. Instead of a Middler, which I now realize is really just another name for servant, or even slave.

My eyes begin to tear up again. I feel a newfound sadness for him that I'm just beginning to realize. It's almost unbearable. I have to stop thinking this way before I begin to cry. Not out of sadness for Ben, but for myself. I physically shake it off, remembering that I'm not just taking the exams, but I am on a mission that there is no turning back from, and I need to stay focused.

Together, as a family, we walk outside where the wind caresses my face with heavy scents of lavender from our garden. The misty clouds hover around the city. I breathe in the fresh, clean air, grateful for the privilege that until yesterday, was a right.

Sebastian darts over to my side and nuzzles up against my leg. I reach down and pet him. I whisper softly, "Bye, sweet Sebastian. Take care of everyone, OK?"

He purrs and licks my hand. Tears threaten to fill my eyes once again. I honestly don't know if I will ever see Sebastian after today. I tell myself to be strong. Be composed.

"Keep it together, Jena!" I say underneath my breath so only I can hear.

Our chauffeur is patiently waiting by the Bullet. It's one of the latest designed cars that glides along the streets of San Sun on magnetic vibration. Bullets are different than standard cars in San Sun because it can also convert into a skyrocket to travel from one Sky City to another. Very few people are allowed to have a Bullet.

Before yesterday, I would have just assumed that it was by choice, but now it's yet another reminder that even within our society I have privileges that others do not because we have inherited a Hundred-Percenter bloodline.

We all fold our legs inside the Bullet and sit down in comfy bucket seats that face each other. The Chauffeur presses a button and we begin to zoom off to join the exam procession. Dad, who has always been a pillar of strength and conviction, looks anxiously out the window as we passed crowds of onlookers joining in the celebration. He has barely said a word since we left the estate.

When he does look at Alexander and me, he struggles to produce a fake half-smile. He returns his stare to the window. Mom takes his hand and squeezes it, silently reassuring him that his daughter will be OK. So much is riding on the exams. So much is riding on me. And today is only day one of the three-day event.

I follow in my father's suit and watch the families waving at us as we drive past them. A buzzing starts in my head, and I know what's about to happen. This power has always revealed itself to me, which is unusual because typically powers are only activated during the exams, not before. I don't know how it's possible. I didn't even tell my parents last night that it's been happening for a couple weeks.

The buzzing starts to dissipate and as clear as day I begin hearing Alexander's thoughts, his inner voice. "Why is Dad so nervous? Is he worried we won't pass the exams? I guess no one thought Ben would fail either. Surely, we'll do well. I mean, our bloodline is pure! Look at everyone lined up on the streets waving at us, how cool! Damn right we're cool..."

I don't say anything, but I reach over and pat Alexander's shoulder. I can tell where his thoughts are starting to wander. When I'm in his head it's like he's having a one-sided conversation. It reminds me of overhearing him talk to himself when he's staring into the mirror and doesn't realize anyone is watching.

"Looking good Monsieur de Fenace', looking really good!" he would say. But he doesn't know I can jump into his mind, or that sometimes, without consent, his thoughts intrude on my own without warning. Sometimes it goes beyond hearing his thoughts, and I can literally feel everything he's feeling. It's like we share the same body.

I used to think we had this sixth sense as twins but Alexander doesn't seem to share it. I haven't said anything to him either. I don't want to freak him out that I can read his thoughts and probably, if I tried hard enough, could control his entire body. But mostly, I don't want to say anything because I shouldn't have any powers before the exams. Maybe he can do it too and isn't saying something for the same reasons. But knowing him, he'd be so proud of himself that he'd definitely say something to me.

Several other Bullets—some silver, some orange, others yellow—join us as our procession turns into a parade down the main corridor of San Sun leading us to the Panathenaic Stadium, a replica of the original from a place once called Athens.

"Good luck!" people are cheering. Some are waving multicolored balloons along with little flags of turquoise, crimson, and lavender as a kaleidoscope of tiny fireworks explode above them. Percenters share a strong bond with their alma mater. Each prep school is named after their founders: Markus Briarsley, Justine Stillstone and Leah Freelinn.

Each flag, each pattern of firework, represents one of the three prep schools that await all Percenters after the exam. Turquoise is the color of Grand View's Briarsley Prep, the largest school accepting the majority of candidates with the most common of powers. Briarsley produces Percenters with average powers that many share, nothing extraordinary.

Stillstone Prep, located in Crystal Sky, is known for graduates that often turn out to be Sky City leaders. While some may have advanced super powers, many are average but come from more pure Percenter bloodlines. Stillstone Prep's color is Crimson; synonymous with wealth and power and long associated with the Stillstone legacy.

Freelinn Prep is represented by lavender and considered to be the most prestigious of all three. Only candidates possessing the most advanced powers are accepted. The most powerful of all Percenters attend Freelinn. If that wasn't reason enough for Alexander to want Freelinn, it's also where our parents met and where Father serves as the president.

It's kind of a family legacy. Alexander would be devastated if he didn't get accepted. But he knows that just because Dad is the President, that doesn't guarantee either of us a spot. It really is based on our exam scores.

There are no flags or fireworks to represent the other possible designations from the exams: Middler or Barren. Every year a couple candidates end up without activated powers and are banished to the Ground, or if saved, become Middlers, like Ben. Neither will go to a prep school nor receive any continued education. If there were a color for those without Percenter powers, it would surely be black.

More children begin to run alongside us, screaming and shouting with excitement. I remember doing the same thing at their age. The exams are the beginning of the rest of your life and are draped in celebration. For a moment, I wonder if I should roll down the window to wave to them. Alexander decides for me.

"Screw this," Alexander says. He taps the glass sunroof and grabs my hand to pull me up with him. Our upper bodies emerge from the Bullet and the crowd erupts in even louder screams. Alexander smiles and waves at each and every person as if he's running for public office. He loves being the center of attention. He's like a kid in a candy store. Maybe Stillstone wouldn't be the worst thing to happen to him.

I have no choice but to do the same, so I put on my best smile and begin to wave.

"This is it, Sis!" Alexander looks over at me. "Just a couple days until we get our powers!" He grabs my hand and lifts it high in the sky, catering to the crowd's applause. I can't help but feel butterflies of excitement in my stomach. We are finally here. Right now. Alexander and I have been talking about this moment for years.

"Yup," I say humbly. "We are finally here." My voice trails off as I concentrate to keep my mind clear. I look around at all the faces. I see some of our neighbors, Mr. and Mrs. Ward and their three young boys. I always forget their names. Our weird neighbor, Mr. Hampton sticks out like a sore thumb, standing there so calmly when everyone else around him is jumping and screaming.

We catch eyes briefly, and he lifts his hand slowly to wave, but all he really does is lift his hand to his shoulder and tighten the corners of his mouth ever so slightly, as if he's trying to smile but just doesn't know how.

I laugh a little to myself and whisper in Alexander's ear, "There's our weird neighbor!" and give a head nod towards Mr. Hampton. Alexander's laugh helped mine get louder.

Within seconds, other candidates stand in their Bullets and follow our lead. They all smile and wave to the crowds excitedly, some even jumping up and down. It truly is a joyous occasion in San Sun. I wish I could turn back time and somehow avoid the conversation with my parents last night. Maybe if I pretended to be asleep, they would have talked to Alexander instead.

I wish I could share in Alexander's blissful ignorance to the true order of the Sovereign Sky Cities. But I can't. I will never be able to feel that kind of bliss again. *Dammit!* My thoughts were transparent once again. I have to get stronger, better. I have to cloak at all times, no exception.

"Let's make this our exam," Alexander says. "Let's do it the way we want to, not the way they expect us."

"Isn't that the point?" I shout to him as we whiz by the crowds. "Our powers dictate that we do it the way we want to!" I realize that my voice has defiance in its tone. Alexander has never known me to be defiant or even the slightest bit rebellious, so I understand it when he asks me, "Are you alright, Jena? You've been a little...off today."

He looks at me quizzically. The wind is blowing his hair back from his forehead and for a brief moment I see a look of great concern. It's hard to hide my true feelings from him. As twins, we have a bond that is closer than most siblings, I think. At least now I know he can't read my thoughts like I can his.

"Of course," I shout back to him. It is so noisy we can barely hear each other. We've been talking about this day for years. Prepping for the day we officially become adults and gain our independence. I had been excited, extremely excited, and now all I feel is trepidation for the unknown. Life is not going to go as planned for any of us, but there's no reason to rob him of this joy today.

We are finally approaching the Panathenaic where the three-day exams will take place. It is newly constructed every year–more grand and opulent than the previous one. Our driver slows down and prepares to enter the queue before the colossal titanium clad gates. As we enter the archway, an announcer introduces each car by the family name. The first car to arrive, and the first family to be featured on the big screen, is our cousin, Jezebel, Ben's sister.

A sound emanating throughout the air for all to hear begins: "Ladies and gentlemen! Please welcome Jezebel Stillstone, daughter of Caroline and Philip Stillstone. Niece to Lady and Lord de Fenace'. Please give Ms. Jezebel a warm welcome to the exams."

Spectators clap their hands and shout in Jezebel's honor. I couldn't. I wonder how many Percenters would clap if they knew she disowned her own brother for not having powers. But I realized it probably wouldn't matter to anyone. This has always been a part of our Sky City tradition. It's nothing new. I'm just finally seeing it for what it really is...privilege and persecution.

As soon as I see the screen, my mouth drops open in shock.

"Do you see that?" I say to Alexander, pointing at the family photo on the big screen. It's only Jezebel and her parents, no Ben.

"I know," Alexander says. He has a sad look on his face. He has always considered Ben a best friend, not just a cousin.

"Ben is dead to them, Alex. He has been erased. You know this isn't fair!"

"He failed his exam. He didn't die," says Alexander. "I wish they would change that rule. But Ben..." He pauses, questioning himself for a split second before he continues. "Ben isn't a Percenter, he's a Middler." He continues waving to the crowd not giving a second thought to Ben's injustice or the injustice of all Middlers. I wonder when he started to think of Ben more like a Middler and less like an equal.

"Exactly." I shake my head in dismay. I trail off under my breath. "That's my point."

"And now, entering into the stadium is Jenavieve de Fenace' and her twin brother, Alexander," The announcer's voice is polished and smooth.

"Arriving with them are their parent's, Lord Abraham de Fenace', President of Freelinn Prep and Lady Annabelle, one of our elected Sky City Chancellors. Please wish good luck to the de Fenace' twins!"

A portrait of our family can be seen on the big screens throughout the Stadium. Alexander and I continue to wave to the crowds. The crowd embraces us with cheers only suitable for royalty. I play the role brilliantly, curtsying and blowing kisses. Inside, I'm beginning to seethe with anger.

"Alexander! Jenavieve! Come back inside, please!" Father calls out to us. "You're going to appear pretentious."

We do as he says, without hesitation. We know not to disobey father. It's not that we're afraid of him—nothing like that. It's more that we respect him. And for me, it could be the last day I ever see him if things don't go according to plan. Which is starting to feel like a huge IF. I'm actually glad to get back into the car and out of the spotlight and drop down without hesitation.

I am curious though. Both Alexander and I are eager to see the rest of the families and our peers from all the Sky Cities who are joining us in the exams. Until now, most of our lives have been spent behind the walls of our estate, hidden from public life outside of the occasional glib social affair.

Our Bullet pulls up to a parking space within the walls of the stadium. Our chauffeur gets out first and opens our doors. He directs me and Alexander to the door on the left and my parents to the door on the right.

"Alex, my son, I love you. Be yourself. Do not let anyone intimidate you. But promise me you will only show them only what they need to see, nothing more. Do you understand me? You do not have to expose all your powers. Not now anyway," Dad says in a very stern, yet compassionate voice. "You'll understand what I mean shortly." He begins to turn away to face me but turns back to Alexander.

"And I know you will get into Freelinn, Son. I just know it! Good luck!"

Freelinn is the school both he and my mother attended. They met there during their first year and have been together ever since. Like most parents, they have always wanted us to enjoy the same experiences they have been fortunate enough to have. And going to Freelinn has been a family tradition for generations.

"Of course, Dad. I will do my best," says Alexander. "I mean, not my best, but close to it. You know what I mean. I love you, too." He gives Dad a little punch on the shoulder, then turns to Mom and gives her a kiss on the cheek before running to get through the door.

"We love you, son," Mom says. She has reluctant tears forming in her eyes.

"Jenavieve, are you ready?" Father turns to me. "This is a very big step for you—for all of us." His eyes are stormy grey. His words are layered with multiple meanings. He doesn't say it but I can tell he's thinking 'Our lives literally depend on you.'

"Yes, Dad. I can do this." I look back and forth from Father to Mother. I am trembling slightly.

Mother reaches out and puts her arms around me. In a low voice, she whispers in my ear, "I love you, my darling daughter. Be strong. Remember that as you face these exams. They will try to break you. But also remember you are strong and courageous, and we believe in you!"

"Hey, don't worry about Jena," Alexander yells back with a smirk as he peeks his face out from behind the door. "I'll watch out for her. And let's just be honest, she'll probably get the highest possible score anyway."

Dad hugs me. "We're counting on you, love."

Mom and Dad stand back to look at us both. They are brimming with pride. I can see this. But they are also hiding their fear. I'm sure this escapes Alexander. He probably just thinks they're nervous for us.

I embrace my parents one more time. The doorman patiently waits and finally says, "It's time."

Alexander and I take one final look at our parents. He mockingly blows them kisses, and I manage a weak smile and courtesy wave. Carefully, we step into the doorway to a new life… a new beginning. Out of nowhere, a violent shudder wracks my entire body as I realize the full meaning of what's about to happen.

The door slams shut behind us.

Chapter 5

"Come this way, please," says someone dressed in what looks like a bright orange tuxedo, with cream lapels and checkered tails on his jacket. An usher, I assume. I'm already on high alert, noticing and observing every detail. I'm sure it will pass, but right now, I'm starting to feel a bit freaked out. Luckily, everyone else is so excited they aren't even noticing my anxiousness for anything more than exam fright.

Day One of the exams and already I feel like an outsider, like a non-Percenter.

"Two lines please. Left sleeves up. Follow the candidate in front of you," is being repeated from the speakers. I peek ahead to see where we lemmings are being led. It looks like there is a nurse at the end of the line. She's dressed in all white with this weird white hat with a red cross in the front center. If she's not a nurse, she should be. I decide to try and bypass the line and sneak my way past the nurse. There really isn't any where to go that I wouldn't be seen but I have to try.

"You! Stay in line!" says a loud voice. "You are not allowed into the arena until you are triggered!"

"Bullshit! I know exactly what that tracer is for and it's not to activate my powers!" I want to say.

But, instead, I respond with a simple, "Sorry!"

Alexander looks at me with a confused expression on his face. Whispering, he leans over to my ear and says, "Jena, what are you doing?" He gently grabs my arm and merges me back into the line with him.

Fuck! How am I going to get out of this now? I think.

The antigen has been used since The Oze for every adult, Percenter or not. Even the Barrens are injected when they turn sixteen. It became so normal for everyone to get it that for generations no one has questioned its purpose. But I know it's not really to trigger the activation of our powers like they are telling us.

According to my dad, Phineas Riley, and his groupies called the Cleansing Coalition, are using the antigen to track everyone so they can continue to control our societies and ensure Percenters are the reigning species. The antigen is actually some type of organic compound that maps your DNA. Mom and Dad called it a Tracer. At its very basic function, it will archive the results of our exams and record our Percenter powers to some type of digital library. It is stored and monitored by the Archivist or Keeper of Records. The Archivist is the only one with unlimited access to all the DNA data in the Library. But it does way more than the Chancellors are admitting to the rest of the Percenters. Part of the problem is that not all Chancellors are even aware of the antigen's real functions. And definitely not it's intended uses by the Cleansing Coalition.

The Tracer allows the Archivist to locate any individual adult, whether a Percenter, Middler, or Barren, at any time. If I get injected, they will be able to trace me. If I get injected, I've failed my mission before it even begins.

I ignore Alexander and walk directly to the nearest usher and begin rolling up my sleeve.

"Hi. Sorry." I pull back my sleeve quickly now. "I have already received it. I just had to run back to tell my friend something about a really cute boy." The lie is so obvious I'm not even convincing myself. But I figured I should go with something stupid that embarrasses everyone at the same time, especially the usher. It's easier to go unnoticed that way.

She looks at me cautiously and slightly perturbed. This probably doesn't happen often. She takes her scanner and waives it past the inside of my forearm, gripping my wrist more sternly than I think she does most. My palms turn clammy. I'm so nervous.

"Fuck! Hurry up machine!" I whisper under my breath. My nerves are completely on edge as they test the substitute antigen my parents injected last night. It's supposed to throw off any antigen scanner but this is my first scan.

"What did you say?"

Ding! Ding! blurts out of the scanner. Scaring the both of us but saving me in more ways than one. I release my breathe and my shoulders collapse in an obvious decrease of tension.

Looking disappointed, she nods at me to advance.

"STAY IN LINE!" she reinforces the message with an unmistakable hand signal.

I take a deep breath, "OK, sorry! Won't happen again." I avoid looking back at my brother, who is clearly confused by what just happened. Knowing Alexander he's biting his tongue and squeezing his eyebrows together. Even without looking at him, I'm a hundred percent positive he is doing just that.

I see a portrait of Jude Stephens, one of the Chancellors from Grand View. Clearly embossed on the nameplate beneath the photo, "Archivist for the Sovereign Sky Cities." Jude alone has access to unimaginable information. The Archivist is able to identify each person who has Percenter powers and what those powers are and where the person is located at any given moment.

There is no real privacy in our world. Once you are injected, the antigen immediately enters your bloodstream and binds itself to DNA markers. Your blood powers the antigens, like fuel to a fire. Once administered, there is no way to reverse it. Data collected by the Tracer is transmitted to the Sovereign City Mirror, an impenetrable system that only the Archivist can access.

Originally believed to only identify powers recorded during the exam, the Archivist is also able to identify those with undiscovered powers. But, as Father emphasized to me last night, and Alexander this morning, it's critically important to hide some of our powers from being recorded. Even though we need them all to be activated.

Father warns, "Jena, there is no easy way to say this. If you are discovered…if they learn how powerful you truly are, you will be treated like a threat. The Coalition does whatever it takes to swiftly eliminate every threat against them."

I close my eyes as I am reminded of the risks I'm taking for people I never knew existed until last night. If they learn that my injection has been faked, I don't stand a chance of making it out of these exams alive.

Sweet, amiable me. The girl who gets along with everyone. The girl who is respectful and kind. The girl who excels at everything she does. I am, after all, part of a royal Hundred-Percenter Bloodline and destined for great things. So they say. That girl. That's who is expected. That's who I must be. No exceptions. No wavering.

My body is still shaking from the adrenaline as we enter the arena. Alexander catches up to me and mouths, "What's going on? Are you OK?"

I nod. And I mouth back, "It's nothing."

He whispers in my ear while subtly touching my wrist with his fingertips. "Where did you get that?" I make eye contact with him and hold his gaze without saying anything for longer than a moment.

"Not now," I finally affirm.

A filmy black shadow appears on the periphery of my eyesight. I shake my head and look again, directly at it. It is still there. Blinking to make it disappear, fear, a dark fear, takes over for a brief moment. I place the palms of my hands over my eyes, and I try to refocus on the attendant's voice. I take a deep breath before reopening my eyes. The shadow is no longer there. I'm starting to break. My mind is playing tricks on me already and we haven't even begun the exams.

"I can do this!" I say in a rushed breath inaudible to anyone else.

Another usher begins talking, "At the end of the day, after you finish Part 1, you will be escorted to the candidate quarters. You'll get settled in. Meet your mates. And dress for the opening ceremony. You are not allowed to leave your quarters until the opening ceremony, and you are not to be late for this. Is that understood?" He pauses.

The usher sternly glances at everyone, looking uncomfortably at each and every one of us directly in the eye.

He continues, "These exams determine the path you take for the rest of your life. Take this seriously. Be prepared for extreme challenges. These exams are testing you all the time, even when you think they aren't. Don't be fooled. And consider yourself warned."

My ears perk up. At first, I think this guy is about to give us a useful hint, but then I notice the look of fear on everyone else's face, and I realize he's scaring everyone instead.

"Today will be the easiest of the three. The tests are designed to assess your intelligence and won't necessarily require any physical prowess, unless it's an exercise for you to think." His back now turned to us, "'But the tests get harder as you move forward." The usher speaks in a monotone voice as if he's said the same thing over and over a hundred times in front of the mirror.

I glance over at Alexander, and he just smiles at me. He is so excited he can barely stand still. I envy his innocent optimism.

"Now, go and begin!" The usher finishes with, "And good luck. May you strive to *Surpass all others before you!*"

"See you later, Jena," Alexander says to me. "Good luck, as if you need it!"

"You, too." I watch my twin brother walk away. He is so confident, so self-assured. He knows his place in our world, and he is comfortable with it. He does not question the order of things even though, sometimes, he is slightly bothered by it, especially after what happened to Ben. But he's one of the good guys and his heart is as pure as gold. Alex has a good conscience, after all. He will eventually be forced to realize this for himself. But that's not going to happen today, or anytime soon.

To be fair, I never questioned our world either. And now, I can't stop questioning everything. I am suspicious of everything and everyone.

I step into an expansive room that's lined with metal lockers, each displaying a life-sized image of a candidate. A voice similar to Buzz is speaking in repetition. "Find your locker. Change. Good luck." I quickly find mine and change into the sleek, all white stretchy bodysuit that's hanging inside my locker. I look around and see everyone else grabbing the same thing out of their lockers. I turn my back and start changing. I find the final zipper and just as I pull it up, I notice myself in a mirror.

The jumpsuit fits perfectly, hugging every curve of my body comfortably as if it was couture design with me as the muse. It's quite embarrassing. I don't like showing off my body. I'm aware that my curves are in all the right places, according to my mom, but I'm still pretty shy

I look at myself in the mirror or a little bit longer and realize the bodysuit will be perfect for the athletic parts of the exams, but it's a bit overkill for today if we aren't doing any physical activities.

A couple lockers down, I notice Jessica Piston. I've met her a couple of times, but I don't really like her that much. To be fair, I suppose, I don't know her very well, but she just rubs me the wrong way, and I can't pinpoint it just yet.

She notices I'm staring at her. I quickly look away but not fast enough. "You're Jenavieve" she pauses as if she's thinking of what to say next, "Jenavieve de Fenace', right?" asks Jessica. She looks pointedly at me with small, dark angular eyes.

"Jena, actually," I say surprisingly as she walks over to speak with me.

"I recognize you from the last soiree my parents held. It must have been six months ago. Remember?" Jessica asks.

"Oh," I respond in an uninterested tone. "Jessica, right?" I say as if I'm just recognizing her for the first time and barely remember her name. "Correct. Jessica Piston" She wrinkles her nose in an attempt to be cute. In reality, she's stunning with long straight black hair and the quintessential petite body every teenage girl yearns to have. Nothing like mine.

I return my focus to getting dressed, remembering that Jessica has a bit of a temper and could be a total bitch if she wanted. I've seen it happen to unknowing victims at her parents' parties. I have no interest in becoming her next one. She reminds me of someone who is always looking for attention. Or trouble. Or both. Exactly the type of person I need to avoid. I have no inclination towards befriending anyone, especially someone who is a potential loose cannon. I need to fly under everyone's radar.

"Good luck today," I say and turn to leave before she has the chance to start a conversation.

Once I'm outside the changing room, I follow a group of congregating candidates being escorted to the individual rooms flanking both sides of a long corridor. We all look more or less alike in our fitted white bodysuits.

It's a bit too reminiscent of our Middler Staffers, or every Middler really. We look sterile—too clean—too alike.

I notice Jessica joined only a couple people behind me. She walks with her head held high, her long hair bouncing on her shoulders. Her stature reeks of self-confidence and privilege. She is not a conformer, that's for sure. I walk forcefully, wanting to get this started as quick as possible. I notice the annoying shadows in my peripheral vision again. I turn sharply. They quickly dissipate into nothing. I still have no clue what they are, if anything, and chalk it up to stress and nerves.

Inside the exam room, the ceilings are high and glow with a brilliant white light. It's almost too bright for me. I place my hands arched over my brows to dull the brightness for my eyes. I peek around to assess my entire surrounding while my eyes adjust. The glow is so unnatural it makes me feel like the lights will expose my innermost thoughts. That would be beyond dangerous.

I realize I'm being a bit dramatic and have to keep myself in check. I close my eyes and remind myself I'm just like every other candidate. I am no different! I blink one more time so my eyes can fully adjust. I can see everything clearly now.

The room has a sterile, disinfectant like smell, as if the whole place had been scrubbed with rubbing alcohol moments before we walked in. It's not a pleasant smell and reminds me of the Infirmary. I've only been sick once. I hated being probed by the doctors and certainly didn't enjoy the smell...or the bright white lights for that matter.

We are all directed to individual pod-like chairs. Several ladies stand by, wearing light blue frocks and a monitor's badge on their lapel. One turns towards me.

Speaking to the entire room, she says in a voice that projects enough to fill the entire space, "Candidates, please take your seats and make yourselves comfortable." Her voice is pleasant and matter of fact.

I walk over to the pod with my name and family crest engraved along its side. I sit down in the white padded chair that automatically reclines once my body makes contact. It's comfortable. More comfortable than I was expecting. My head falls easily back into a cushioned headrest. If I wasn't so nervous, I would probably fall asleep. I feel weightless, almost like I'm floating but floating on a soft cloud. A monitor walks over to me, sits down and begins to place a myriad of copper electrodes onto my forehead and temples. I squirm uncomfortably. Mother and Father didn't warn me about these.

"Don't worry, honey," the monitor says. "My name is Michelle. I promise you, this won't hurt." I notice that her badge says Michelle Lohrenz. I try to remember if I know anything about the Lohrenz family, but I don't recall ever hearing that name.

There are so many Percenters in the Sovereign Sky Cities that aren't from notable bloodlines and virtually anonymous in society. The de Fenace' bloodline is known as a Noblesse Oblige. Families of nobility that are one hundred percent direct descendants of the Founding Chancellors. Families who generally assume leadership roles in the Sky Cities and harness the most powerful of Percenter abilities.

I squirm again, wishing they would turn off the blinding light. I feel too exposed, almost as though I'm in a laboratory and being used as a test specimen. I just want to get this over with. For a moment, I regret being so agreeable with my parents last night. For a moment, I want to pass all my exams with flying colors and attend Freelinn Prep with Alex. Like I'm supposed to. Like everyone else in this room. Like every other sixteen-year-old. In so many ways, I wish I could go back just forty-eight hours and avoid my parents completely so we never had any conversation about the end of the world as we know it. Back to when I was as naïve as Alex. To when I was just Jenavieve. Not Jenavieve, the savior, who has the fate of the world resting on her shoulders.

Although my parents gave me a choice, and it was ultimately my decision, how could I say no. I chose to play this role. To stop the Cleansing Coaling and save all of humanity. But it was a heady, overwhelming decision. And now, all I feel is fear and regret, and I don't want to go through with it.

Michelle scans my forearm and populates my profile on her display. Success. It's working as my parents said it would.

"I'm simply connecting these electrodes to areas that will monitor your brainwaves." The monitor seems oblivious to my nervousness. "They're designed to scan and fuse data from your mental responses to the information we download. These responses will then overlay with imagery that the computer has pre-selected solely for you based on your antigen markers and unique DNA. Scanning your brain this way will identify your intellect and aptitude. Essentially, it's going to determine a baseline for your true Percenter powers. It helps us assess your capacity for harnessing your powers. Very exciting stuff but don't worry yourself too much if you didn't understand all of what I just said."

I can't help but feel everything she is telling me is a complete and utter lie. She seems authentic, so either she's telling the truth, or she's just as ignorant to the true purpose of these tests as everyone else in the room. In either case, I proceed with caution.

"Oh, I understand perfectly!" I retort.

Michelle leans closer to me and whispers, "I expect, dear–knowing your family's bloodline– that this test will reveal intelligence of the highest order." She smiles brightly and offers a wink. "After all, your family is one of the Noblesse Oblige." I got the answer I needed to feel comfortable. She's a believer, not an enemy.

I don't care about nobility or prestige, not anymore. To be fair, I never really have. I know our family name is synonymous with an elite segment of the Percenter society, but what I didn't realize is just how powerful a name could be. And just like all other Noblesse Oblige, I am born with privilege that can either better society or ruin it.

There is a humming from the machines as Michelle places more electrodes to my forehead and temples. From the corner of my eye, I see Jessica nearby. She is squirming, too. But many of the other candidates are smiling and eager to proceed. Oblivious to any harm that may be coming their way.

"How long will this take?" I ask, biting my lower lip.

"Not long." She fidgets with the display screen before me. She then takes a needle out of her pocket, flicks it, and gets it ready to inject my arm with a silver liquid. "Well, it won't feel too long, but you'll be under for several hours."

"Wait. What? Under?" I am suddenly alarmed but so strapped in I can't move. "What's that?"

"Why, dear, this allows you to enter the exam. It's all in your head silly girl and this here" She raises the needle containing the liquid, "is essentially the exam! It won't hurt, I promise."

I manage to grab her wrist, stopping her from proceeding. I look around and notice everyone else accepting the injection. I look Michelle directly in the eye to determine if she is really to be trusted. I have no choice but to hope so. I've been on edge since I stepped into my family's car. Thinking I am going through this alone. Unwilling to allow myself to trust. But I won't survive if I don't. I have to be willing to trust some people.

She injects my arm, and my eyes reluctantly close on their own.

Chapter 6

When my eyes open, I feel like I just woke up from the best dream. I was relaxed, yawning, forgetting everything about the pressures of these exams. I look around to get my bearings. I'm standing beneath some type of massive structure. It's so majestic with massive white pillars soaring into the sky. Walls extending into the clouds on each side. I can only see enough to know I'm not seeing it all. Pink sandstone walls are dotted with floor-to-ceiling archways allowing sunlight to stream into the room, creating beautiful rays of light dancing across the polished stone flooring. The floors are a white marble, layered with different shades of grey veins, just like ours at home.

I walk through the first archway into the expansive room. All around me are exquisite paintings I have never seen before. Some must be fifteen to twenty feet tall. They remind me of an ancient time, the Renaissance period, if I'm remembering my art lessons correctly.

I think the Renaissance era is when people first applied mathematics to theorize nature. It was also known for gaudy oversized oil paintings, just like these. I've always preferred Impressionism to the Renaissance period.

I laugh a little, thinking of how Alexander used to try and act so worldly when he first met a girl by saying something as cheesy as that. "I've always preferred the beauty and complexity of Impressionist works, like those of Monet," he would say while putting one hand in his jean's pocket.

I walk around the never ending room a bit more, looking for clues to what I am supposed to do next. After looking around for what feels like an eternity, something inside me, like an inner voice or a gut feeling tells me that I need to solve some type of puzzle. I look around at the different pieces of art, hoping for a hidden message or clue, at least. I wish that gut feeling would be a little more specific. You know, like "Hey, girl! Read this first." kind of specific. I'm not sure what puzzle I'm supposed to solve, if that's even what I am supposed to do. I just feel it. Not like an intuition or anything, more like a memory.

I walk really close to one of the paintings. I feel an urge to reach out and touch it. I focus on the women with the soft eyes, yet her facial expression says she's defensive and almost...scared. As I reach to grace her dress with the back of my fingers, my hand becomes one with the canvas, turning to oils right before my eyes.

I try to pull my hand back, but I can't. It's like I've stuck my hand through a hole that is too small to pull it back out. The woman in the painting turns to face me and reaches to place my hand in hers. She's smiling and at the same time gently trying to pull me closer, into the painting. I wonder if this is the first clue to the puzzle or something completely different, like a trap.

I stop trying to fight her pull and in a blink of an eye my entire arm, all the way up to my shoulder, is now a part of the painting. Using my free hand, I grab the frame and stop myself from being pulled further. The entire painting has now come alive. This is it. This is the challenge, the puzzle. I can feel it!

If I had no powers, I would only see the painting as it merely looks, a piece of art on the wall, not what it could be. Torn between the amazement of it all and the fear of revealing whatever powers this may be, I decide to jump completely into the painting and throw caution to the wind. I'm here, I'm going to enjoy it as much as I can.

With the sensation that I'm walking on spongy air, I step into a garden that's filled with flowers of every color of the rainbow. The beauty is overwhelming. Light extends from somewhere in the heavens and forms slanting rays upon the grounds. I feel the warmth of this light all around me. I stare longer at the rays of light and start seeing laser-like lines, all vibrantly piercing the landscape around me. They start to look more solid and less transparent.

I reach out and grab one of the rays of light. It pulses in my hand as if energy was moving from one end to the other. I pull on it, but it flexes like a massive rubber band. I grab it with my other hand and tug as hard as I can. Nothing. It's not moving. I look around to make sure I'm not missing something. All I see now are fields of flowers blowing in the wind, wiping everything else away into multi-colored dust particles.

I turn my attention back to the rays of light. I pull myself on to one like you would a tree branch and reach for another ray. As soon as I grab it my feet lift off the ground, and I become virtually weightless and start floating.

"Wait! What?" I say out loud as if there was someone to hear me. Quickly followed by a laugh.

I start climbing, well, partly flying, up the light rays like they are a jungle gym. One to the next in any direction. The faster I go, the more light rays appear around me. It feels like I am climbing forever until I finally reach the point where there is nothing except a massive wall. I jump from my last light ray to reach the edge of the wall. I float for a good ten feet and as soon as my fingertips reach the edge of the wall, I feel gravity pulling me back down. I'm no longer weightless, but still not the same as I was before. I continue to climb and pull myself out of the artwork.

The massive wall I jumped to was just the two-inch lip of the frame meeting the canvas. My feet touch the ground, and I immediately jump back up in the air with utter excitement and scream, "I can fucking fly! My Percenter Pow—" But before *power* completely leaves my mouth, gravity once again holds me back, and I unexpectedly land on the cold hard floor. "Ouch!" I say.

"Heh! Nope. I guess flying not so much! What was all that about?" I say as I raise my left hip and begin to rub the point of impact. I look back at the painting only to see the rays of light fading away and it returning to its original artwork.

I feel a strong electrical surge pierce my body, then a brief blackness envelops my vision. I close my eyes to absorb the pain. But my eyelids snapped back open, like when Buzz wakes me.

I'm someplace else. I'm facing a statue of a man I don't recognize. It's larger than any person I have ever met. Smooth, black onyx stares back at me. Making me feel insignificant. I walk around it to see the face. To my surprise, it's a woman.

"No, wait. It looks more like the face of a cat, no, a jaguar...on a human body!"

I continue walking around it. I briefly look away, scanning the vastness of the empty room. As soon as I do, the statue reaches out and grabs me with both hands, holding my shoulders with my back facing it.

"AAAHHHH!" I scream and jump around in an attempt to break free.

It tightly pulls me closer. I continue to scream for help as I inch closer to the statue. I manage to turn my head just enough to see that I am only inches away. I look at the jaguar's face and moments before it drops me, I notice the face change, morph.

I fall to the floor, backing away on all fours as quickly as I can. Panting, I stop, more afraid of what's actually happening and not knowing what to do next. I stare at the statue now turning its back to me. Almost like it doesn't want me to see how the face was morphing.

"All matter is mutable," my father's voice pops into my head.

I stand up, fighting back the tears that I know so badly want to come out of me. I size up the statue from all angels, watching as the evolving jaguar's face turns more with my every step.

"All matter is mutable." I say softly to the statue in a hesitant tone. Repeating a second and third time with more confidence.

"All Matter Is Mutable! ALL MATTER IS MUTABLE!"

I don't really know what that means but I reach for the statue's hand, placing my palm against it. I feel an electrical jolt of power surge within me. Just as I do this, I hear a low growl to my left. An enormous jaguar, its sinewy muscles taut like a rope, saunters slowly towards me. The statue closes its grip on my hand, and I can't move. I look directly into the jaguar's eyes. Its intent is clear. I swallow hard. My heart races, and fear takes hold.

With just one hand free, I position myself to fight the jaguar the best way I can. I feel the power of the statue surge within my veins again. My fear begins to dissipate on its own. It must be my body's fight or flight instinct.

Without warning, the statue pulls me in, wrapping me in both arms again. The jaguar face turns back to the woman's face I thought I initially noticed, but not just any woman, my mother.

I recognize it moments before she says, "Breathe."

Confused, I do as she says. I have no choice really as a real jaguar is charging in my direction from across the room. I melt into the stature and become a part of it looking down at the jaguar. I raise my hands and rays of light begin shooting from my fingertips in all directions. The jaguar slows, approaching carefully. He bows to me as I watch in utter surprise.

He stands and walks away, never turning his back to me. The light from my fingertips evolves into some type of spinning vortex. Without warning, the jaguar lunges towards me, disappearing...into me.

The statue ejects my body, and I fall to the ground.

"Ugh...enough dropping me on cold hard floors!" I say in frustration.

I turn and look at the statue to see my mother's face again but all I see is a motionless statue of a man's body with the face of a jaguar. I briefly worried that Michelle saw my mother too.

A painful buzzing begins in my head. Some type of unrelenting electrical charge, similar to the power I felt when I was part of the statue. I can feel it centering itself in my heart and radiating a sense of warmth outwards to my fingertips.

What happens next stuns me.

"Hi. My name is Xavier."

"Who said that?"

He ignores my question. "Your parents told you about me, right?"

I acknowledge the voice but return the favor of ignoring his question. "Where are you?"

There is no response, just a sensation that he is watching me. No, not exactly watching me, but more like...next to me or all around me.

"Xavier? Is that really you?" I ask in a surprised tone. I didn't know anybody by the name Xavier existed until last night. My long-lost brother that neither Alexander nor I knew existed. That went over like a bag of rocks when Mom and Dad dropped that one on me.

"Yes," he replies.

"How? Where? What are you doing here?"

I hear the same voice in my head. "Stop talking," he says. "They won't be able to detect me unless you keep talking!"

I feel an immediate headache. I put my hands to my ears and shake my head as if I can make everything disappear.

"What is going on?" I say, using my inner voice.

"Breathe. Just take a deep breath and count to three to clear your mind." I do as he says. I close my eyes. I can feel Xavier's thoughts, but know they are separate from mine.

"Good," he says. In a calm but hurried voice, he continues, "Be ready when you get to the Beach. You can't let Alex follow you. Remember that!"

"The Beach? What are you talking about? Why can't Alex follow?"

"I can't explain. You will know when you get there. Just remember, you have to leave Alex on the Beach. Now let go!"

Out loud I say: "Let go? Let go of what?"

"Shhhh…use your inner voice, Jenavieve!" I hear Xavier say directly into my mind.

I follow suit and think, "I still don't understand? I'm sitting on the floor in an empty room?" I opened my eyes, and I notice the statue had disappeared.

"Let go of me. I'm going to let go of you."

"But…but…I have so many questions I want to ask you!" I think excitedly.

"Jena, I know. Me too, actually, I mean, have so many questions for you, too. But not now. Soon, I promise."

"Okay, I'll try." I close my eyes again and take another deep breath, exhaling everything inside my lungs. A weight lifts itself and my headache is no more.

"Xavier? Xavier are you there?" I think.

I wait a couple moments scanning the darkness to hear his voice. Nothing. I still feel the warmth inside me, but at the same time I feel his absence. And just like that, my mysterious, long-lost brother was gone.

Almost immediately after that revelation I stand alone in a new temple. This time, I stare back at myself in a mirror. A wall of mirrors in a golden gilded hallway. My reflection has a silhouette of a lion. I've read about this before. When you gaze into a golden mirror, one that has seen the Earth through many evolutions, it can reveal your truth. The silhouette is morphing into some type of creature. It is definitely me with my long blonde hair and blue eyes but at the same time it's not me. It's a version of me that I have never imagined before. In this instant, I recognize my true strength for the first time.

"Damn right, I'm a fierce lioness," I say under my breath, giggling a little.

I close my eyes. My breaths are low...almost nonexistent. I feel my body drifting. My arms shaking slightly before my entire body jolts. Alex and I often talked about what it would feel like to have our powers awakened. I never imagined it would be like this.

In the distance, I hear a woman's voice whisper, "Jena, Jena, Jena you must wake now." Michelle stands before me. Her eyes are wide in surprise. She is pulling the electrodes from my temples and forehead.

I look up and clear my throat. "Well?" I ask.

"Quite OK," says Michelle.

"How long has it been?"

"You've been out for four hours and twenty minutes." Michelle smiles encouragingly at me. "That's a normal amount of time for this exam."

"Four hours? It didn't feel nearly that long."

"The exams can be misleading when it comes to time evaluations. Just know that you have done exceptional for Day One, Jenavieve. Of course, I didn't doubt for one second that you wouldn't. I'm sure you'll be very pleased with your scores."

"So, nothing unusual happened?" I ask her, trying to figure out if Xavier was detected.

"Unusual? What do you mean?" Michelle asks.

"Never mind. I guess I'm just nervous and want to be perfect." I sit up straight and stare at my hands. I can still see laser-like blue sparks emitting from them. I wonder if Michelle can see them, so I quickly close my fists and the sparks dissipate. I slowly get out of the chair and stretch my arms. Monitors are waking up the other candidates. Jessica Piston looks back at me with a frown on her face. I probably have a similar look on mine.

Michelle turns toward me.

"Please, go into the hallway where someone will escort you and the other candidates to the dormitories. Tonight you'll have a chance to get to know the other candidates and celebrate the exams at the party!" Michelle smiles at me like we are best friends.

As we walk to our dorms, our chaperon tells us about the levels for each prep school and what we must do to achieve them.

"The average Percenter awakens less than fifty percent of their brain's total potential. That's five times as much as…" I look around at the other candidates and see some of them taking copious notes, rapidly. She's not telling me anything I don't already know.

My mind starts to wonder, and I tune her, and everyone else, out. I started thinking about talking to Xavier, my brother! I wonder if he was the jaguar but then confused by why it had my mother's face. I also think about telling Alex. How can I keep this a secret from him? Alexander deserves to know.

"During each part of the exam your brain is measured to see what, if anything, is being activated. The more your brain is awakened, the greater your powers will be. The average human uses just ten percent of their brain's potential. A Percenter harnesses more–a minimum of thirty percent. That's all it takes to develop superhuman powers. Candidates that score between thirty and fifty percent are automatically enrolled in Briarsley. A score of fifty-one percent is required for Stillstone. And seventy-five percent is required for Freelinn. These rankings, of sorts, are based on the powers of each school's namesake."

This chaperon is probably the most boring person I have met in my entire life.

"Everybody already knows this," I accidentally say out loud.

"Excuse me?" she responds with a hint of anger.

"Sorry. I meant…sorry, never mind."

I know there is so much more to it. Father told me that within each school the Cleansing Coalition has placed moles. They are using candidates to hunt other candidates with unique powers. powers they can use to their advantage. These moles are forming army's disguised as prep school clubs. Father knows it is happening at Freelinn but can't do anything to stop it without drawing the attention of the Cleansing Coalition, which he absolutely cannot do.

The Secret Society's biggest fear is that candidates with advanced powers, or those with the potential to unlock one hundred percent, are being recruited before they even realize it. It's even possible that these moles are teaching kids how to harness new powers just like Mother and Father taught me. The most powerful Percenters can awaken one hundred percent of their brain's power, but it's rare.

According to the Archivist, besides our Founding Chancellors who drank the original elixir, there have only been a handful of Percenters recorded as having such powers. My parents, and the rest of their Secret Society, think the Cleansing Coalition has either been kidnapping and brainwashing or killing candidates over the past decade who they feel could be more powerful than themselves. They are viewed as a risk and are using the moles to eliminate all risks.

I continue to get lost in my thoughts as the chaperon continues her diatribe on activating Percenter powers.

Chapter 7

Surrounded by a mob of candidates, Alexander and I begin making our way to the main building. My brother, as usual, is chatting up every girl within earshot. And as usual, I'm in my head. I breathe in the fresh, clean air. I look around and realize no one else is. But why would they even think to, really. I'm so jealous of everyone else's naivety.

Uniformed men stand at either side of a wide gate that automatically opens as the first candidate approaches. We cross inside to a courtyard. There is a long driveway that circles a massive water fountain and leads to the front doors. Guards wearing jet-black tuxedos with the word "Security" inscribed on each lapel stand there motionless. I can't help but wonder, are they here to keep people out, or keep people in?

Its entry isn't just grand, it's palatial. Exotic stone mosaic floors lead you directly to a three-story, spiraling staircase that butterflies on both sides. Now, unlike when I visit with my mother, signs direct us past the staircase to the Grand Ballroom.

The sun has started drifting behind the neighboring buildings. Encased in Turkish stone, a romantic rose-pink glow emanates throughout the ballroom from what is left of the sun's light. Twilight is just around the corner, and the party is about to start.

My cohorts flood the room with unbridled enthusiasm. Even I can't hold back a smile now and then. A sea of white fills the room as our mob disperses to fill the ballroom. All the girls are wearing long white gowns that romantically flow behind them as they dance. The boys are wearing crisp white suits, fitted to perfection, and adorned with the standard bow tie. White is supposed to represent a clean slate, purity, and newness.

We are all equal, today. We're starting anew. A rebirth. After tonight, we are no longer able to rely on the innate privileges of Percenter life. These exams will determine if we have inherited the Percenters' powers...or not. The exams will dictate whether we are to remain one of the privileged and elite...or if we will become a Middler, or even worse, a Barren.

I 've been trying so hard not to think about the ultimate consequences of the exams for everyone, especially for me. And right now, for the first time since I arrived, I'm actually enjoying myself. I'm surrounded by laughter and smiles. Strangers making new friends. Teenagers being teenagers.

A swarm of bustling staff approach us offering drinks and hors-d'oeuvres. Tables are adorned with silken white tablecloths and settings complete with the Percenters' insignia, a percent symbol, and sterling silver flatware. Miniature glowing lamps emanate a soft, ethereal light across the table tops. It's designed to be an enchanting evening for everyone. I decide to partake in the excitement. I can deal with everything else tomorrow.

A couple Lingonberry Lemonades later, my attention is drawn to two black figures hovering in the corner of the ballroom. I stop dancing dead in my tracks. They are beyond creepy looking. Two hulking figures dressed in black robes that look older than the Sovereign Sky. Hoods are pulled down disguising their faces. I stare hard.

I can't figure out if they are real of if they are just in my imagination. They look so real to me but if they were, everyone would be noticing them too. I look around at Alex, still talking to some random girls. It's clear that no one else sees them. Suddenly, one of them looks directly at me as if they just spotted me for the first time. I make what I can only assume is eye contact.

I can't quite make out a face but the eyes were unmistakably fiery red. Like I would imagine in a demon from the fires of hell. I gulp and turn my attention back to dance with Alex and his harem of girls. No one else appears to have noticed them so I'm going to chalk it up as a stress induced hallucination. I grab Alex's arm to get his attention, well, really his affirmation, but he gently nudges my hand away. He's too busy flirting to pay attention to me.

I glance back out of the corner of my eye to see if they are still there. Damnit! Now they both are staring me down with their red eyes. I'm still unable to see any faces. They begin walking, more like floating, on a direct path to me past everyone else. Still they seem to go unnoticed. I stumble backwards, bumping into Alex and spilling his drink.

"Jena! Easy now. Have you met Sonya?" Alex says with his typical happy tone.

I ignore his question and turn my head back in the direction of the approaching figures.

"LOOK! Do you see them?" I say frantically and probably a bit louder than I should. When I turn to point Alex in their direction they are gone.

"Who? Who are you talking about?" Alex says with a bit of disappointment. I stand there, frantically scanning the room but they are nowhere to be found.

"Um, nobody. I thought I saw...never mind." I wonder if this is some leftover residue from my exams but an unfamiliar chill skitters up my back. I start thinking about the silver liquid injected into my arm earlier. It might be a side effect, but I would assume they'd warn us about something like that. Hopefully it was just a hallucination, nothing more. But my gut tells me otherwise.

My hand trembles slightly, and I calm it by picking up another Lingonberry Lemonade. Alex waves me off and puts his arm around Sonya as they wander away from me. I scan the room, one more time. Just to make sure. I catch a glimpse of sprawling gardens outside the glass wall. Darkness has already arrived, and it is interrupted by soft twinkling lights in a starry-like atmosphere. It really does give the illusion of beauty.

Middlers are our event staff of course. It is considered an honor amongst the Middlers to work the exams. Both the men and women are dressed in gray jackets and slacks and carry silver platters filled with decadently prepared appetizers. As designed, I barely noticed them. They are everywhere and nowhere. Like they are hiding in plain sight.

I don't see Ben anywhere and briefly wonder why he wasn't invited to serve. Maybe my parents didn't think it was a good idea because he'd have to see his family. That would be awkward to say the least.

Teams of media meander through the room with their drone cameras taking video of candidates. I notice there are big screens throughout the ballroom playing live footage. It's probably the same video the rest of San Sun is watching outside of the Capital. I avoid them as if they are a plague coming for me. There's no way I'm talking to them. I need to be as much of a wallflower as possible, as my father would say.

"Jena! Hey!" Alex smiles at me and hurries over.

His sandy-blonde hair flops long on his forehead. He looks so handsome in his suit. I often feel a sense of pride that he's my brother.

"You haven't told me about your exam yet? How do you think you did?" he asks me.

"Fine. What about you?" I try to smile convincingly. I'm actually not sure if I did well or not. I mean, well…Xavier is a bit of a concern. Michelle could have been lying to me.

"Just Fine?" Alex asks with a questioning look on his face. "I'm sure you did better than fine Jena!" He continues in the same breath, "I'm pretty sure I killed it. Oh, and guess who I saw just a few minutes ago?"

"Who?" I raise my eyebrows.

"Raquel Hawthorn, that's who!"

"So, are you finally admitting you've had a crush on her all these years?"

"Let's just say she is clearly the most beautiful girl in all of San Sun tonight! Do you think she'll get into Freelinn? That would be perfect!" Alex's eyes twinkle with mischievousness.

I punch him in the shoulder. "Most beautiful?"

I wink at him while I put my hands on my hips, briefly flaunting my own sexiness.

"Present company excluded…of course, Sis!"

"OK, then I'll just whisk my magic wand and make sure the two of you end up in the same classes!"

Alex reaches over, putting both hands on my shoulders and looking extremely serious says, "Can you do that? Is that like a real power?" His eyebrows draw together forming a near perfect line. The same thing Father does when he is contemplating something important.

50

"I'm teasing, you knucklehead." I thump him on the forehead and full on laugh out loud for the first time today.

Alexander blushes. "Oh, OK" He pushes his hair back off his forehead and looks around the room.

For a moment, I feel worried for Alex. He is so good-natured, so trusting. Will he be OK? I wonder. I realize there is a chance I may never see him again. My heart clenched tightly. Stop it! I can't focus on that right now. Not tonight.

"Hello, Jena," I hear a voice from behind me.

A voice I recognize. A voice that makes my heart skip a beat. Several beats, actually. I turn around and see Avelino Riley, my childhood crush. I feel my face turn all shades of red. Avelino is part of the Royal Riley bloodline.

We don't actually have royalty, per se, in the Sovereign Sky cities, but if we did his family would probably be it. His parents, like mine, are Hundred-Percenters. Their bloodline possess unparalleled elixir purity, direct descendants of Akshay Riley, the one true first Percenter. Their bloodline is even more pure than our lineage.

His name, Avelino, means powerful and complete. And it suits him perfectly. I've always known Avelino to be inquisitive and extremely smart, but also kind and gentle. Not to mention, he's smoking hot!

One of Avelino's ancestors, Buchanan Riley, was the original creator of the exams when his own son, Nick, was born. My parents told me about this last night when we were discussing the fate of the Sky Cities and the hidden Percenter world in general. The Secret Society thinks Avelino's parents might be the leaders of the Cleansing Coalition.

Of course, I can't hold that against Avelino if it's true. I'm sure he has no idea. I hope he has no idea. I mean, I had no idea my parents were part of a secret society so there is a chance!

I stand there, unresponsive, for what feels like several minutes. My mind jumps to everything from last night's conversation with Mother and Father, to how the original exams were introduced when The Percenters were still a secret society. The members initially used the exams as a celebration of their children coming of age. It was a way to celebrate and showcase their new powers.

But last night I learned a twist to that story. When the Percenters created the Sky Cities after The Oze, the exams became a way to filter Percenters; disguised as a prep-school admissions exam. In short, the exams had become a tool to exclude people rather than celebrate their differences.

The Percenter world is an orchestrated illusion, and a good one at that. We are led to believe the structure of our society is critical to everyone's survival. But in reality, Percenters treat Middlers and Barrens like second class citizen. Our leaders enslave all non-power people to maintain control over them. A cruelty I had never considered until last night.

The truth is that nothing is as it seems and the Chancellors aren't all noble and ethical as they have us believe. There is a seedy underbelly to the entire world and the Cleansing Coalition are the ones responsible. I shudder and honestly wish my parents hadn't told me anything. I want to look at Avelino as I would have just two days ago with complete adoration. But now, now I don't know if I can.

He could know about his parents, maybe even be serving as a spy for them like I am for my parents. My parents mentioned the Cleansing Coalition having moles in our schools, maybe he could be one. I shudder at the thought and drift back into last night's conversation with Mom and Dad.

Chapter 8

We sat in our lounge, drinking tea. Alexander had already retired to his room, and the staff had all gone home for the night.

"You know the Percenter history from our lessons, right?" Mother says.

"Yes. I do."

"Well, you don't know all of it." Mother looked at me nervously.

"What do you mean?" I ask. "What else could there be?"

"Darling, I need you to listen carefully," Father says before looking around to make sure we are alone. "There is a group of Percenters called the Cleansing Coalition. Your mother and I, along with a handful of others, have known about them for a long time. They are bad people doing unthinkable things."

"What do you mean? Bad things like what?" I ask.

"When we were just a little older than you are now, as seniors attending Freelinn, your father and I discovered something about Phineas Riley. He had an unnatural hatred for all non-Percenters. He believed that because we were Percenters, we were entitled to so much more than the rest of humanity. He felt we were a superior race.

He learned this hatred and bigotry from his father and his father learned it from his father. His ancestors convinced several others that Barrens were nothing more than unevolved animals who needed to be enslaved. Slaves whose sole purpose was to provide for Percenters, at all costs. Even at the cost of their own lives.

That was the true purpose of the Barren Pods and the real meaning behind the exams. The exams were created to oust those believed to be unworthy of living in the Sky Cities and enslave them as Barrens.

"About eighteen years ago, Phineas found support amongst several Chancellors who also believed it was important to keep the Percenter lineages pure. They call themselves the Cleansing Coalition and their sole mission is to control, or eliminate if necessary, people who do not harness Percenter powers. It was then that your father and I formed a secret faction, called the Saviors, to oppose Phineas' leadership of our Sky Cities.

"We enacted a plan that, or so we thought, that would prevent the Cleansing Coalition from achieving their ultimate goal of permanent enslavement for all non-Percenters. We wanted to create a new bloodline. A generation of Percenters born of purity of heart and mind. Percenters born from the womb of humanity."

"What are you talking about?" I say with utter and complete confusion. "What on Earth is the womb of humanity? I ask.

"Children that are born in the Sky Cities, like you, like we were, are tested during the exams to demonstrate, well, prove really, that they belong. That they have superhuman powers entitling them to live in the skies and not the uninhabitable ground." Mother says. "No Percenter shares the same DNA make-up as a Barren. Barrens are still considered one hundred percent human. Their bloodlines have not been influenced by the elixir which altered all of ours. Eighteen years ago, the Saviors each chose a Barren surrogate. Humans who represent a non-power lineage, or rather, a hundred percent natural human being with no powers at all and no elixir in their DNA. Together, we were to raise a new generation of children. A new race, really. Children with the DNA and powers of Percenters but with the blood of a Barren."

"The Saviors believe it unjust to enslave people merely because they are different, period." Father says, "That means Middlers, too, not just the Barrens. We should all be working hard to help each other thrive. Our differences make us stronger, together. But because of the way the Sky Cities and the Barren Pods were created during The Oze, it bred division and segregation.

The segregation allowed people like Phineas to infect the minds of other Percenters to believe separation of Human and Percenter was critical to our ability to survive. He used fear to convince many. But in the last couple of years, our informants tell us that there are areas of the ground where The Oze toxins have now dissipated and there is land that is habitable, ready for new life, including human and Percenter alike, to thrive. It's still rare, but it exists.

So, who are we to tell non-Percenters what they can or cannot do with their lives? Where they can or cannot live? How long are we going to force them to be our farmers, our laborers...our slaves?" My father looked genuinely sad.

"What do you mean eighteen years ago you chose surrogates?" I say with a heavy voice. "What do you mean the ground could be habitable?"

Mother takes a big breath and looks at Father.

"You and Alexander have a brother. His name is Xavier."

My jaw dropped in disbelief. I was not expecting her to say anything remotely like this.

"He shares your DNA, but a human woman named Isabel birthed him. Xavier was one of the children nurtured inside the womb of a human surrogate. Xavier is one of nine children born from the Saviors and the humans." My mother says in a cautious yet matter of fact tone.

"A brother? What are you talking about? Who are these nine children?" I ask. "Who's raising them? How could you hide this from me...and Alex?"

"We call them the Secret 9, or S9 for short. They are being raised by the Barrens in a unique preparatory school hidden to the naked eye. We created this school, hidden far away from the Sovereign Sky Cities, but the time to remain hidden has passed. The time is now. The S9, including your brother Xavier, have been training and preparing their entire lives and are almost ready. The Saviors are ready. It is now time to stop Phineas and the Cleansing Coalition. Our fight is coming. And we need you, Jenavieve, to lead the S9 and defeat the Cleansing Coalition and free the Barrens and Middlers from their oppression and potential extinction."

"I-I-I...don't know what to say. This all just sounds so surreal." I was shocked beyond words. Mother took my hand in hers.

"We, the Saviors, have an alliance here in the Sky Cities, and with many Barrens. But we have a lot more enemies and each one of us would be murdered by the Cleansing Coalition if they knew who we are and what we were doing. So far, we believe our identities have been protected. But the Cleansing Coalition knows the Saviors exist, they just haven't been able to identify us... yet! We have been waiting for this moment for a long time, honey. You are the final piece for our revolution.

"I don't even know what you are talking about! Act? Act on what?" I basically screamed at them.

"I'm sorry that we have to tell you this now. I'm sorry that we have to ask so much of you," says Father.

My parents continue to explain the oppression and how they needed me to help. I sat there and listened. Confused mostly, but also angry. I had been too shocked to even speak for a while. I just sat there and listened. Absorbing about every other word, at the most.

My parents and I talked long into the night, ultimately discussing my role in their grand plan. How I must help the S9 and the Saviors defeat the Cleansing Coalition. While they repeatedly insisted it was totally my choice, how could I deny that something needed to be done to right all the wrongs and free those unknowingly enslaved.

Chapter 9

After daydreaming about the state of our demoralizing world, I come back to reality as Avelino pokes me.

Gorgeous Avelino. Standing right in front of me.

"Earth to Jena? Are you OK?"

It would be a particularly dramatic event if one of the Rileys did not possess Percenter powers. But stranger things have happened during the exams. I've always felt a deep compassion for Avelino. His parents divorced several years back, and his loyalties have always been split. His father lives in Crystal Sky and his mother lives here in San Sun. He gets shuffled back and forth at his parent's will, used as a pawn in their ongoing feud. Poor guy has never really known his place; who truly loves him or where he belongs. But Avelino doesn't seem to be too bothered.

I have always admired Avelino for being so thick-skinned and positive. He has an infectious kindness and a generous heart. If only those traits weren't such an anomaly in his family. I'd be a wreck if my parents shuffled me back and forth, never having an actual place to call home. But I guess it's better than his parents asking him to leave the sky cities all together, like mine did.

I finally turn to face him. Before I speak, I actively study him from head to toe. He notices and with a pleasant 'OK, so that's how you want to play this' look on his face; he takes a step back inviting the observation. He has grown taller, probably over six feet now, and he is even more gorgeous than I had remembered. He's muscular, with broad shoulders and bulging arms almost too big for his shirtsleeves. He has jet-black hair and beautiful deep brown eyes, with specs of green. His skin is the color of melted caramels.

My heart beats a little too fast. He's definitely stunning.

He repeats with a chuckle in his voice, "Um…Earth to Jena!? I've been standing here watching you in a trance for like ten minutes! What in the world are you thinking about? It must be really good! But you might want to…just…" He winks. Closing with the biggest smile of perfectly white teeth I have ever seen. And he reaches over and gently uses his fingers to lift my chin and close my gaping mouth.

I shake my head suddenly realizing I've taken this silence a bit too far. Not to mention I was literally looking at him with a dropped jaw! "Oh, I'm so sorry. Yes…I was just thinking about… Aw, it doesn't matter. Hi, Avelino," I say, louder than I intended. "I was wondering if you were here. I mean…I was wondering if you were… Um… I forgot if we were the same age or if you were a year younger." I cringe. My cheeks are on fire. Next time, I should just keep my mouth shut after I say hi. My heart is pounding a thousand beats a minute. It's so loud it wouldn't surprise me if he could hear it. I had no idea I'd be this nervous to see Avelino again.

He's kind enough to pretend that I'm not being totally lame. "It's been awhile since I've seen you, Jena. You look…breathtaking as usual."

My cheeks are flaming red hot now. "Thanks. You look nice, too."

Out of nowhere, Alexander walks up, slapping Avelino assertively on the back. Just in time to rescue me.

"Good to see you, AV," says Alexander.

"You, too, Alex." He offers his hand and they shake like teenage boys do, making simultaneous shapes with their fingers and using every part of their arms and side bodies, ending in a "woah!" from both of them.

"How did your exams kick off today?" Alexander asks.

"I think I did OK." Avelino smiles at me and something in his eyes makes me feel like one of his Percenters' powers might be telepathy.

If that's the case, I'm in trouble because there is no way I can stop thinking about his lips, his eyes, those bulging biceps! Even if he can't, it was a good reminder that someone might be able to. I cloak my thoughts preventing him and everyone else from being able to read my mind. It took practicing with Mom all night, but I finally figured it out.

She said it would come in handy during the exams. She also said it will come in handy with boys one day, but I suspect she wasn't thinking today. I guess it doesn't really matter. I can't risk anyone peeking into my head. Anyone could be a new enemy so everyone has to be kept at an arm's length.

"I'm sure you did really well, Avelino," I add to the conversation. I try to keep the attention away from me and redirect the conversation to Alexander who is usually happy to steal the attention.

"Alex thinks he did extremely well. Don't you brother?"

"Ah-hem!" Alexander says. "Wowza! I mean, holy bananas! Who is that sexy woman over there?" Completely ignoring me.

I look in the direction Alexander is starring. I don't see any exceptionally looking women, but I do see one of, if not the most, gorgeous men I have ever seen. Tall with black hair and soft brown skin, he could be AV's older brother. He is dressed in a handsomely tailored tux and from where I'm standing,

it appears that he's wearing an unusual ring on his right hand. Most guys don't wear jewelry of any kind, but especially not on their hands. Still, he is stunningly attractive. There is something about him drawing more glances than just mine.

"Who is that gorgeous women? Come on, you have to know! She is absolutely beautiful!" Alexander says.

I scan the room again in the direction he's facing.

"I don't see any beautiful girls, Alex," I tell him. "So, settle down your hormones." I think about mentioning the attractive man on the stage, but I don't want Avelino to think I'm interested in someone else.

"Are you blind, Jena?" asks Alex. He leans and raises his arm directly in front of my face. "Her. Over there!" He uses his finger to serve as a direct line to the person he is referring to, "in that stunning long dress is probably the most beautiful girl I've ever seen. How can you not see her? I think you need glasses, Jena! She's got some massive ring on her finger. The kind every girl dreams about."

"What are you talking about? You are pointing at a guy," I say. "I promise you. I know the difference." I laugh slightly, my cheeks reddening as I turn to Avelino.

Avelino looks towards the object of both our affections and grins. "You are both right. I take it this must be your first time seeing Hayden? Jena, what you and Alex don't realize is that Hayden possesses the power of desire."

"Power of desire? Hayden?" both Alexander and I say simultaneously.

"Yes, that means that whomever we desire is who Hayden will appear to be to each of us," Avelino explains. "Believed to be the most powerful Percenter power in the world, Hayden looks differently to each person depending on what attracts them. For example, I see a strikingly beautiful blonde woman…"

I stare at his mouth as he continues talking.

"Desire, however, cannot create actual love, that would be impossible. But it does cause a, how do I say this, a powerful obsession or infatuation. For that reason alone, Hayden is probably the most dangerous person in this room, not just the most powerful. This kind of power over people can make almost anyone do almost anything. No one knows if Hayden is actually male or a female because everyone sees Hayden as a reflection of what they desire, never Hayden in true form. So, Alex, you might see a beautiful girl where, Jena, you might see a tall, dark, and handsome man, or not. I don't presume to know your desires." Flirtatiously winking at me.

"Oh. Definitely women!" Chimes in Alexander. "Definitely women!'

I don't say anything to confirm or deny Avelino's assumptions. Especially since Hayden looks like a slightly older version of Avelino to me. They could almost be twins they look so similar.

"Wow, that's an incredibly useful power. I've never heard of it," I say.

"But that's not all. Hayden is an Oracle," Avelino continues.

"What kind of Oracle?" asks Alexander.

"Hayden is someone who can predict the future," says Avelino. "Who has visions of what is to come. Hayden serves as the Percenter's main Oracle. A role created to help guide our society down the right path, so they say."

"Oh yeah," I added, "I read about this. The power of the Oracle has always come from one family bloodline. It's something to do with the way the elixir manifested in one of the founding chancellors.

No one outside of their bloodline has ever had the power to see the real future with such accuracy. It is foretold that the Oracle will one day be instrumental in determining the future of the Percenter society. The story goes something like this. There will be a great war and the Oracle, seeing the future as if both sides had won, chooses the winning side, and helps them defeat the opposition victoriously. It is the Oracle who ultimately wins the war."

Pausing with a deep breath before I continue, "It's amazing," I say. "But I don't know if I'd want that kind of power. You know, to determine the future of everyone! That's a big responsibility." I half joke.

"Right! So much power. You know, they say that only a Percenter who has reached a certain level of mastery over their own powers can truly see Hayden for who or what she truly is, but so far no one has lived to tell the tale!" says Avelino with that sexy laugh.

"Well at least we know you see Hayden as a female," Alexander jokes.

"What does the Oracle look like to you?" I ask. Deflecting from my brother's ridiculousness.

"Why she looks exactly like you, Jenavieve!" he says. He looks at me and smiles big. Then he turns to Alex and does one of those head-nods guys do to affirm each other.

"Nice. I'm going to use that one AV. You're too clever for your own good," says Alexander, laughing. "But, hey, if everyone desires Hayden," says Alexander. "I think I'll move on. Not to be rude, but I don't need competition, to many options without," says Alex. He glances to his right. Raquel lingers nearby. He winks at me and Avelino. I know he will be devastated if he and Raquel do not get into the same Prep school. But I also know he'll get over this crush and move on to another girl in no time.

"You're excused." I laugh lightly, but my laugh is hollow and not carefree.

Avelino yells behind Alexander as he walks away, "Never underestimate the power of desire my friend!" Alexander moves towards Raquel and they soon engage in lively conversation.

Taking my hand in his, Avelino asks "If I can turn your attention away from Hayden for just a moment, can you promise to save a dance for me later?"

His fingers are long, yet strong. The fingers of the musician I remember his parents parading in-front of guests at every party. I always felt bad for Avelino, but he didn't seem to mind.

I would have been horrified if my parents made me perform in front of strangers. I wonder if he still plays the piano. I hope so. I look up at him, noting his eyes are more the color of emeralds than brown in this light. "I'd like to catch up on all the latest," he continues. "It's been awhile since I've seen you."

"Of course. I'd like that." I suddenly feel self-conscious, wondering how my hair looks…wondering if he likes my dress…wondering about everything. I feel stupid for worrying about these petty things. In a couple of days, none of this will even matter. No one will be looking at me for those reasons anyway.

The orchestra begins playing and suddenly parents crowd through the entrance of the ballroom and begin looking for their sons or daughters.

"I guess we'll have to catch up later," says Avelino. "I have to go find my mom and dad. Don't forget our dance!"

I smile as big as I can, showing teeth but not too much teeth like Rose showed me, and watch as he drifts away looking for his parents. No words escape my mouth.

"Hi, Jena."

I turn and there's my cousin, Jezebel.

"Oh. Hi, Jezebel," I respond curtly. "How are you?"

"Me? I'm fabulous, Jena. Really fabulous. It's been so long since I've seen you!" Jezebel says. "Where's your brother?"

"Alex?" I pause for a split second thinking the world knows I have two brothers. "He's talking to some girls, I think. How's Crystal Sky?"

"I'm so glad you asked. It's soooooo much nicer than San Sun. I mean, San Sun is fine and all, but I just feel like Crystal is just more…you know…" and she lowers her voice to finish her brag, "sophisticated! You know, with technology and stuff. Of course, I plan on getting into Stillstone, duh, so I guess San Sun will have to do for a while. At least until I meet a dashing young Percenter, get married, and move back to Crystal."

Jezebel thinks she is the most beautiful creature alive. Yes, she's attractive, with long red hair and porcelain skin. But there are dozens of girls who look better than her. I can't stand her arrogance or her nasally tone when she talks. She'll definitely be a mean girl at whichever school she attends. I guess that's one silver lining. The thing I dislike most about her is the way she disowned Ben. I could never, would never do that to Alex. No matter what.

"By the way, since you asked," I say snarkily, "your brother, Ben, remember him? Yeah, he's doing great at our house," I continue, unrelentingly sarcastic, throwing my hands on my hips. Reminding her that she has a brother and that she's not the only one who can throw shade!

"Oh…um…really?" Jezebel frowns. "That's good." Jezebel looks around nervously. It's clear Jezebel has no interest in discussing Ben. As if Ben's name was never mentioned, she continues. "Oh, Jena, pray tell, who is that gorgeous young man over there?" She points to a tall, curly blonde-headed guy who's standing in a corner of the room by himself.

I roll my eyes and decide it's probably easier to just play her game and let her move on. "That's James Bellini," I say. "He's from Grand View. Would you like me to introduce you?"

"Oh, would you?" asks Jezebel. "That would be so cool. He's simply darling. Is he from a Hundred-Percenter family?"

"I don't know, does that matter?" I say, trying hard not to give her a look of complete and utter disgust. "He is very smart and super sweet. Jez. You couldn't go wrong with him." I say this wanting to get rid of her, but hoping she doesn't take me up on it. James is just such a nice guy. I wouldn't want her to taint him.

"Ooooh, look at that one!" Jezebel points to another candidate in the corner, also standing by himself. He must be at least six feet tall and is extremely thin with soft brown curls falling around his face. He's actually unassumingly handsome.

"That's Trevor Fitch," I tell her.

"I might have to go introduce myself to him," Jezebel says. "He is the most beautiful boy I've seen here so far! He must be a Hundred-Percenter looking like that!"

"I think he prefers boys, Jez" I tell her. I raise an eyebrow. "Or maybe not. Why don't you go find out?"

"Really? Just my luck!" she says. "What's a girl to do when all the gorgeous ones are gay?"

"Just go introduce yourself to Trevor," I tell her. "Maybe you'll turn lesbian and be paired for co-ing" I continue to display a smug smile, hoping she will just go away.

"What's co-ing?" She asks innocently enough.

"You know, when gay men and lesbian women decide to co-parent a child together. But I guess you wouldn't know much about that. It's more common in San Sun and Grand View. I think Crystal Sky attracts a different kind of gay and lesbian. Ones who are more focused on their careers than..." I pause for effect, alluding to how wrong her family is for disowning Ben. "...raising a family."

"Hmmm, we do like to focus on our careers in Crystal. Well, maybe I'll meet him later, but I really don't think I'll be lesbian. So, tell me this. Do you know if James Bellini is gay or not?"

"I don't think he is," I say. "But don't take my word for it. I can't speak for everyone, but James keeps looking your way. That's a good indication he's not if you ask me."

"Well, what are we waiting for? Take me to him, Jena." She flips her hair back on her shoulders and sucks in her cheeks to give her face a sultry look. She is desperate to be seen and recognized as a woman of high stature. At sixteen she's already a social climber. Something I'm sure her parents are praying for after Ben.

"Sure, c'mon," I tell her.

Jezebel follows me as we head over to James. He's handsome with mysterious eyes beneath his black-framed glasses. He looks up with a smile on his face, happy to see me.

"Hi, Jena, how are you?" His smile shows his brilliantly white teeth.

"Good, James. How about you?"

"I'm doing very well if I do say so myself." Stumbling over his words. He's either nervous or just awkward.

"I'd like to introduce you to my cousin, Jezebel Stillstone. She's from Crystal Sky."

"Hi, James," says Jezebel, batting her fake long eyelashes obnoxiously.

"Nice to meet you, Jezebel." He takes her right hand and brings it to his lips and kisses it lightly. Jezebel swoons, slightly.

"Jena tells me that you live in Grand View. I've actually never been. I'd love to learn about it," says Jezebel.

"Sure, what would you like to know?"

I can see that James likes her too, so I decide to leave.

"Look, I'll let you all talk while I go and find my brother," I tell them. "Talk to you later!"

"Sure, Jena," says Jezebel. "See you later."

"Bye, Jena, see you soon!" James adds but his eyes are fixed on Jezebel.

I quickly move away from them and look for other friends, anyone really.

I walk out of the ballroom and back to the butterflying staircase in the main entrance. I don't know why, but I started up the stairs. Once I get to the top, I hear voices in a room down the hall, both male and female. Whoever it is, they are speaking in excitable tones, almost fighting. Curious about who's there, I make my steps as light as possible and walk quietly towards the room.

"Did you hear that they're going to be really strict this year, and some people, even those with limited Percenter powers will be demoted to Middler status?"

I stop in the hallway. These voices are coming from a room to the left. I recognized one of the voices as Reece Davenport. We met at a dance last year, and he has this unusually raspy voice for a teenage boy, very distinguishable.

"How do you know?" The question comes from a girl's voice I'm unable to place.

"I can't say," he says.

"But the rules for the exams have been the same for years." the girl says. "They can't just change now and start doing whatever they want. Percenters are people with powers, so if you have even just a little power, you are one of us. It's the others that don't belong!"

"I know," says Reece. "But I'm telling you, I've been hearing things. Things about population control and what not. You know what I mean Rebekah?"

'Rebekah? Who could that be?" I wondered.

"Oh, that's just ridiculous," says Rebekah. "You've been hearing lies, Reece."

"Mmm, I don't know," says Reece. "I've also heard rumors that some of the Barrens are secretly being kidnapped from the Pods and left on the Ground to die. Apparently, there isn't enough food for all of them in the pods. The air is so toxic they die after just a few minutes of excruciating pain!" He makes a choking sound as if he's pretending he can't breathe.

"No! That can't be true either! You're making this stuff up, Reece Davenport," Rebekah says.

"Shhh. Promise me you won't say anything about what I just said," Reece says.

"I don't believe you for one minute, you crazy goose. I'll be quiet...for a kiss!" Rebekah laughs.

For a while, I hear nothing, so I assume they're making out. I have to agree with Rebekah. Even though our society has its problems, what Reece told her is a bit ludicrous. It's one thing to outcast citizens to lower levels of society because they have no super human powers, but to leave them on the Ground to die is a totally different kind of cruelty.

Even after everything I've learned in the last forty-eight hours, I just can't believe that it's true. I can't allow myself. And plus, the Barrens grow all of our food so if we have food, they should have food too. Reece's story doesn't make sense. He's probably just trying to impress Rebekah.

My attention is directed to another set of voices from a room at the far end of the hall. There whispers are much lower than Reece and Rebekah, which makes me even more curious. I creep towards that room looking to uncover more mysteries.

"Young lady, where do you think you're going?" a booming voice rings out behind me.

I'm startled, and the voice makes me jump an inch off the ground.

I turned around abruptly and see a security guard standing there with his hands on his hips. A posture I'm sure he feels makes him much bigger and stronger than me.

"Oh, I'm sorry, sir," I apologize. "I was just looking for the bathroom. Do you know where one is?"

"Hmph," he growls. "There are several on the first floor, next to the ballroom. Where you should be." He stands there, hands firmly on his hips, glaring at me.

"Sure, sure," I say. "No problem. I'll just go back downstairs."

I make my way back to the staircase. I can feel my cheeks are flaming red but I try to play it off. I feel like a child who has been reprimanded, scolded for taking too many cookies. I try to put it out of my mind but now I'm even more curious about the missed conversation I started to overhear. I start down the marble staircase, determined to find Alexander or any familiar, friendly face in the crowd.

"I know what you're doing," a male's voice speaks low behind me, almost a whisper.

I whip around. A stranger stands before me. I have never seen this boy before. He's paper-thin with skinny arms and legs—just a facsimile of a boy, really. His jet-black hair is swept up high on his head with straight sharp edges. It gives him a strange, wild appearance. He's dressed in the same suit as Alexander so it's obvious he's a candidate.

"What do you mean?" I ask, throwing back my shoulders defensively.

"I know who you are, and I know what you're doing," the boy says. There's something menacing about him. He has sharp, almost pointed teeth and a scowl on his face. But the scariest thing about his face are his eyes. They're dark and the pupil looks more slanted than circular, like a reptile. He looks at me as if he is about to attack and suck the blood right out of me like a vampire. I turn back down the stairs and continue walking away from him.

"I didn't know the second floor was off-limits," I say as I walk away. "I didn't hurt anything." Something about him is just...off. I pick up my pace.

"I'm not talking about that," he says. "I know what you're planning."

My heart falls to the floor. There is no way he could know anything. I barely know what I'm doing. But the fear of *what if* creeps into my mind. If anyone even accused me of cheating the exams, I'd be found guilty by the Chancellors, and they would have no choice but to take immediate action. There are too many members of the Cleansing Coalition that would know exactly what I was attempting to do if they caught wind. My parents, even Alex, would be persecuted alongside me to set an example.

"And just who are you?" I try to act confident so he doesn't know I'm afraid of him.

"You won't get away with it, Jena" he says. He balls up his fists. They look like little rubber erasers on the ends of a pencil.

I stop abruptly and face him. "Look, I don't know what you think you know, but I'm not doing anything wrong. You have me confused with someone else." I say. "Now, if you'll excuse me, my friends are waiting for me." Maybe if he thinks I'm with a bunch of people he'll leave me alone.

I turn back down the stairs and start walking away from him for the second time. He grabs me by the wrist and holds it so tight, it hurts. "Look, J…e…n…a…vieve, you're getting in over your head. Remember, this is your one warning. Next time it won't be a warning but someone getting hurt!"

"Let me go, you brute, or I'll scream." I struggle, but I can't free myself. Of course, there is a security guard to keep me from using the bathroom but not to save me from this nut job.

"Remember, I warned you." He let's go of my wrist and disappears back up the stairs, no security guard stopping him.

I just stand there, rubbing my wrist, too shocked to move. The night has just taken a turn for the worse. First, I saw weirdly morphing black-robed shapes that disappeared into thin air. Then I hear Reece and Rebekah whispering about a plot by someone, or multiple someone's, to murder innocent people. Next, I'm reprimanded for going to the second floor. And now I'm being threatened by a strange boy with beady red vampire eyes! I have no idea who he is, but he definitely gave me the chills. After all, he threatened me. I admit it, he rattled me a little. Maybe he's right. Maybe I am in over my head. I don't even know what I'm supposed to do next.

I am absolutely relieved and thrilled when I see Alexander coming my way. He's holding Raquel's hand. "Hey, Jena! Remember Raquel?"

I deeply exhale and look at my brother, fully expecting him to read my mind. If he could, he would hear me say, "Really Alex? As if we weren't just talking about her?" Seriously?" But instead, I say, "Of course I remember Raquel. How are you?" I lean in to give her a gentle hug and kiss on both cheeks.

"Nice to see you again, Jenavieve."

"You, too, Raquel."

I can see why Alexander is so enamored with her. She's truly beautiful. She has sparkling turquoise eyes, dimples, freckles, and long brown curly and bouncy hair. There are so few Percenters with those same recessive features.

"What did you think of day one of our big exams?" asks Raquel.

"They weren't quite what I expected," I respond. "But they were interesting to say the least."

"My sentiments exactly," Raquel says, winking at me

Before we can say anything further, I see my parents rushing towards me and Alex.

"Darlings, there you are!" Mother hugs me and Alexander as if she hadn't seen us in years.

"Hello, Mother," says Alexander. "May I present to you Ms. Raquel Hawthorn, the most beautiful women in the Sky Cities!"

Rachel's cheeks turn crimson.

Without thinking, I say, "Really, Alex? Laying it on a bit thick now, aren't you?"

Mother gives me a look of disappointment and then turns towards Raquel. "Of course! Hello, Raquel. How are you, dear?"

"Just fine, Mrs. de Fenace'." She turns around to my father. "And hello, Mr. de Fenace'. It's nice seeing both of you again."

My father smiles simply and nods in Raquel's direction, acknowledging her comments.

"You look lovely, Raquel," my mother says.

"Thank you. And you...of course...I mean, as well." She looks around the room. "Now that parents are arriving, I must go and find mine. Please excuse me." Raquel says, almost bowing as she curtsied. It's actually really adorable.

Clearly she feels about Alexander the same way he feels about her and wants to make the right impression on my parents. Maybe Raquel could be the one that actually steals my brother's heart someday. I guess I wouldn't hate it if she did. My parents, on the other hand, might disagree.

"Alright," says Alex, "Save a dance for me?"

"Of course. I wouldn't have it any other way." Raquel grins. She accidentally catches my parent's eyes and quickly looks away, slightly embarrassed. She has a deep dimpled smile that lights up her whole face. As if she's floating on air, she turns and walks away.

Yup, totally wouldn't hate it!

The moment Raquel is outside of earshot, "Oh be still my heart!" Alexander says in an exaggerated, theatrical manner as he clutches his heart with one hand while reaching for her with the other.

"Give it a rest," I say, trying to be lighthearted. "You're going to have all the girls eating out of your hand by the time the exams are over."

"But Raquel is the only one for me!"

"Son, Raquel is sweet, but you're too young to think about your one and only right now," Mother says with a smile. In truth, she'd be happy if Alexander settled down sooner than later. I think she's a bit worried that Alex will never pick just one girl. But really, she knows our world isn't going to stay like it is for long and it might be easier for Alexander if he isn't in love. A loved one is always a vulnerable spot or weakness an enemy can exploit. I'm sure mother just wants what is best for Alex.

"How did day one go?" Father asks a bit nervously. Although I know he's concerned for Alexander, too, his question is clearly intended for me.

I pause, my mouth slightly ajar as if I'm intending to speak.

"Wonderful!" says Alex, saving me from going first. "Trippy with all the visuals inside these pod-like capsules, but weirdly wonderful. And it's been so much fun seeing old friends..." He pauses, winking at Dad while his eyes follow a cute girl who is clearly staring back. He continues, "And...making some new ones!"

"It's been an interesting day, to say the least," I jump in. "And yes, it's fun seeing old friends. I didn't think we would get to see you tonight."

"Well, it's not sanctioned that you keep your exams a secret, but at the same time, it's frowned upon to discuss your actual experiences," Father says. He frowns himself as if to demonstrate. "That being said, the reason parents are allowed to attend tonight's gala is to give you one chance to ask questions. After tonight, we won't see you again until the..." Stumbling a bit, my father continues, "The ceremony."

I look at Alex, raising my eyebrows. As soon as we left our parents at the Grand Reception, we agreed to do the exams our way, on our own terms, and that included leaving our parents in the dark at least until it was over.

"We'll learn our scores soon," I remind him. Signaling to Alexander that I am keeping my word, and he needs to as well.

Alexander excuses himself to go talk to some guys I have never met. He's so good at making friends. I wish we could trade shoes sometimes. Father does the same. It must be a male de Fenace' trait.

Mother motions for me to take a walk so we can talk privately. "Honey, how was it...really?" Her eyes squint together, and she searches for my face.

"It was fine." I don't want to say too much. "I-I...think."

"What do you mean, you think?"

"I'm just rattled a bit. Some kid approached me a little bit ago and told me that he knew what I was doing and that he was warning me to be careful or someone is going to get hurt."

The blood immediately drains from Mother's face.

"Did you recognize him, or do you know his name?" she asks.

"No, but he was scary looking, Mom," I say. "Evil, really. He had these weird eyes that when the light hit just right, looked red. Do you have any idea who it could have been? He's gotta be my age because he's dressed like a candidate."

"We were afraid of this happening. There have been rumors that the Cleansing Coalition has been recruiting families in the Sky Cities for some time now; probably as long as we have been planning this rebellion. They are breeding hatred and using our own government's laws against us to defend their actions. He could be a spy. Just like we have you. They've been trying to breach our group for years, unsuccessfully. It's possible that someone's son has refined his powers to seek out our savior, you!" Mother looks more than worried. She looks frantic! And a bit desperate! "Or he might be trying to scare everyone the same way to see who he can rattle the most. Just in case, you need to stay cloaked at all times."

"Don't worry, Mom, I can handle this," I assure her. "Please, don't worry. I only mentioned it because I thought you might know who he is."

"Can you point him out to me?" she asks.

"I don't remember much about his face other than those weird eyes. But if I see him, I'll let you know. I won't be able to forget those eyes."

Father walks up and joins our conversation.

Mother nods in his direction. "Darling, I worry that your father and I have placed a terrible burden on your shoulders. This is so dangerous, more than we may have realized." She looks around quickly to make sure no one can hear us.

"Based on what you guys told me, I don't think we have a choice," I say. "And this is my decision, you gave me a choice. It's no longer on you. If I don't do this, Mom, more people are going to die! Innocent people will die." I look around, my arms open to the lavish lifestyle we Percenters enjoy. "It's exactly how you said, the way Middlers and Barrens are being treated is unforgivable. People without powers are still people!" I confirm for both of my parents that I am on board. That I am going to fight this as long and hard as I possibly can.

Mother nods. "Did your tests today reveal any new powers?"

"I don't know, really. I'm not totally sure what exactly happened. But something interesting did happen" I pause, making sure no one is close enough to hear me "I met Xavier."

"What?" My father's eyes grow wide with alarm. "You...met...Xavier? B-b-but, aren't all of your cognitive thoughts recorded?" he stutters. "What if he's discovered by the Proctors? Or worse, the Coalition?" Dad acts as if saying the Cleansing Coalition will automatically make them appear. Maybe it would. What do I know?

"Don't worry. I cloaked, or I think I cloaked."

"What did he say?" Mother wrings her hands, then clasps her fingers together. "Is he alright? How does he look?"

"He seemed alright. He basically just introduced himself. That's really all the time we had. He didn't want the proctors to see him, so we spoke telepathically. I think I protected him...I think. But the odd thing is—"

"What, honey? What was it?" Mother interrupts me, her brows furrowed as if every word that came out of my mouth was going to be a game changer.

"He was...he wasn't a boy. He was a..." I can't help but look around the room, as if I was expecting to see him "a statue of a boy with a jaguar's face."

My mother faints and falls to the floor.

Chapter 10

Father immediately leans down to help mother.

"Mom! Mom!" I scream as I fall to my knees and cradle my mother's head in my lap. People begin to cluster around us, asking what's wrong.

"I'm alright," Mother says as she comes to. She sits up. She expels a simple laugh to dissuade the onlookers from asking any questions. "I just think I need some food."

A Middler quickly brings a towel and a glass of water for my mother. Dad takes them and offers the water to Mom. She takes a sip.

"Honestly, I'm alright, Abe. I think it's just a bit stuffy in here."

Out of the corner of my eye, I see the Vampire Eyes kid over to my left. I quickly look and notice he's laughing, a calculated and methodical laugh. Staring directly at me. I want to wring his neck, but I'm frozen.

I try to tell my mom that the weird eyes guy is over there, but I can't bring myself to say it. I blink my eyes rapidly before I close them hoping to erase him from my sight. I pretend he's gone by not looking in that direction. I don't want to upset her any further.

Father helps Mother to stand up and compose herself. After satisfying their curiosity about Lady Annabelle fainting, the crowd disperses and heads to the Grand Dining Hall where dinner is being served.

"C'mon, Mom, let's get something to eat," I say and put my arm through hers. Dad takes her other arm and we head to the dining room. We sit together at a table that's covered with white silk tablecloths, napkins, and sterling silver. Servers begin bringing endless plates of food, one after the other. Mother, Father, and I are quiet as we eat. Still unable to read any minds other than Alex's, I'm too afraid to ask either of them what they are thinking. Alexander finally joins us, bubbling with excitement and smiles as usual. Exactly what the three of us needed to lighten the mood before we find out our scores from Day one.

The flags for each of the prep schools are positioned throughout the dining room. A magnificent turquoise flag represents Briarsley Prep University, the largest school with manicured quads, majestic brick buildings and endless fields for athletics. Most candidates expect to get into Briarsley because it represents the school with the most common of powers and skills. But if you asked any one of us, no one would say they *hoped* to get into Briarsley over one of the other prep schools.

A crimson flag represents Stillstone Prep, and it is by far the most prestigious socially of all the schools. Crimson represents the wealth associated with most Percenters that graduate from Stillstone.

Lavender is the color of the flag for Freelinn Prep. It is considered to be more intellectual than the other schools. Candidates with the most advanced powers tend to go to Freelinn. But even if you qualify for Freelinn, you can still choose one of the other schools if you wanted.

One of the moderators, a man with too much product in his hair and a dark suit that's too tight and revealing a pudgy stomach, introduces himself as Elliot, and begins addressing the room.

"Welcome, candidates and parents." Elliott carries a grandiose air about himself as he speaks to the room. "Candidates, you have now come of age and have started to activate your powers. A person with access to at least thirty percent of their brain's cortex unlocks the ability to have superhuman powers known as Percenter powers. A score of fifty percent is required to attend Stillstone Prep. And sixty percent is required for Freelinn Prep. All other candidates unlocking over thirty percent will be admitted to Briarsley Preparatory. These percentages are based on the percentage of the school's namesake's powers.

"However," Elliott continues, "as you know, if you do not pass your exams with the minimum to attend Briarsley, you will be sent to the Ground or, if you are lucky, you will serve as a Middler."

There is unrest throughout the dining room as people begin to squirm uncomfortably. No one wants to go to the Ground. And no parent wants their child to be sent there.

"And now, candidates, good luck and *may your powers surpass all others before you!*" Elliot concludes.

You could hear a pin drop in the dining room as everyone anxiously waits to hear their name or their child's name being called. Elliot may not be that much to look at, but he sure knows how to create suspense that can capture everyone's attention. If the orchestra was in this room, there would undoubtedly be a drumroll at this moment.

"In first place, Alexander de Fenace'!" Elliot finally exclaims. The room erupts with cheers and excitement.

"I don't believe it! Jenavieve de Fenace' is second!" Elliot cheers and the room continues screaming in my honor. I was hoping to be more in the middle of the crowd not wanting to draw any unnecessary attention, but even though I am a bit embarrassed to have my name being shouted, it does feel good to score so high! Even Jessica Piston seems proud and gives me a nod that I take to mean as "Well done." I wish I could say the same for her. Jessica was one of the last few names called.

As usual, no candidates fell below the line on Day One and everyone scored the minimum points to move forward. If your score falls below the line at the end of the exam, you are at risk of being Barrened and kicked out of the Sovereign Sky forever. Tomorrow is when we can expect to see the first couple candidates in trouble. While I don't want to be top again tomorrow, I definitely don't want to be below the line!

All the parents are escorted out after the announcement of the last few scores. My parents hug me and Alexander. They wish us well.

"We'll be here on the final day to hear all the scores. Good luck you two!" Father says.

"Good luck, my darling," Mother says before she leaves.

I nearly choke up with tears, but I compose myself. This is not going to be easy.

All the candidates head into the Ballroom for an evening dance. There is a full orchestra playing classical music. The music is more heavenly than anything I have ever heard before, yet my heart really isn't in the mood for dancing.

I don't know why, but Jessica lingers at my side.

"Are you alright?" I ask her.

"You heard them call my scores, right?" she asks me.

"Um...yes, I heard."

"Then you know. I'm worried," she says. "That's all."

"There's no need to worry," I try to be supportive. "I'm sure you'll do much better tomorrow."

The Vampire Eyes kid lingers in a corner to the right of the room.

"Hey, Jess, can you look in that corner over there. Do you know who he is?" I ask her, nodding towards the corner.

Jessica looks and thinks for a moment. "I believe his name is Hunter. Hunter Sebring, I think," she says. "He's bad news, Jena. You want to stay away from him. He's the last of his Hundred- Percenter bloodline and is a complete jerk. I've heard he's pretty antisocial and weirdly secretive. Basically, a freak. But apparently his family are old friends with the Riley family, maybe Avelino knows him. He graduated like four or five years ago, I think."

"Why's he here and wearing the same outfit as a candidate then?" I ask, a little annoyed.

Jessica shrugs her shoulders. "Hanging on to his youth maybe?"

"He's totally creepy," I say.

"That's an understatement," says Jessica. "I've heard that his dad, Marcus, can jump into people's thoughts. And you never know, Hunter might be just like him!"

"I guess I'll stay away from him at all cost." I don't tell her that Hunter has already approached me with an off the wall threat. The less I share with Jessica, the better.

Avelino approaches us. "There you are!" he says. "Are you ready for that dance, Jena?"

I look at Jessica. For some reason, I feel bad for her and don't want to leave her alone.

"Go," she says. "Have some fun, I'm fine. Seriously. Go!"

I'm surprised to find that I'm actually liking her.

I turn to Avelino and smile brightly. "Alright, I'm all yours."

The orchestra plays a piece from Beethoven, and the crowd thins out on the dance floor. Most of the candidates prefer current music. But I like the romantics from the past. But right now, I'll take any song that allows me to be closer to Avelino.

Avelino wraps his big arms around me and holds me close for a waltz. I can hear his heartbeat. I lean in closer. He smells of lavender, which makes me smile. It reminds me of playing in the gardens amongst the flowers in the springtime. I wish I could stay in his arms forever, or at least through the night.

"You're trembling," he says. He leans back a little and looks into my face. "Is everything OK, Jena?"

"I'm just tired," I say. I look up at him and his eyes sparkle an emerald green.

"I know what you mean," he says. "The exams are…intimidating."

"Avelino," I say, "do you ever wonder about all of this? What it's really for?"

"What do you mean?"

"You know…do you ever wonder about why we separate Percenters from Middlers and Middlers from Barrens…you know, anyone who fails the exams. No power sorta thing. You know?"

"Sometimes," he says. "But it's not really our place to worry about those things. It's for the Chancellors. We'll be in charge someday, but not today!"

"You're right," I say. "We're young and should just enjoy life."

I don't know If I brought this up because I was feeling bad for Jessica, or myself. I know it's dangerous to talk about…even to Avelino, someone I think I can trust.

"You know something, Jena?" he whispers in my ear. His breath is hot on my cold neck.

"What?" My heart is beating a little too fast.

"I think we should forget about all our worries and just focus on dancing. Right?"

I have to smile. "I think you're right. Thank you AV."

I lean back into his shoulder and enjoy the moment. I swear, I think I can hear his heart beating fast, too. I close my eyes, enjoying the simultaneous movements in his arms for as long as I can.

Minutes later when I open them again, the same shadowy hooded figures appear in my peripheral vision again. Every time I see them, they are sneaking in the corners of my eyesight, as if they're trying to watch me undetected. Just as fast as I saw them, they disappeared. For a split second I almost asked Avelino if he saw them too but I can't risk him finding out about me. I especially don't need him thinking I see ghosts when nobody else seems to see these hooded figures.

Avelino and I keep dancing, cheek to cheek as if nothing is unusual. Every now and then I catch a glimpse of Hunter lurking in and around the shadows. He seems to be taunting me; more like stalking me. Maybe that's part of his ploy to catch me off guard. I focus to ensure my cloaking is working. I need to make sure Hunter doesn't hear or feel my thoughts. Jessica could be right, and he might have inherited some telepathy powers from his father.

Chapter 11

I wake up after one of the worst nights of sleep in my life to Day Two of the exams. I try to remember my dreams from last night, but they're sketchy at best. Red vampire eyes, mysterious hooded stalkers, jaguars, and Avelino. My mind reaches to tease yesterday's reality from last night's visions.

In one dream, I was running down a cobblestone path and someone or something was hunting me. In another, Avelino was pleading with me, "Don't go! Please don't go, Jena! It's not safe!"

Needless to say, I'm still tired. I wake up early, eager to get this day over. I'm in a dorm room where there are no windows, and I have no Buzz to wake me with a pleasant view. It doesn't matter, really. I must focus, anyway, on the exam. It's going to be even more challenging than yesterday.

The trick for me is to be able to experience all parts of the exams so my full powers will be activated, but not traced. Today and tomorrow, I can't score as high as yesterday. I didn't mind passing Day One with flying colors–even though I hated being celebrated as having one of the highest scores. But if my departure from the exams is going to be believable, I can't be ranked as one of the more powerful candidates. Of course, Alexander would think I was crazy if he knew what I was doing. And Avelino would probably think that I have betrayed everything Percenters stand for. Our people. Our purpose. No doubt about it, I will indeed betray the sanctity of the exams with a heavy heart. But only because I know what the exams are truly about, oppressing humans without Percenter powers. Once Alexander and Avelino learn this to be true, I don't think they will consider me a traitor. At least I hope not. My heart aches a little knowing that I'll be disappointing Avelino, and he won't really know why. I don't want to think about what failure would look like staring into Avelino's eyes.

We're all wearing our white bodysuits like we did yesterday. In our dining room, I gulp down a rather bland vanilla protein shake while my fellow candidates eat a hearty breakfast of bacon, eggs, fruits, breads, and cereals. I can't stomach a lot of food early in the day. And even though my protein shake is bland, in comparison, it's exactly what I want. Everyone is quiet. No whispers or conversation to fill the room. It appears that I'm not the only one inside their own head today. I think the reality of the importance of the exams starts to hit everyone at the same time.

After breakfast, we're escorted to a different building than the one we were in yesterday. The building we're headed towards is a tall stone building with few windows. It's a nondescript office building with no defining characteristics at all. It's the kind of building you wished you never had to step foot in for fear of never getting out.

Jessica Piston walks quietly behind me. Her face is dark and pinched, as if she's terrified of what's coming next. I feel for her, really I do, but buck up, girl. It's time to be confident, not afraid. I smile as I hear my own advice.

"Right!" I murmur under my breath so no one can hear me.

Inside the building, we step into a massive room that has glowing white lights protruding from the ceiling. Instead of pods, there are cubicles stationed throughout the room. Monitors direct us to a designated cubicle. Today, my monitor's name is Kree.

"Good morning," Kree says. "I hope you're ready for a strenuous day."

"I am." I stand while she places numerous wires and electrodes on my forehead. "What are these for?" I ask.

"While you're going through this part of the exam we'll be able to record and assess your rhetorical and critical thinking skills." Kree is wearing bright red lipstick that makes her mouth look oversized and garish. She is probably about twenty-five years old, but the bright lipstick makes her look much older.

"What can I expect?" I ask.

"The first is actually synchronistic with yesterday's exam. And then Part Two of today's exam will link to the first part. They're all in synchronicity with one another. These exams build to Day Three—the one you'll be taking tomorrow." Kree looks at me sideways, her eyes tiny slits. "Only a select few will be chosen to participate in Part Two today, but you certainly will be one of them Ms. de Fenace'. I'm sure of that!" She ends with a schoolgirl giggle.

"Umm... You didn't really answer my question," I say to Kree under my breath.

"What's that, Jenavieve?" Kree says to me in response.

"Nothing. Never mind," I say back to her more audible.

What she's not saying that I already know is that Part Two is the Xapiri, spirit guide, test. Xapiri is one of the most unique and coveted powers. That's why they have a test specifically for it and exclusively for the candidates with the highest DNA/Elixir percentage in their blood. So, basically, it's a birthright.

It is believed no one can possess the power for an Xapiri without at least being a Seventy-Percenter. Xapiri gives you the ability to be anywhere at any time. You can teleport through time and space. Your Xapiri Spirit is the embodiment of your ancestors. Imagine what the Cleansing Coalition could do to the human race if they harnessed this power. It's too scary to think about.

"Most candidates have studied Cellular Memory with private tutors, and while you may not have recognized it in yesterday's exam, you experienced a bit of it already. Today's exam involves a great deal of Cellular Memory." She readjusts all the electrodes on my forehead to make sure they're securely fastened. "But not many candidates can recall the data stored in their cellular memory, their DNA. That's a special power."

"Yes," I say. "I know." What I don't explain is that I also learned Cellular Memory is the complete blueprint for our existence. Of course, with Percenters, there's much more to it than that because of the Elixir. At the very basic, Cellular Memory is an energetic expression of humans' bodies. The labels of mind, body and spirit are just representations of our multidimensional existence on earth.

However, because of the Elixir, the Percenter powers that defied science and natural law, were born. And thereafter, each cell harnessed the new altered DNA with the power of the Elixir. It is Cellular Memory that allow the power of the Elixir to pass from generation to generation, just as our DNA is passed on.

Kree smiles at me as if she just heard my thoughts. I again remind myself to be careful. Very careful. Everything I think could be used against me, or at the very least, expose me. I focus to cloak my thoughts, making them incomprehensible to anyone who tries to enter my mind.

Once Kree moves to the side I notice a lounge spanning the entire side of one wall. Three senior looking members of the exam Council sit behind a massive table covered in papers and binders stacked high. My mother would have flipped out if I ever let my desk get that messy. Two are elderly men and one is a middle-aged woman with white hair piled high on her head.

They look a bit odd to me. Almost like they don't belong or that they don't do well socially. Or more like they are...confused. My cousin Jezebel would call them dowdy-looking and immediately want to do beauty makeovers. But, apparently, based on the nameplates in front of each of them, they are each a distinguished professor from one of the Prep Schools. I guess it's made more obvious by their clothing, each in their school's unique colors.

So, for that, I'll pay them the respect they deserve. Plus, they most likely know my Father, so I have to play the good daughter role too. Regardless how disheveled and kooky they appear, I need them to like me. As judges, they have control over whether or not I'll be called for the Xapiri test.

The professor wearing dark-framed glasses and a mature handlebar moustache, asks me my first question, "Ms. de Fenace', I am Professor Kinsey from Stillstone Preparatory School." His tone is deep and raspy. Almost like he has a cold. He is probably one of the slowest talkers I have ever heard. I would definitely fall asleep during his lectures.

"Welcome, and let's begin. Could you explain the origins of the Percenter Society and the Sky Cities?"

I take a deep breath before I begin reciting everything my parents have taught me.

"Hundreds of years before the Great Ozone Event, humans were only able to access ten percent of their brain's capacity. Today, what defines a human is someone who can only activate up to twenty-five percent of their brain's capacity. A secret elixir, discovered in a remote region of the Southern Cascade Mountains, activated one hundred percent of the brain's cortex by removing neurological impingements and altering DNA. It afforded limitless potential of everyone who drank even a drop of it. This Elixir was shared amongst twelve people who discovered it and those twelve became the Founding Chancellors of a secret Percenter's Society.

I stop briefly to catch my breath.

Professor Kinsey quickly says, "Go on, Ms. de Fenace'. There is more is there not?"

I speed up my talking pace to get it all out before I have to take another breath. "The families who drank the Elixir soon manifested Percenter powers–superhuman powers that defied science and natural law for the human race. Each cell harnessed the new altered DNA with the power of the Elixir. Those who have the right percent of Elixir in their DNA are born with Percenter powers," I continue squeezing out my last bit of air. "The intensity of those powers vary from bloodline to bloodline. The most powerful members of our society are the Hundred-Percenters, direct descendants of the Founding Chancellors. We..." The Proctors are all smiling. Proud of me. Proud of our heritage.

I couldn't make it. I had to gasp quickly for more air to wrap it up with a slower pace to drive home my last point. "...as a Percenter Society, we have inherited the Elixir's powers through generations. It is an honor and a privilege to be a member of the Percenter Society," I conclude with a subtle but noticeable bow of the head.

"Great job, Ms. de Fenace'," says Professor Kinsey. "Clearly, you have studied our history books and know them well."

"Thank you," I say. I smile as authentically as I can muster. I know this is just a romanticized version of how our Percenter Society came to be, but I refrain from saying anything controversial about our evolution and who we have become today. Instead, I continue rambling about how the Secret Percenter Society formed the Sky Cities as a place for civilization to thrive and the Ground Pods for human survival, barely.

I was in the middle of talking about the Farm Pods when a bright flash almost knocks me over, my body jolts and like a ghost, I begin to float. But not all of me. My spirit or my consciousness starts to float out of my body. It feels like a parallel reality. The room transforms into a great library where the shelves are filled with books from floor to ceiling. I look back at the judges, they still see me standing before them, smiling, and discussing some boring rhetorical theories about the Sky Cities and their engineering and magical marvels.

I walk through the door on the opposite side of the room. The door slams behind me. I turn and reach for the handle to try and open it. The handle is gone. I look around and all I see is an empty desk, nothing more. A split second later, I suddenly find myself sitting at the desk. At first there is nothing else in the room, just me and a desk. Then I'm sitting in a chair at that desk that wasn't there a second ago.

I scan the room again and return my eyes to the top of the desk. There is a massive book with a worn leather cover and hand carved wooden bindings. The cover reads: Go! A Guide to Cellular Memory.

I open the book to find the first page empty. I flip through and quickly realize that all pages are empty. I close the book in frustration. Almost yelling, I speak directly to the book, "Are you serious? What the hell am I supposed to do now?"

I look around the empty room to see if I have missed anything, a clue to this book, or even a new object. The room is so expansive in every direction that it appears to be endless in the darkness. I open the book again to the first page and stare at it for a few moments longer. Nothing. What am I missing? I check the desk drawers. All empty.

I close my eyes to calm my mind and continue to talk to myself out loud, "No one is here. No one can hear me." Suddenly, the book opens and pages shuffle on their own. It lands on a blank page and the words "Passphrase Accepted" appear, and then disappear just as quickly. Images begin to appear, replacing the former text. The images get clearer and clearer. Vivid images of colors I have never seen before. I move my hand closer to touch the images on the page.

Just before I run my fingers across the ink, I feel the book pulling my hand towards it. I pull back a bit. Massaging my hand as if I were trying to warm it up, I stare back at the page. No words. No instructions. Nothing except these brilliant evolutions of a color prism appear. I bring my hand closer to the page and feel it pull me once again. I look around the room one more time.

Nothing. I decide to give in and place my entire palm in the center of the page. The book holds me close like a magnet would to metal.

I feel the pages wrap themselves around my fingers, then my hand. It's grasp becomes stronger. I decide not to fight it. I watch as my arm disappears into the book before I am completely swallowed. I feel warm, as if I was receiving one of my mom's morning hugs. I'm crossing into a different world. Definitely not the Sky Cities.

I don't know where it is, really. I don't recognize anything. It could be fake, like a fairytale. Or even some computer-generated reality. But I have this uneasy feeling that it's not a mythical land but…an actual place. Mysterious shadows pop-up in the corner of my eye, but every time I look in that direction, they are gone.

Grey clouds wisp across the sky and block the light of the moon that has now appeared. I'm surrounded by varying shades of black, unable to decipher any shape. Silver beams of light begin emanating from stars that cut through the clouds to reveal a structure in the distance, a castle .

In the time that it takes for a breath, I am suddenly at the base of the castle. I notice a myriad of turrets and windows set amidst snow-capped mountains and trees in the background. I climb the castle's winding steps with only the flicker of starlight on the stone walls lighting my way.

I'm taken back by the romantic setting. It's like every fairytale my parents ever read me. And just like in those stories, I feel this unrelenting need to continue forward to find my prince charming…no, to rescue him. I feel like he is my long lost love, yet I've never seen him. I don't even know his name.

But still, I must find him. My heart pounds as I run aimlessly through the castle. Fear creeps in as I slow my pace. Wind whispers around the corners, and I feel the need to step lightly. Then I notice him. He's standing on the other side of the room ascending the staircase.

"Wait!" I yell to him. "Wait! "Who are you?" I scream at the top of my lungs. Never able to see anything more than his back, my pace matches his as I begin the chase.

By the time I reach the top of the enormous staircase, he has vanished. In his place, the black-hooded demons who have been plaguing me. Directly in front of me, I can finally see them clearly. They begin running, no floating, towards me.

I think about escaping, being anywhere but here. And there's a snapping like a massive rubber band being pulled and released on the walls of the castle. I'm transported again. Utterly exhausted, I slowly walk down an avenue of vines to the edge of a vineyard and sit in the shade of an old fig tree.

It's dusk, but the day's sun still feels hot. I see the shadow of a young man in the distance. I perk up. I'm drawn to him like a curious cat. But who is he? Could it be the same guy from the castle?

He turns in my direction. I still can't make him out. I remain quiet. Watching his every move. He approaches me as gentle as dew falling on a meadow. I still can't see his face, but I can feel him. His aura warms me. He continues toward me, picking up his pace. It feels like he should be covering more ground than he actually is. Almost like he's running in place. Then I notice it. Behind him the black-hooded demons appear, chasing him. "Run! Run! Behind you!" I scream. "Behind you!"

NO! I hear screaming back at me in my mind.

I look up. For a brief moment, a wave of dizziness consumes me. I am in front of the Proctor and Professors again. I'm disappointed that I'm back. I sway just a little, trying to catch my balance.

I'm continuing my diatribe and speak in a monotone voice to the Proctors as if I have been there the entire time. "Buchanan Riley was one of the Chancellors who implemented the first ever exam in which children become candidates to activate their superhuman powers. The exams are a coming of age celebration for sixteen-year-olds to embrace their new powers."

I stop talking, watching as the professors transform into the black-robed hooded creatures right before my eyes. It's them, I just saw them! A smell of decay floats my way. I'm frozen, wondering if this is part of the exam or my imagination getting the best of me. Are they going to attack me? I wonder why the Proctor doesn't see them, too!

The demonic shapes move closer, I'm beginning to think I need to get out of here real fast. My heart is pounding so loud and hard, I'm sure that everyone in the cubicle can hear me. I prepare myself to run. Just as I position myself to jump, the black shapes disappear back into the professor's bodies just as they had appeared. It all happened in less than five seconds.

"Jenavieve," says Professor Kinsey, "you have done very well. We are going to move you to the room down the hall where you will participate in Part Two of the exam: The Xapiri."

Kree removes the electrodes from my forehead and gives me a half-smile. I don't think she is as impressed with my scores as she thought she'd be. But I smile to myself because I realize I have just outsmarted them. Or, at least, I think I have.

"Come with me," says Kree.

Chapter 12

Kree and I walk quietly to a room at the end of the hallway. Other candidates are being escorted by their monitors to the same room. One after another, candidates enter the room. Most come out just as fast as they entered with a few barely even getting the chance to shut the door. Disappointment appears on everyone's face. It's obvious no one has seen an Xapiri yet or activated phasing powers.

When we get to the door, Kree says, "Good luck, Jenavieve. May you surpass all others before you!"

"That's it? Aren't you going to connect me to video monitors or give me a tracing antigen or something?" I ask half-sarcastically.

"It's not necessary," says Kree. "This room has been masked in a way that will transport you directly into the experience with the Xapiri, if you have one."

"But I'll only see the Xapiri if I have phasing powers, right?" I ask.

"Yes. If you do not have phasing powers you will not see the spirits. It is very rare, so we aren't exactly sure what happens once an Xapiri appears. But it is understood that your phasing powers are automatically activated, and you will have an experience that is unique to your percentage of powers and your Xapiri spirit. And because of the transport masking of the room, a digital imprint of all that happens will be recorded and be tallied with everything else at the end of the exams."

I take a deep breath. This is going to be tricky. But it's unlikely that I have this Xapiri spirit thing anyway. And I definitely don't think I have these phasing abilities Kree keeps talking about. I've never even heard of them before. And yet, I remember how I was a Lioness in yesterday's exam. So, I guess anything is possible.

"Good luck, Jenavieve," Kree finishes.

"Thanks." My voice is dry and small.

I step inside the room. The door behind me seems to close more slowly than I noticed for other candidates. I look around before the fading light is completely gone. The four walls are painted a dark grey. There is nothing that I can see other than empty space. It's just a room that looks like an empty box. And then I feel it. Like a ton of bricks falling on my chest. The room is thick with all sorts of Percenter's powers. It's so heavy, it puts pressure on my chest and almost smothers me. I gasp for air.

A strange new white glow begins to form in the corner of the room. As the light becomes brighter and brighter, I see a tall man standing before me, leaning on a walking stick. He looks like a wizard with long white, silky hair, a rough and curly beard, and a golden silk robe that grazes the floor behind him. "Don't be afraid," he says to me in a calm and patient voice.

"I-I-I'm not afraid, but who are you?" I ask.

"I'm your Xapiri Spirit. You can call me Za."

"You mean I actually have phasing powers?" I ask.

"Didn't you already know this?" Za returned my question.

"I-I-I didn't think so. I mean. It's so rare. But Xapiri...I mean, Za—" I begin.

"Jenavieve de Fenace," Za interrupts me, "you have phasing powers, an extremely advanced Percenter power, but you must keep this hidden from the Proctors and everyone you know. Reaching into his robes, he pulls out a small vial of something bright orange.

"Quickly, drink this. It will hide your experiences for the rest of the exams from being recorded properly. You must excel at the exams to fully activate your powers, but we need everyone to think you failed and have no real powers of significance. Or you will die before you have the chance to achieve your mission." He pushes the vial in front of my face. I pause, but only briefly. I instinctually believe and trust Za. I drink the entire vial.

"You know about my mission?" I ask.

"Of course," Za, the Xapiri Spirit says. I've kept an eye on you for a very long time. Sixteen years, to be precise." He smiles.

"In fact," Za says, "I was your grandmother's Xapiri when she was alive. You not only inherited her kindness but also me, her Xapiri."

"My grandmother?" I ask. "I have so many questions!"

"Oh, yes," Za says. "I was her guide from the moment she completed her exams until she was no longer. And now, I'm yours. I've been waiting a long time for you, Jena."

"For many years, I hoped she would be reincarnated and that one day we'd meet and become best of friends."

"Her spirit will always be there for you through me," Za says.

"I don't really understand what you mean," I say.

"It doesn't matter now. You'll learn in time. But just know that for now, your grandmother is always with you," Za says. "Now then, let's get started. We have to be quick. I've frozen time on the other side of the door but it won't last much longer. We have to make it appear as though you weren't in here long enough to activate an Xapiri Spirit. The Xapiri power is so desired that the Cleansing Coalition doesn't want to miss out on the opportunity to detect it in a candidate. They must not know about me or that you have an Xapiri!"

"OK," I say. Confirming I am taking this as serious as Za's tone is conveying.

"Most Percenter's don't know this, but there are only thirteen Xapiri Spirits. Each one, including myself, was born once a Founding Chancellor died. We were born first of their spirit, and then from generation to generation we have chosen our next worthy Percenter."

"Wait? Why thirteen? There were only twelve Founding Chancellors that originally drank the Elixir."

"There have always been, and always will be, thirteen Founding Chancellors and thirteen Xapiri Spirits." Za says with a bit of a firm tone. "Regardless of what your history books taught you."

"Likewise, there will always be thirteen Percenter's with phasing powers and an Xapiri. The Percenter Oracle, able to track all Percenter powers, has been the only one to know this throughout time. But less than twenty years ago, the Percenter Oracle at the time was murdered by the Cleansing Coalition in an attempt to uncover all of the twelve Xapiri that they thought existed. Several of the Xapiri Percenters were also killed in the same attack and forced to choose new Percenter's. The thirteenth Xapiri was able to vanish forever, with no other records existing to prove the thirteen Founding Chancellor existed.

"I, Jena, am the Xapiri of Jack Kiang. The unknown thirteenth Founding Chancellor.

"Holy shit! This is huge. Oh, my God. OK." My hands are in my hair as fast as they are pushing against the sides of my temples. I begin pacing in circles trying to comprehend all of this.

"OK. So, the other Xapiris. Do they know about you? Can they find you? Are you friends? Are they now my friends? How does all this work?"

"We'll get to all of that in time. But time is not a luxury we have right this moment. I must warn you, Jenavieve." Za looks at me intensely with silvery eyes. "With such powers comes tremendous responsibilities. And it's a slippery slope. You will be tested more than most. I have been an Xapiri, a phasing guide, since the beginning of the first Percenters. Our roles may have evolved as Percenters became more and more powerful, but one thing has always remained the same. People can be very jealous of one another's powers. And there will be those who try to steal yours. Who try to stop you. And it may take you a while before you learn to control all of your powers, and that's how I can help you. You may find yourself phasing from different times in the past or even future, spontaneously and without control. And you won't know how to stop it or control it. You will have to learn how to control this because there is always the danger of getting stuck forever."

"Stuck? Forever?" I ask confused and a bit scared.

"You'll learn more about that in time. Come now, let's get started."

Za places his hand on mine, and I feel a tingle zing through my body.

"Jenavieve, I'm going to give you something—a kind of talisman. This talisman is very special and carries a unique vibration that pairs me to you. As long as you have this, I can find you whenever you need me."

He hands me a stone, amber in color. It's lighter than anything I have ever touched, almost like it could float right out of my hand if I didn't hold it save. I look closer into the stone and notice a pulsing from it's inner core. It's heart beat like pattern mesmerizes me.

"Alright," I say. "Anytime, anyplace?"

"Yes," he says. He waves his hand over mine and the amber gemstone is set into a thin gold chain. "Wear this pendant. It is your key during your times in need. It contains a life force that can transform into energy and can only be activated by you."

Za explains. "With this special pendant all energy can flow through it in one direction. It will help you call on your powers more efficiently. The more balanced you are, the more energy you can transmit through this talisman. And you will be able to consciously connect with the very source of this life force to access your multitude of powers. And Jena, you have many to be discovered!" Za winks at me like it's something he's impressed by.

He latches the pendant around my neck. I tuck the dangling stone beneath my white bodysuit. Thankfully the chain is long enough so the entire thing can remain hidden.

"Keep this with you always," Za instructs. "Some call this a healing stone, as well. You must wear this amber pendant with you at all times if you want to access the greater gift of the Elixir running through your veins."

"Thanks, Za. I'll keep it with me always." I nod in confirmation.

"Ready?" And within in a blink of an eye, Za pushes me, and I fly backwards through the door. I immediately put my sad face on to help make it appear as though I was as disappointed as all of the other candidates. No one seems to react differently to me than anyone else. I guess what felt like ten minutes to me was actually less than a second to everyone else.

"This concludes the Xapiri Part Two of your exam," says Kree. She has a blank look on her face. I wonder if Za was right. Did his potion really help prevent the monitors from discovering my abilities? If so, they won't think I have an Xapiri.

"Thank you, Kree," I say as she escorts me back to the main cubicle.

"You're welcome, Jenavieve. Her tone different than before. You may go back to your dorm now and get ready for dinner tonight. The scores will be tallied and presented tomorrow night at the end of Day Three. That's when everyone else will discover how much Percenter power they possess and which Prep School they'll attend." She lowers her eyes as if embarrassed for me. Did she just say, "everyone else," and, "they?" The potion must have worked. She's probably thinking I'm not scoring well.

"I understand," I say.

When I get back to my dorm, I approach the door to my room, eager to be alone with my thoughts. I hear someone crying next door. I knock on the door. "Hello? Are you alright?"

"Go away." It's Jessica Piston's voice.

I don't really like the girl, but at the same time, she clearly doesn't have anyone else. "Jessica? Are you alright?"

"I said go away."

"Please, if I can be of help..."

The door opens.

"Jessica, what's wrong?" I ask her. She's standing there, sobbing. Black mascara streaks down her cheeks. She blows her nose while still managing to chew that annoying gum she always has in her mouth. So frustrating. It's like nails on a chalkboard to me.

"I-II don't know what to say," she says.

"May I come in?"

"Sure." She steps aside, and I go into her small room and sit in a chair across from her bed. She flops down on the bed.

"Look," I say, "I don't know you very well, but something must be wrong. You can tell me."

"I don't think you can help," Jessica says.

"That might be true, but if you tell me what's going on, I might be able to help. Why are you crying?"

"Jena, I'm failing miserably," Jessica says. She blows her nose again.

"How do you know?" I ask her.

"My scores were very low yesterday," says Jessica. "and they didn't even let me take the second half today."

"They didn't?" My eyes open wide.

"No, they didn't. They said that it wasn't necessary, and that they would see me tomorrow for Day Three. My monitor said that if I score high tomorrow, then I have nothing to worry about."

"Well, see? I told you that you'd be alright." I try to comfort her.

"But what if I don't?" Jessica says. "What if I flunk and I'm sent to the Ground?"

"Well, all you need is twenty-six percent to be considered a Percenter. Do you think you can pull that off?

"I honestly don't know. Everything seems to be too hard for me. I'm lost, and all I'm doing is breaking down and crying all day."

"Oh," I say, not really sure how to respond to her whining. I've never understood people who act like victims when they are anything but. Just make it happen. "Do you think one of your relatives would Middle you? You'd at least get to live in the Skyscrapers as a Middler...one of my cousins, Ben, is a Middler in our home, and he doesn't seem to mind so much," I lied to make her feel better.

"I don't think I could bear it!" Jessica says, sobbing, grabbing a pillow and hugging it. "I couldn't bear being a Middler! You see what they wear and how they cut their hair!" she screams out in utter agony at the thought. "And I've been such a bitch to everyone all my life, I doubt anyone would save me—ever! I wouldn't save me."

"Look, you still have tomorrow," I try to assure her. "You'll do fine."

"I'm sorry to burden you with my problems," says Jessica. "It's just that...well...it's just that I simply can't live that way."

I want to reach out and either hug her or slap her, I'm not entirely sure which one so I do neither. I sit with Jessica for a while longer, trying to reassure her that all will be alright. I know it won't. If she wasn't even allowed to take the Xapiri exam, that meant her score would be extremely low. It could be impossible to score high enough for a prep school. Or maybe I'm wrong. I guess we'll find out tomorrow. Even though I have my own issues to worry about, it's nice to be distracted by someone else's for a change.

Finally, Jessica calms down. I tell her that I'm just next door if she needs me. I'm surprised I actually feel a little bit sorry for her, but I'm even more surprised that I'm starting to like her. I realize her haughty personality has always been a cover-up for the weaker side. She has simply been an insecure girl in a world where power was heavily prized over everything else.

"Look, if you need anything, Jess, I'm right next door," I tell her. "Come and get me."

I go to my room to be alone with my thoughts. I'm not hungry and do not even go to the dining hall for dinner. I just want solitude. I have to think over everything that happened today. Only one more day to go. Only one more day as a true Percenter.

Chapter 13

After slipping into my formal dress and brushing my hair, I walk slowly towards the magnificent Royal Hall where the Gala is going to take place. This building has been here for as long as San Sun has existed. It is separate from the buildings where the exams took place.

Those buildings are erected every year. But the Royal Hall stands always. This is the final place of our weeklong event. It is the place where the results of our exams will be revealed and where all of us sixteen-year-old candidates will be assigned to a prep school. And where some will be cast out of the Percenters' society and exiled to the Ground.

The sky is a twilight periwinkle blue with just a hint of rose from the drifting sun. It looks lovely. It looks perfect. How the grounds of our Sky Cities exist tethered to skyscrapers below us is both an engineering and a magical feat. I am reminded that this world of the Percenters is a fabricated world. An illusion. A facsimile of what life is like for the Middlers and Grounder below.

My dress is long, soft, and silky, the color of brilliant, sun-glittering gold. After my bath and quick nap, I had dried my hair and pulled half of it up with ribbons that I had brought from home. They were gold and glittery, too, and matched my dress. I slipped on the pendant that Za gave me and hid it under my dress. I did not want to draw attention to it.

I had dabbed on a bit of mascara and lip-gloss, but that was all. I do not like to wear much makeup. I still have a couple scratches on my face showing, but I'm going to wear them like battle scars. It's interesting, but with only mascara and lip-gloss I feel almost too artificial. As though the beautiful dress and glittery ribbons do not belong on me. As if they're fake. Like everything else around me.

The magnificent Royal Hall has been a landmark and source of pride for San Sun residents since its very beginning. It is so beautiful that many of the other Sky City residents visit San Sun to vacation at the Royal Hall Hotel, part of the vast Royal Hall estate. It has been a favored getaway for vacationers and celebrities alike amongst the Percenters.

A stately palm-lined walkway runs in front of its entrance. Ground lights illuminate the path. The Royal Hall has been a discriminating center for social events year-round, a prestigious destination for visitors from the Chancellors and other Sky Cities.

Tonight, the red carpet has been rolled out, connecting the walkway to the Royal Hall's canopied entrance. As attendees arrive at the front of the Royal Hall and Hotel, they invariably look up in awe at the ornate façade. It is leafed in gold and accented by silver cascades, artistic and beautiful.

Sauntering down the runway on the arms of their escorts, many stop to point out the unique turreted corners of the palatial building before passing through the stately doorway. It is a bit ostentatious for my taste.

The parade of the top designers' fashions of the Sky Cities are unending as party goers fill the main lobby of the Royal Hall. Every designer wants his or her designs worn by the wealthy and the royalty. Gorgeous gowns are worn by the mothers of the candidates, by the leading faculty of the exams, and by female leaders in the Sky Cities. The gowns swish delicately against the marble floors amidst the friendly din of anticipation in the domed room. My parents told me last week that many of the candidates' families will stay in the hotel tonight and continue their celebrations late into the evening. Mine will not.

I am a little late because of my nap. Mostly, everyone else has already arrived. I step gingerly through the doors to a place that will change the course of my life. There, inside the Royal Hall, there is a buzz of excitement. It is palpable. The boys are all dressed in white tuxedos, with their hair slicked back with gel, and look handsome, although I prefer boys to be natural with no sticky gel in the hair.

The girls are all wearing gold dresses similar to mine with their hair curled and jewelry glistening. The candidates are all nervous, chatting and fidgeting. They are all worried about their fates.

We are supposed to mingle in the foyer of the Grand Royal Hall and Solarium before going into the auditorium-like room where we will face the exam Board. The Chancellors from all the Sky Cities will sit there and judge us as they read our final scores. They will then assign us to our prep school or dismiss us to the Ground as a Barren. And for those who didn't pass the exams, some will be given the opportunity to become a Middler and Servant to a Percenter family.

After this, everyone will gather into the Royal Hall Dining Room for dancing and celebrating with family and peers. The ones who do not pass the exams, will be led away by guards and sent to their dismal destination.

I shudder. What is that like? I wonder. Do they put handcuffs on them? Does anyone protest? Does anyone kick or scream? Do the parents have the opportunity to say goodbye? Or, is it such an embarrassment that the parents ignore them altogether? That's what Ben's parents did.

They wouldn't even speak to my cousin after he was expelled from the Percenter's Society. After he was given the assignment to become a Middler and Servant. I had felt so sorry for him. The pain and anguish in his face from his parent's treatment had been heartbreaking. I had been so relieved when my parents spoke up and said they would employ him in our household.

I am worried. I have not seen Jessica anywhere and this frightens me. I visualize her somewhere in a hospital in a catatonic state and this makes my stomach lurch in pain. Even though I have not known her long, I have grown to like her and do not wish for anything bad to happen to her.

I look around for my family. For my friends. I see Alexander talking animatedly to Raquel over to the side of the room. He looks handsome, and she is beautiful. I smile happily. I can just imagine that he's telling her all about his heroic exploits to save me. He looks so happy. I envy him.

Jezebel, Ben's sister runs over to me. "Oh, Jenavieve, how were your exams?"

"Interesting," I say. I do not feel like talking to her. I kind of hate her.

"I honestly believe I scored very high. I can't wait to get my scores." She twirls in her golden dress. "Don't you just love our dresses? They are soooo gorgeous!"

I look at her like she's an idiot. Her own brother, Ben, didn't score high enough to get into a Prep School and is now our family's servant. Doesn't she realize she could very well end up with a low score? I don't say anything though. It would serve her right.

"Well, good luck to you," I tell Jezebel.

"You, too," she says. "Hope we get into the same prep school!"

I want to scream, "No way would I want to be in a prep school with you!" But I say nothing.

I start walking around the room, too nervous and fidgety to stand still and make insignificant small talk with some of these idiots.

"There you are!" I feel a hand on my shoulder.

I turn around and there is Avelino. He has cuts and bruises on his face like I do. If this were not such a serious night, I would have laughed. We must look like quite the pair. He is regal in his white tuxedo. And gratefully, he does not have gel on his hair.

"I'm glad you're here," I tell him.

"You look lovely, Jena," he says, slipping his arm through mine.

"You like nice, too."

"I look like I've been in a cat fight," he says, laughing lightly.

"Well, you have. But not a cat. A real demon. We all have." I try to laugh lightly, too.

"Your scratches look good on you, though," he says.

"At least I got out of there, thanks to you...and Alex."

"Your exam was one of the more difficult ones, I believe," says Avelino.

"What do you mean?" I had never considered that.

"It's just that neither Alexander nor I had that extreme of an experience. I think they consider you one of the more advanced ones with extremely high Percenter's powers," says Avelino. "That's why they made your exam so brutal. You're special, Jena."

"Well, all I can say is that I'm glad it's over." I shudder one more time.

"Everything's alright now," says Avelino. "You're safe. You must be excited about tonight, right? Are you nervous?" He leans in closer to me. He smells so good. So clean and fresh like sunshine.

"Yes, I am. But, honestly, I still haven't recovered from that last exam." I tremble as a chill skitters up my back.

"I know. I haven't either. Let's try to not think about it right now, though. Tonight, it's all good and we are going to have a lot to celebrate."

"You're right. Let's make the most of our evening." I smile at him.

Avelino and I are standing by the floor-to-ceiling windows in the Solarium. He reaches out and takes my hand.

"This is really a beautiful place, isn't it?" says Avelino.

It's as if we don't want to talk about the reality of the night's events. That we'll be separated. That our friends could be sent to the Ground. But I can read between the lines and we're both thinking about the awful tunnels from earlier. Or, maybe he's not. Maybe he's only looking forward at what's going to happen next. I am sure Avelino will get into one of the best prep schools available. And I am sure I may never see him again.

"The marble columns are very regal," I say. "This place is like a palace."

"The excitement around here is infectious, isn't it?" says Avelino. "You can't help but feel excited about tonight and proud of our city."

I want desperately to tell him everything, but I can't.

"Have you seen Jessica?" I ask, biting my lips.

"Jena, last I saw her, she was over towards the back of the room," says Avelino. He motions towards one end where there are long dark curtains that would be good for hiding. "She's not doing very well."

"C'mon, let's go find her."

We find Jessica standing alone by one of the tall columns facing the window. She's staring at the scene outside where trees and flowers adorn the garden. She is wearing a long gold dress like all of us girls are wearing, and her long black hair is trailing down her back. But her shoulders are slumped, and she looks like she has been crying.

"Jessica, are you okay?" I ask her as Avelino and I approach.

"Oh, hello," she says, straightening her shoulders. She wipes her cheeks.

Her mascara is slightly smudged.

"We've been looking for you," says Avelino.

"Yes," I say. "Jess, did you get through that last exam alright?"

"I was pulled out," she says, sniffling. "I didn't pass it, Jen. I don't think I did very well at all through any of the exams."

"At least you got out," says Avelino, looking over at me. I know what he's thinking. I almost didn't make it out!

"That's just it," says Jessica. "I think they pulled me out before I even had a chance to try and get out myself. They preempted me from finishing the exam and I'm not sure why."

"Do you...do you mean that you think the exams were rigged somehow?" I ask. I honestly have never thought about that.

"I don't know," says Jessica. "It just seems like someone didn't want me to even complete the exam. Like their minds were already made up about my fate."

"It's probably just your imagination," says Avelino. "There's no way they wouldn't want you to uncover all of your Percenter's powers. That's the way of our society. Our world. What good would they gain from not letting you uncover your new powers?"

"I know," says Jessica. "You're right. It is probably just my imagination. What about you two? Did you all do alright?"

"I didn't do so well," I say. "Alexander and Avelino rescued me."

"That's nice," Jessica says. "It's nice that someone was there for you."

"Yes, it was nice," I say, squeezing Avelino's hand.

"Look, I'll meet you all in the main auditorium." Jessica looks around the room. "Right now, I need to find someone."

"Alright, see you later, Jess," I say.

We watch as she disappears in the crowd.

I turn back to Avelino. "Do you think she's OK?"

"I don't know, but right now, I don't want to think about her. We only have a few moments before the Grand Reveal in the Royal Hall Auditorium, so let's go where we can have a little privacy."

We discreetly pull away from the crowded hallways and stroll out onto the

Royal Hall's wide wraparound columned terrace. I remember some of the older candidates at San Sun City had often talked about couples going out into the gardens on the evening of the Grand Reveal and sharing intimate moments. Maybe that's why Avelino has brought me here.

Avelino pulls me close as he waves to a friendly group of acquaintances and leads me over to a private area against the terrace balustrade. At first, we stand in hushed tranquility, breathing in the fresh clean air of San Sun. A warm breeze gently rustles through the trees.

I finally let out a contented sigh and glance at Avelino. He is so handsome. And so naïve. So kind and generous of heart. In the twilight, his green eyes look coppery and matches his hair. If possible, his shoulders are even broader now than when I first saw him earlier this week. He takes my breath away.

Leaning against him, we both search the clear night sky. We are high above the poisonous ground below and in this world in the Sky City, everything is perfect. Avelino silently points out Orion, the Hunter with Belt and Sword, in the sky. I follow as his finger moves to the moon, a sliver of golden-gilding suspended in the sky. Then he points to the most famous love star, delicate Venus, twinkling like a dancing pixie just under the moon's right side.

"Jenavieve," Avelino says softly, breaking the silence. "I-I...well, I don't know how to say this exactly, but have I told you how beautiful you look tonight?"

"Yes," I say. For the first time in my life, I feel flirtatious. Girly. Silly. Frivolous. "You've told me a couple of times!"

"No matter what school we get in, I want to see you again," says Avelino. "Do you think that's possible?"

"Yes, Avelino," I say to him. I'm lying, but I don't want to ruin the moment. "The prep schools are always competing with one another. And they have joint dances and lots of sporting games. We can still see each other no matter where we are."

"It seems like we've been through a few lifetimes together after our exams. I never dreamed I would have the opportunity to get to know you this well through these tests."

"I know," I say. "It does seem like we've known each other a long, long time, doesn't it? Maybe those exams are designed that way. To help us find true allies as we move on to prep schools."

"I don't want to brag, but Jen, I learned that I'm a shape-shifter," Avelino barely whispers.

"A shape-shifter?" I ask.

"Yes, I know this sounds like I'm bragging, but I'm not. I can shape shift! Or, at least I could while in the exams. I know I still have lots of learning to do in the Prep School I get into. But it's exciting. Did anything like that happen to you?" His eyes light up with sparkles. I can see his excitement.

I'm not sure how much I should share. "Yeah, sort of. Did you meet any Xapiri Spirit guides?"

"I did!" He seems excited that we have this in common. "So, you did, too? Wow! Maybe you and I have similar Percenter's powers. Wouldn't that be great?"

"It would."

He looks at me intently, then tenderly traces the deep scratch on my cheekbone with his forefinger.

"Does that cut hurt?" he asks.

"Yeah, a little," I say, dropping my eyes. I know it still has some clotted blood on it. I couldn't get it all off in my shower.

I feel butterflies fluttering in my stomach, and close my eyes, swaying a little bit. I love being with him here in this moment.

"Are you sure you're okay, Jena?" His voice is so gentle, it makes my chest hurt.

"I'm just a little tired after today."

He pulls me close as if he's done this a thousand times. He cups my chin in his hand and leans down. He tilts his head and kisses me on the lips. Softly. At first. But then, I feel an urgency. Knowing this is going to be the last time I ever see him, I wrap my arms around him, pull him even closer to me, and kiss him hard.

I open my mouth and feel his tongue inside mine. My legs turn to flimsy strings, and I do not know if I can remain standing. He grips me in his arms.

He feels the urgency, too. Even though he doesn't know what is so urgent about the moment, he feels it.

I do not want this moment to end. Ever.

"Ouch!" I moan as I rub my elbow from falling out of bed. First, I realize it was all just a dream. Then I realize I haven't finished the exam yet.

Chapter 14

I t had all happened so fast. I was so excited just a week ago. *Was* being the key word. Today should be more fun since I won't be alone. For once, I wanted to just act like a regular candidate and not worry about the fate of our world being in my hands. I want to be a regular sixteen-year-old having fun with friends. This is the beginning of the rest of my life, after all.

We finished our breakfast and we all begin to congregate in the Grand Hall. Strangers surround me yet everyone else is familiar to one another. Everyone is laughing and joking with their friends. As usual, I am not in on the joke. Today's exam is intended to unlock all of our remaining powers for activation. It is the final phase to access our powers and learn how to harness control over them. When the simulation is over, we will awaken with full use of our powers. Maybe not well, but all powers will be activated.

Russ, the lead Proctor, stands at the podium. "Quiet, please." He briefly pauses. "Shortly, you will enter a shared reality that before today, did not exist. You have randomly been divided into teams." He points to a large screen announcing the names of team members on each team.

Clearing his throat, Russ continues, "Find your teammates and meet in your assigned simulation room, now."

Everyone begins to cheer and shout as they find their teammates. I look back to the screen to find my name. I find it. I couldn't be more relieved. It's almost too perfect. Either the Gods are looking down on me or these assignments aren't so random after all.

Russ continues, "Each of your individual experiences through these exams has been combined to create a new virtual world. If you succeed in reaching The Numinous, you each will face challenges that will help unlock your true Percenter powers. But know this... The Numinous, while omnipresent, will not easily reveal itself to you. Trust nothing and no one but each other. Remember, you must work together to find The Numinous..." He pauses briefly... "together! What happens next, is up to you."

His caution could not be more palpable. His tone could not be misinterpreted. This is going to be like some sort of weird mind trip, I can already tell.

He continues after what felt like an unusually long pause that quickly created a chill in the room, "Few Percenters can overcome the full force of The Numinous, and only those with the most advanced Percenter powers will ever truly understand The Numinous. If you do not succeed in reaching The Numinous, your powers will not be activated. And consider this your warning...you will face many challenges unlike anything you could ever imagine and if you fail to overcome them, we cannot save you. You will be forever trapped in The Numinous, like a genie in a bottle. We will all be watching you so good luck, and may you surpass all others before you!"

"Ummm... excuse me?" Jessica raises her hand and says in the most pissed off tone I have ever heard from her, "Did you just say that if we don't succeed, we could be trapped...forever?"

Nodding his head as he continues to walk away, Russ says very matter of factly "Yes. That is what I said."

"Couldn't be more matter of fact about it!" Alexander says as he slaps Avelino on the back while looking at the rest of us with a huge smile, like he's about to have the time of his life.

As luck would have it–or maybe it wasn't luck at all–Alexander, Avelino and Jessica were my randomly assigned teammates. Along with Jacob Johnson and Sven Krouse. Three boys and three girls. Not so random I'm thinking. But as far as I'm concerned, I couldn't have picked better teammates; even though Jessica is clearly not going to win MVP of the year awards anytime soon.

Obviously I trust Alexander, but I oddly trust Avelino too. I just hope that when push comes to shove, Jessica isn't going to be a loose cannon out to save her own skin. I guess we'll find out. Trust isn't going to be my biggest issue. Hiding my true powers from my teammates and the entire Percenter society watching, on the other hand, is.

"Hi there, Jena," Avelino says to me, smiling. His eyes locked with mine, and I knew he was thinking the same thing I was. The other night. Our dance. Just the sight of him warmed me from the inside out. I wanted to throw my arms around him and kiss him right then and there, but of course, refrained. I'd probably scare him away if I did.

My thoughts interrupted, Jessica whispers in my ear "Please. Don't say a word to them about, you know, what I said last night!" I could almost feel her intense fear. I had mixed feelings about Jessica. I was authentically worried for her. I think I'm starting to realize how vulnerable everyone is, including me. But I'm also starting to understand how people can do whatever it takes to survive. Fear is a powerful motivator.

"Of course," I says showing actual concern by putting my hand on her shoulder. "Are you really *OKay* though, Jessica? I mean, really?"

She just threw her chin up and tried to act confident as she normally parades around, but I knew she wasn't. She brushes my hand off her shoulder. 'Uh, yes, Jena. I'm fine! Jeez." And just like that, she's back to being her normal bitchy self.

Alexander was looking over at Raquel, longingly with puppy dog eyes. I couldn't help but smile at the idea of their ridiculous crush. I knew he was probably hoping she'd be on his team, probably even more than he wanted me. Sadly, for him, she's on a team with Thomas Roberts. I'm not sure if Alexander sees it that same way as I do, but he's probably his biggest competition for Raquel's affection.

I, on the other hand, couldn't be more thankful she's not on our team. Not that I don't like Raquel or I don't want them to be together, nothing like that. Now, I know Alexander will be able to focus on what's important...making it to The Numinous instead of making out with Raquel.

We slipped into these weird body suits that had fabric connecting our arms to our waists, and our legs together from ankle to crotch. They called them wingsuits. They fit perfectly. As if they were custom made to fit each of our bodies.

"Are you ready?" Avelino says to me.

Those dimples. How could I not be ready with those dimples on my side. "Don't worry about me! I'm more worried about you. Are you ready?" Catching myself giving him the most flirtatious wink and smile I could muster. After all, I was very happy he was with me… but he didn't need to know that! I quickly refocus on tying my laces.

"Do you have any idea of what to expect?" I ask Alexander.

"Of course! Virtual worlds, combined experiences, blah, blah, blah."

Alexander never seemed to worry about anything. He especially could not be bothered with details. Maybe if he had been the one attacked by mysterious hooded creatures he'd feel differently, maybe!

"I can't wait for this!" Alexander continues trying to rally the team. "This is going to be awesome! Seriously. We are going to kill it! Who's with me?"

He puts his hand in between the rest of us, trying to secure our commitment to kicking ass as good as any cheerleader would have done.

"C'mon!" Alex says, looking at each of us directly in the eyes with his confident and ridiculously handsome smile no one can refuse.

We simultaneously look back at him with mild amusement turned excitement. We all join his hand and repeatedly chant "Let's Kick Ass!" loader and faster until it devolved into just "Kick Ass!"

After some jumping up and down in anxious excitement, we begin walking down a brightly lit corridor, passing one closed door after another. Each door must lead to an unimaginable world other candidates will face. There were no windows, just clandestine lights illuminating the hallways. A red or green light on the door signaled if it was in use or not.

As we approached the second to last door, it opened slowly with lights directing us to enter. Alexander, first. Then Jacob and Sven entered. Avelino and Jessica stepped into the room just before I did. I followed, hesitating slightly more than the others. The door sealed shut behind us with a noticeable *clink*, becoming seamless with the walls and completely hidden.

Barely breathing with anticipation, we waited as there was a noticeable change in air pressure. The lights went completely dark. We all backed up to each other to form a misshaped circle, looking out into the complete darkness.

The floor drops suddenly from beneath our feet. There was a roar and a huge wind-tunnel sucking sound. We don't drop into the chasm. Instead, our feet begin to lift and our suits catch the air. We are flying! The room's ceiling transformed to the night sky. Stars spread out before us like jewels thrown askew on black velvet.

I looked down, all I could see were swirls of clouds as we passed them, lit only by a round silver moon that has now appeared in the distance. We position ourselves face-to-face in a circle, reaching out to hold hands. We are all grinning, lips and cheeks flapping uncontrollably in the wind. For the first time in the exams, I was actually enjoying myself. It's like we were dropped from the bottom of the Sky Cities and flying to the Earth's mysterious surface.

Reading his lips, I could make out the nearly inaudible cheer coming from Alex.

"Let's do this! Let's find The Numinous. Let's find it in record time!"

Alex the eternal optimist. Avelino and Jessica nodded, then we all lean forward, using our wingsuits to free-fall to Earth, gliding like the crows Sebastian watches outside our window.

I stretched out, held my arms close to my body, and tilted down, guiding my way to a toxic free looking Ground. All I could hear was my wingsuit flapping against the wind. I could see Avelino's mouth move, but I just smiled in response having no idea what he's saying. Moments ago we were in a square, dark box of a room, inside a building in San Sun. It was unbelievablehow lifelike this virtual world was. Surreal really.

I felt light and weightless at first. The wind rushing against my face felt cold and blustery. As the air transported our bodies, we careened like birds down through the remnants of wispy clouds, and soon, a sprawling landscape came into full view. There were mountainsides, cliffs, trees, and valleys.

In the distance was a gushing waterfall that streamed a silvery path of light filled water down what seemed like miles and miles of rocky, jagged cliffs. I signaled to everyone and tilted my body to head in that direction. Avelino, Jacob, and Sven followed first. Then Jessica and Alex trailed behind.

We were approaching rapidly, and I wasn't sure where to land. I was afraid of the waterfall, yet felt it was calling to me. Halfway down the cliff, I notice a dark spot behind the evaporating water. I signaled to everyone to keep following me. Avelino and Jessica shook their heads no and pointed to a flat grassy area at the head of the waterfall. I ignored them, and I quickly angle my body and turn abruptly, forcing them to follow me or get separated.

I saw what looked like an opening in a mountain ridge just to the right of the falls. I begin diving into the waterfall, confident there is a cave to land in but afraid of what's inside. I look back to make sure Alexander is following. I don't want to lose anyone from our team, but I definitely want to keep Alexander close. I peek back to see that everyone is continuing directly toward the waterfall in single file.

As I watched the water gushing down the ridged cliffs, I sucked in a deep breath and whisper, "Trust yourself." I was determined to make it, though.

For a brief moment, I felt the cold spray of water on my face and then, almost instantaneously, it was over. My fingertips graze the opening walls of the cave as I make a last minute turn. I just flew through a waterfall! My heart dropped into my stomach as I watch everyone sail through the waterfall and enter the opening safely behind me. Besides some basic scrapes and bruises, we all appear to be unharmed. For now, at least.

"Wahooo!" we all yelled at the top of our lungs repeatedly. The adrenaline clearly in overdrive.

"What a rush!" Sven exclaimed. "That was better than the first time I kissed a girl!"

"I know!" says Avelino. "Me too!"

We all laugh a little.

"Seriously. Unbelievable!" Avelino reaches of to give Alexander a high-five. Such a guy thing to do.

I smile at Jacob, who I barely know. "I can't believe we made it!" I grinned, giving him a stranger hug.

"How did you know this was here?" Jessica asks. I couldn't tell if her tone was amazement or skepticism, but I was leaning towards the later.

Optimistically I say, "I didn't, really. I saw what looked like a shadow, or dark spot, and just, kinda, guessed it was a cave."

"Oh, that's great, Jena. You just guessed with our lives."

"She was right, wasn't she?" Avelino chimes in.

"Whatever. Next time, Jena…" Jessica rolls her eyes and decides not to finish her sentence.

A subtle yet completely noticeable squeal interrupts her and we all rapidly turn to look into the darkness of the cave in complete silence.

For a few moments we stand perfectly still only hearing the rush of the water behind us.

"What the Fuck was that?" Jacob exclaims. It was hard to tell if there was fear or excitement in his voice.

"Whatever it is, it probably isn't good," Sven says.

We strip out of our wingsuits and turn on our flashlights. Without saying another word, we all begin walking away from the waterfall and deeper into the cave. We hear the squeal a couple more times but each time, it sounds further and further away.

"Oh… My… God!" Jessica says just loud enough for us to hear. Her flashlight illuminating what looked like bloody claw marks on the walls of the cave. Fresh claw marks. We could tell because the blood was still dripping. We stop, looking all around us. There is nothing else on the walls, but about ten feet in front of us we see drag marks in the loose dirt, layered in more blood. Our eyes all meet. I take the lead.

"Wait!" Avelino yells at me. "You don't have any idea…I'll go first!"

"Like you do. I'm fine AV," I say, a little put-off.

"I do, actually. Let me lead. I've…I've been here before. I think." Chimes in Alex with shock and surprise in his voice.

Before I knew it, the ground beneath my feet disappears, and I slide down a hole barely wide enough for my body. I push my hands, painstakingly, against the walls to slow myself. Ripping the skin off my palm and tearing several of my fingernails, I begin to slow and eventually stop. I'm exhausted and suddenly feel the intense rush of pain on my hands.

"Jena! Jenaaaaa!" Avelino yells in panic.

I hear him, but don't respond immediately. After a couple big gulps of air, I catch my breath. The walls are inches from my face, but I can't see anything below me. While I can see Avelino's light shining down the hole, I can't see him.

"Jena? Are you alright? Can you hear me?" Avelino continues.

"Yes", I yell with the air I can manage to manipulate into sounds.

"Did you get hurt?" Jessica says with mild concern in her voice. Part of me felt like she was hoping I'd say yes.

I regain my composure. "I'm fine. I'm going to go down a little further."

"Don't!" Alex screams at the top of his lungs with complete urgency. "I feel like I've been here before. I think."

"Well...If you have, what is down here?" I respond.

"I don't know. I just feel like you shouldn't. You know, in my gut. Like it's a trap or something."

"You feel like it's a trap or you know it's a trap?" I say, patronizing him a little but frustrated he's being so vague and slow.

"Can you climb back up? If you can, it's probably better to be safe than sorry," Avelino adds.

"Probably. But maybe I should explore. It seems to go pretty deep."

"No," Alex protested. "We need to go this way. I've definitely been here before!" he responds with what felt like urgency in his voice.

"That's impossible. No one has ever been here before," Jessica chimes in.

"I don't mean *here* here. I mean in this cave, or in a cave like this." Alex walks a couple feet further into the cave and shines his light on the walls, using his free hand to rub the dirt off the wall to expose the surface more clearly. "No. I've definitely been here before and if it's like before..." He shines his light towards a spot in the cave that leads to a vast opening. "we need to hurry the fuck up!"

"No...way!" Avelino pausing deeply between each word.

"What? What is it?" I yell up.

"Just get back up here. You are making me nervous!" says Sven.

I look down the hole one more time. I can't see anything. I lower myself another feet or two, still nothing. I look back up to the light above and begin climbing, reluctantly. I know something is down there, but I better stay with everyone else.

Jessica grabs my hand to help pull me out as I make it to the opening.

"What did you guys find that is so important?" I say.

"It's not what we found, per se, it's where we are." Avelino leads me down the cave to another opening where Jacob, Alexander and Sven are standing. Jessica follows closely behind us, almost in between the two of us.

"What is that?" I say.

"That? Oh, that's just Grand View." Alexander says. "Which means we…we are in the Barrens outside of it."

For the first time in a while, I hear something besides excitement in Alexander's voice. What isn't he telling us?

"How can we be outside of the city? That's not even possible Alex!" Jessica says with so much sarcasm in her voice you could tell it was masking something else, probably fear.

"If that's Grand View, then where exactly are we supposed to go now?" I ask, as if anyone is going to know the answer. But surprisingly, Jacob does.

"We… Need… To… Go… Anywhere… That's… Not… Here… That's where!" Jacob exclaims as he points back towards the waterfall side of the cave.

The rest of us turn back to look where he's pointing. I don't see anything but I hear the weird squealing sounds again and they are getting much louder. Suddenly I could see the outline of black figures rapidly crawling and jumping out of the hole I was just in moments ago.

"Go now!" Jacob screams at all of us. "Now! Now! Now!"

Chapter 15

"Faster, Jessica! They're gaining on us!" Avelino yells as he reaches for Jessica's hand.

"If we don't get down before they get us, we are screwed!" Without looking back, Alexander chimes in and continues to lead us down the cliffs towards Grand View.

I briefly pause, turning to check on Avelino and Jessica. The screams get louder, and I squint, trying to focus my vision and see whatever is making the sound. Still, I can't see anything except for the tee canopy illuminated by the moonlight. No leaves, just bare, dead branches. Whatever is terrorizing us is clearly a master of disguise. I continue running, looking all around me. The impact of The Oze can be seen for miles. Everything looks so barren.

"I can't breathe," Jessica finally offers as an excuse for her tardiness. She adds a couple coughs to reinforce how difficult it is for her. "The whole area reeks of decay and smoke."

"You are fine," Alexander retorts. "It's all in your head. Yeah it smells, but the air is breathable."

"How do you know so much about where we are Alex?" I ask cautiously.

No response from Alex. Avelino and I exchange a quick glance. He signals to me that he has no idea what's going on either. The screeching gets louder. Whoever, or whatever is chasing us is getting closer. Much closer.

With heavy concern in his tone, Alexander forcibly says: "Let's just keep moving. We are running out of time to make it to the door!"

"What door? Why do we have to find a door? There is nothing for miles out here," I yell back at Alex. "Stop being so vague and tell us what is happening or we will..." And just like that the ground below our feet starts to shake uncontrollably. We all run as fast as we can but, within seconds, we are flying through the air as the ground crumbles below our feet. We scramble to climb and hold on to anything around us. Dried brush that crumbled upon touch. Brittle branches that snap under any pressure. And each other.

We land in a loud crash knocking the wind out of all of us.

"Alex, MOVE!" Sven chokingly yells.

I look over in the direction Sven is pointing and see a massive tree about to crash on top of Alex. Alexander looks over his shoulder to see what clearly has both Sven and I panicked. The tree is starting to fall faster, picking up speed as its balance begins to pivot. Alex, buried up to his waist in crumbled earth, futilely tries to claw himself out.

"I can't move! I can't get out!" Alexander begins to panic.

Sven and I seem paralyzed, for a few seconds before we begin running in Alex's direction.

"Alex!" I say as if the power of his name will help ease both of our pain if the tree isn't stopped.

Out of nowhere, Avelino appears in a blur just feet from where Alexander is trapped. He reaches his hands above his shoulders and catches the tree trunk, stopping it in its place. Alex, shocked even more than the rest of us, looks down and notices the slightest scratch on his newly exposed skin. A jagged branch presses him against the ground that with a few more milliseconds of force would have easily pierced Alexander completely through his chest. Avelino saved his life.

Avelino continues to hold the tree with one hand while using his other to latch grips with Alexander and pull him free. He drops the massive tree to his side and brushes the dirt, leaves and loose bark from his hair and his outfit. He continues to clean himself while the three of us are frozen in utter shock.

"That was a close call," Avelino says as if my brother didn't just about die.

"How did you do that! That was fucking awesome!" Alexander explodes with excitement, jumping up and down in circles until he embraces Avelino into a bear hug.

"I don't know, really. When I saw what was about to happen, my body just kind of..." he pauses as he chooses the right word in his head, "responded. I guess."

"Responded? Like fight or flight...and you picked FIGHT! Ok, I'll go with that!" Alexander continues to celebrate that he's still a live and even more impressed by Avelino's strength.

"But...that tree had to be like a 10,000 pounds. And you just...like appeared out of nowhere," Jessica says in a way that I couldn't quite tell if she was envious or flabbergasted.

"No really Jessica. I actually ran. I must have been so fast that you couldn't see me," Avelino responds.

"Oh. So, you have superhuman speed *AND* strength. How nice for you," Jessica adds. She sounded extremely envious. I don't really blame her, especially since she hasn't had any powers activated yet.

"Well, Avelino, looks like you just started to activate powers! Congrats!" Jacob adds in his two scents.

"Totally, Congratulations AV!" I say. "And thank you for saving my brother."

"Any time!" Avelino says so cavalierly. But even in the darkness lit only by our dimming flashlights, I could see him blush.

"OK. We need to start moving before they catch us!" Alexander reminds us all.

"No. I'm not moving until I know what is going on and what you think is chasing us!" Jessica folds her arms in a stance of defiance. Avelino and I shrug our shoulders and join her. Sven and Jacob fall in line as we all force Alexander to tell us the whole story.

"Fine. Yesterday, during the exam, I was being chased by these creatures that were small, like three or four feet tall at the most. Gremlin looking lizard-like creatures with razor sharp teeth that killed everything in their path, and I mean every...thing! And it was in a tunnel just like the one we were in. Okay! Does that not tell you what you need to hear to be a bit more motivated to run? Can we pleeeeaaaase keep moving?" Alexander throws us a look of petty frustration and condescension.

Looking into each other's eyes, we all silently agree to trust Alexander.

"Which way?" I ask. We all look around clearly convinced Alexander has told us enough to keep moving.

After what felt likes hours of running, we reached what appears to be an old railway tunnel. The cement opening leading into the tunnel had '1938 Battery Davis' engraved at the top. The walls and ceiling covered in layers of graffiti and earth. The tracks around us are mostly covered by piles of sand and brush. But further down the tunnel it looks like something else is strewn across the ground.

"Look at this!" says Avelino "Pointing to something on the wall."

"What does it say?" Sven asks not able to fully see it from where she was standing.

"It's kind of a map, of sorts, I guess. Left, with an arrow pointing left. Right, with an arrow pointing right," Avelino explains.

"And 'Up' crossed off," Alexander reads as he approaches.

"And *down* with a question mark," I finish.

"No. No it can't be?" Jessica screams as she finally sees what everyone is staring at.

"What? What's wrong?" I ask.

"I've seen that before. I...I saw it yesterday. Right before...before my exam ended. Before I chose the wrong one. Before... I failed," Jessica cries out.

"OK. So, you failed yesterday," Avelino says. "Now you know which way not to go. So, which way did you choose yesterday?" he asks her like a father would ask his daughter. "Which way, Jessica? Which way did you choose yesterday?"

"Left. I chose left"

"Well we clearly can't go up," I add. "So, that leaves right or down."

Screams. Terrible screams rapidly getting louder. Whatever was chasing them from Alexander's exam is still behind us.

"They've found us!" Alexander exclaims "We have to move. NOW!"

"Anyone see a hole or a tunnel or something that could lead us out?" I decide to take lead as it's clear Jessica is nearly catatonic.

"Nothing here," Avelino adds.

"Or here," Jacob responds.

"Jessica? Do you see anything?" I ask her pointedly.

"No, I don't think so."

"You either do or you don't. Which is it?" Sven snaps at her, obviously as frustrated with her as I am.

"No! I don't see anything like that." Jessica quivers but says with conviction.

"Right it is! Let's go!" I say, ushering them all in that direction.

We climb through the fallen piles of rock and dried dead trees. There must be half a football field that collapsed with us. The screams are intermittently hushed by heavy breathing and grunts as we run with every bit of energy we have left. The creatures that Alexander told us about are now in the tunnel with nothing but air between us.

"Run! Everyone, run faster!" Alexander bellows.

"What are those?" Asks Jessica as the moonlight from the end of the tunnel begins to illuminate the ground before us. "It looks like...?" she adds.

I get close enough to see. "Bones. Human bones. And lots of them. Keep moving!"

Without hesitation, I kick a skull out of my way. "Let's hope they aren't because of whatever is following us! But I don't know about you, I have no intention to find out!"

"We are almost there!" I yell to the rest of my team. "We are almost to the end of the tunnel!"

More bones cover the ground. The train tracks have completely disappeared. Each step closer to the opening crushes more bones beneath my feet. I reach the opening only to find the moon has disappeared into the thickest fog I have ever seen. The train tracks reappear only just to disappear into the fog as they lung over the cliff's edge. Whatever used to hold them has clearly been gone for a long time. Alexander is running with such speed I have to catch him before he would have leaped into oblivion.

"Stop!" I yell at Alex. "Stop! There is nothing beyond the tunnel!"

Avelino and Alexander come rushing to the edge nearly tripping over each other. Jessica arrives a few seconds later.

"This can't be!" Jessica exclaims, "This just can't be!"

"What? What can't be?" I ask

"This is where I went. This is left! This is what happened when I went LEFT!" She continues. "This…just…can't…be!" Jessica falls to the ground on all fours. Her head between the thumbs of each hand. She begins wailing "No. This can't be!" over and over again. Tears flow from her eyes uncontrollably. "I failed again!" Jessica cry's out and continues to weep tears.

"Umm…OK. Great. So, what do we do now, guys?" Alexander says looking away from Jessica in somewhat disbelief and back down the tunnel. In a much more calming voice than he had used earlier, he says, "Believe me when I tell you, we don't want those THINGS to catch us."

"Can we fight them? They must have a weakness," Avelino says, preparing himself to defend us as he picks up a branch that must have been only six or seven inches long.

"I don't want to stick around to find out," Alexander re-issues the warning. "There are dozens of them if not more."

The five of us continue to strategize when suddenly we all notice that Jessica isn't crying anymore. We turn our attention to where she was on all fours. She's on her knees now, looking at the ground silently.

"Jessica? Are you OK?" I ask to no response. "Jessica?"

We all exchange glances and begin walking closer to Jessica.

"Stop!" she says. "Don't come any closer."

Jessica stands up and backs away slowly. Between her palm prints in the loose dirt is what looks like a tiny pool of water, no more than a puddle a couple inches in diameter. Could Jessica have cried that much?

"Are those your…your tears?" Avelino asks Jessica in surprise.

"Damn girl! We knew you cried a lot but…you can seriously cry!" adds Alexander in his usually poor timing for humor.

The little starlight makes the pool of tears shimmer before they are rapidly absorbed into the ground, as if being slurped through a straw.

"Wow, did you see that?" Jacob asks.

The screams behind us have stopped. We are standing at the end of a tunnel with nowhere to go. The creatures should be here by now. I hear bones scraping against bones and quickly turn my attention back down the dark tunnel. My flashlight catches the reflection of bright yellow eyes, much larger than a humans.

"Um...guys? Guys? We have a problem. Well, actually lots of problems!" I say as I notice more sets of eyes appearing.

Suddenly, the silences evolves into a new screeching sound. A much more aggressive growl. Whatever they are, they are getting ready to destroy us. I hold my hands up to cover my ears as Avelino, Alexander, Jacob and Sven start chucking human skulls like tennis balls. The skulls crash feet in front of the creatures, holding them back momentarily, but only antagonizing their appetites.

"Look!" Jessica says. "Look!"

Turning their heads while continuing to throw bones towards the creatures, both Alexander and Avelino's eyes go wide. In the exact location that swallowed Jessica's tears, something is moving.

Simultaneously, they both say, "What is it?"

"It's grass," I say. "New grass. It's growing. And growing way faster than it should."

Jessica takes a couple steps back and has a smile as wide as her face. "It's brand new grass!"

The grass begins to grow all around us. Fresh Ivy begins to cover the wall of the tunnel. Nearby bushes start to flower and sprout leaves. New vines encase old ones. It looks like an area of no less than twenty feet in diameter from where Jessica's tears were swallowed by the soil has come back to life.

"Check this out," Alexander says as he continues to throw bones into the darkness to ward off the creatures.

Vines with enormous thorns begin to grow from one side of the tunnel to the other.

"They are building a wall for us!" Jessica says with her smile continuing to grow.

"You can...communicate with plants!" Avelino skeptically congratulates Jessica.

"Kind of. It's not like we are talking to each other or anything. But I feel like I can influence them somehow. Like they belong to me. Like…I'm their creator that they would do anything for."

"Cool. OK. So, you can communicate with plants. So, you are a Horti. Whatever it is you are doing, tell them to get us the fuck off this mountain! Can they do that?" Alexander sarcastically asks Jessica.

"Just be quiet for a second, Alex. Give me a moment to think." Jessica starts to walk away from Alex, towards the end of the tunnel, but stops in her tracks. "What's a Horti?" Jessica whispers as she leans over to Sven's ear.

"It's something Percenters are called with the power of a Horticulturalist, you know, someone who," using air quotes "communicates with plants."

"Oh, that's just great. As if I'm not odd woman out enough already. Now I'll be known as the Plant Lady. I'll probably live alone surrounded by hundreds of books on plants, and all of the plants in the books."

"Well, at least you finally have a power activated, officially making you are a Percenter. And you are alive! Now hurry if you want to stay alive! They are gaining on us!" I add.

"And think of it this way, if you can save us all now, then being a Horti will become

cool!" Alexander adds his normal positive spin on life.

Jessica walks to the edge of the tunnel and shines her flashlight down the cliff's edge into the darkness. No bottom in sight. The fog is too thick to see more than ten feet.

The creatures are getting angrier as they try to fight their way through the thorny vines. Screaming and grunting more aggressively now than they were just a few moments ago. I see a slimy little arm break through the wall of vines with its razor sharp fingernails. It's oozing something that I can only assume is it's blood from being cut by the thorns. The wall quickly regrows to strengthen itself, but it won't last much longer against their surprising strength.

"Whatever you need to do Jessica, now is the time to do it," I say encouraging her.

The ground begins to vibrate. Trees are sprouting from the side of the mountain with vines spanning from one to the other, creating nets from one tree trunk to the next. It's like they are building some sort of ladder for us to climb down.

"Jump," Jessica says

"Are you crazy?" Sven responds

"We all need to jump together, at the same time," Jessica continues.

We slowly join her at the edge of the tunnel. I look down the mountain with my flashlight. It looks like one cargo net after another stacked on the side of the mountain for as far as my light will shine.

"Ready? One... Two..." We all grab hands "Three!" And jump. We land about 10 feet below the cave opening in the soft netting of vines without thorns.

"Now what?"" Jacob asks Jessica. "This didn't help much. Now we are trapped on the side of a mountain with gremlins preparing for dinner...and that dinner is us!"

"Calm down Jacob. Just wait for it," Jessica says with a slight arrogance as she relaxes back into the vine netting with her hand clasped behind her head.

"Wait for it?" I say just loud enough for Jacob to hear as we exchange a glance.

"Wait for.... Whaaaaaaaattttt????" Alex and Avelino say in unison as the net wrapping our bodies crumbles to dust and we drop another ten to fifteen feet before we land in a second net of vines. Within seconds, just enough time for the air to get back into our lungs, it also crumbles and releases us to drop again.

Screaming over the noise of wind rushing past our ears, "I told you to just wait!" Jessica says. So proud of herself for unlocking a power that saved us all from being eaten alive. But I'm sure her grin is merely due to the fact that she has unlocked a Percenter power. It doesn't mean she can't still fail her exams, but it does mean she has power and isn't barren.

We continue to fall from one vine net to the next, each new one appearing as quickly as the one we are on crumbles. Our last drop lands us on a bed of sand. No, a beach of sand. The ground is starting to flatten out and as it does, the cloud of air around us gets thicker and thicker. The wind is so strong the sand begins to pelt our faces. Everything that grew anew alongside the cliffs of the mountain have once again returned to dust.

Alex catches Jessica fondly gazing at the side of the mountain that just moments ago sprouted plants simply because her tears gave life and her mind willed it, "Hurry! I'm serious! We only have a little bit of time left before it closes."

"Before what closes, Alex?" I ask.

"The door. The door into H6."

"H6? OK, enough mystery. We are in this together. What aren't you telling us?" Avelino says what the rest of us were thinking.

"Fine. Yesterday, during the exams, I was led here by some sort of…I don't really know what it was…like a guiding force or something. I can't explain it. All I know is that when I was here, I didn't get to the door in time and…" Alexander trails off.

"And WHAT?" Jessica screams

"AND…" Alexander continues, nervous to say more in fear of how we'd react, "those screaming creatures following us, let's just say they don't have the warmest of greetings."

"Meaning what exactly?" I chime in.

Suddenly Jacob falls to the ground with a big thud as he lets out a scream of his own. He gets to his knees and uses one hand to pull what looks like a dart out of his neck.

"RUN!" Alexander says as he and Sven lift Jacob and put his arms around their shoulders to carry him. Jessica grabs my arm and we start running in the same direction. The air was so thick that I didn't see her for long. As slow as she was in the tunnel, she's making up for it now. I think she has a renewed spirit now that she has activated a power.

"Jessica? Jessica? Where are you?" I scream.

Alexander is someplace behind me with Jacob half on his back and Sven running alongside. Whatever was in that dart has made Jacob unconscious and completely limp now.

"Keep going Jena!" Alexander encourages me from someplace in the fog

"We are almost there!"

When I turn around to the find the others, they are all gone. I begin walking through what feels like rubble. I start calling their names, searching behind crumbling buildings and blocks of stone. Smoke added to the fog and together were as thick as midnight, and I could barely see my own hands. Alexander mentioned a door. I have to find a door. What door?

Standing in the thick smoke, I hear Jessica scream "Help!"

I immediately run towards her voice and about 10 feet away from me, the smoke is settled, and I see Jessica across a wide cavernous chasm in the center of an asphalt road. Bombed-out warehouse buildings flank either side of the hole, making it impossible to go around. Two soldiers with guns and helmets that conceal their faces have Jessica cornered on the other side.

A voice either in my head or out of thin air, speaks to me as I wonder who these soldiers were.

"They are with the Cleansing Coalition. Do not let them know you are here. Do not let Jessica know who they are. They have mind control capabilities. They can seize your fear and crush you with that fear. They will make you go crazy. They will bring you to your worst nightmare slowly followed by your death. Cloak now, Jena!"

I don't hesitate. I don't care where that voice came from, I'm not taking any chances. I draw in a deep breath from my solar plexus and numb my consciousness like my mother taught me. I close my eyes as I exhale, feeling my thoughts float away. I feel every hair follicle on my head tingle. I did it!

The game, or whatever this is, has just taken a very real twist.

"Please, someone help me!" Jessica screams.

My heart drops to my feet. If Jessica dies, I will not forgive myself.

"Please, help me!" shrieks Jessica again. "What do I do?"

Jessica's eyes are wide with fear.

"I'm coming!" I shout. I scan the surrounding to see if there is a way to reach Jessica unnoticed. Appearing in the distance, I see one of those cloaked figures beginning to take shape out of thin air. It can't be! That usually means Hunter is nearby. But I doubt even he has the skills to invade our simulation, but I wouldn't put it passed him. I can smell the burning flesh of the cloaked figure as it starts towards me. The stench is suffocating.

A second and third cloaked figure appear just as the first had. I know how powerful these demons are and that many more will probably appear if we don't act fast.

Full of adrenaline, I crouch and then jump high into the air. I fling myself across the gaping hole, just barely making it to the other side. As I land, with great speed and force, I conjure up an orb of energy in my hand, and hurl it at the closest demon. An explosion of green-tinged red combusts against the metal of his armor and blazes into the air. The soldier drops to the ground and withers into hissing ash.

Before I let myself think, I spin around in a circle and hurl another energy orb at multiple black-hooded demons now flying towards me.

Out of nowhere, Sven comes around the corner and begins attacking the remaining soldier. She's throwing massive rocks and rubble at him. After being hit, the soldier turns his attention to Sven just long enough for Jessica to escape and run down an old alley away from the fight. He begins firing his gun at Sven.

Avelino, in the blink of an eye, darts over to Sven and brings her over to where I'm fighting the cloaked figures. We quickly run back into the covering of the thick fog, the opposite direction of Jessica.

"Where have you guys been?" I say with the little breath I have left. "Where are Alex and Jacob?"

Before they have a chance to catch their breath and respond, Alexander appears.

"Jena? Is that you?" Alexander whispers. "Thank God it's you!"

I reach for Alex, hugging him as soon as I can feel him. "What happened? You told me to run, and I thought you were right behind me."

"I know, sorry. I had to get Jacob through the door. If I didn't, well, let's just say it's a good thing I did."

"What door are you talking about? I didn't see any door," I ask him. "Everything has been destroyed here."

"Turns out, the door isn't really a door as much as it is an idea of a door."

"What are you talking about Alex? You need to start filling me in, now!"

"OK. So, yesterday, during the exams, I was here. Except, in my version of here, the city wasn't destroyed. There was a door, a gateway, that once I crossed it, I was transported back to San Sun. I found the gateway but I don't have any idea of where, or when, we are now. All I know is that Jacob is still in a bad way but he's not here. He should be safe in San Sun once someone finds him."

Shit. I was so happy to see Alexander that I forgot about Jacob. "Oh, my God! I forgot Jacob!"

"Do you think any of his powers activated before he left?" Sven asks Alexander.

Shaking his head and still catching his breath, Avelino says: "I hope so, for his sake. But I couldn't tell."

"We have to find Jessica. She ran the opposite direction during the attack. And we probably don't have much time before they find us again," I say.

"What were those things flying around all mysterious and shit?" Sven asks the group, looking at each of our faces to see which one of us recognized them.

"I'm not really sure, but I have seen them before. First at the exam's opening celebration, and then again during my simulation. I'm not sure who or what they are, but they always seem to appear with…" I trail off, not sure if I can tell the group about Hunter or not. I'm starting to trust everyone, but I'm not sure they need to know about anything they don't see for themselves. "With…" I'm searching for the right words to say to throw them off the track, "horrible B.O.!"

Everyone laughs, amused by the fact that I called it on the nose.

"And OMG!" Sven continues. "Those energy balls or whatever it was that you threw…so cool! What are they?"

Instead of answering her, I take this opportunity to move the conversation forward. We still have to find The Numinous after all.

"Thanks Sven. I'm not really sure. What do we do now? How do we find Jessica and The Numinous?" I ask, looking at Alexander.

"I don't know. Like I said, the city didn't look like this when I was here.

"I know," musters Avelino

We all look at Avelino with curiosity.

"What?" I say back to him as if I didn't hear him correctly.

"I know what we need to do. I've been here. I know where we are."

"What do you mean, like yesterday, in your exam?" I say.

Avelino takes a deep breath, struggling to say anything at all. "No. I've been here. Right here."

Hesitating as his memories come back to him.

"But I remember now. This wasn't my exam. This was real."

Avelino looks around at the ruins and continues telling us his story.

"I was here when I was just a boy. Maybe four, five at the most. I stayed in the Bullet playing games but I peeked out the window, even though I wasn't supposed to."

Avelino's memories are coming back to him in pieces as he talks them through, one by one.

"I saw my dad. I saw my dad yelling at someone, he was really upset. Wait, there was a woman next to my dad that wasn't my mom. She said something to my dad and then the woman gently touched the man on his temple, and he fell to his knees in complete agony. My dad just turned away and started walking back to the Bullet. I quickly turned my attention back to the toys, and that's the last I remember.

But I think I know where to find The Numinous."

Chapter 16

Before any of us have a chance to respond to Avelino, the room we are standing in returns to normal. The simulation has ended.

We all look at each other with expectant faces. Sven, Alexander, Avelino, and I grab hands and move together to form a solid circle, back to back. No Jessica and no Jacob.

"What? That can't be it, we didn't reach The Numinous! What's next?" asks Alexander.

We all stand there, waiting, holding our breaths. We can see nothing except a bright white light that appears in every direction, no matter where you look. There is no answer to Alexander's question.

"Hello? Is anyone there?" I ask to a completely silent room.

A few more seconds pass in silence when a small crackling blue light, almost like mini-lightning, begins to form directly in front of me. It's no more than one or two feet in diameter and emanates a blue pulse from within its core. I'm mesmerized by it, almost hypnotized, and before I ask can muster my words to everyone else I am hit with a jolt of energy attaching me to the source. Alexander, Sven, and Avelino disappear from my touch and all I feel is the energy of this thing coursing through my body. The energy lifts me into the air and then releases me.

I feel a strange sensation. Instead of falling, I feel light as a feather. A complete weightlessness overtakes me. It is an odd sense of wonderment, joy, and happiness. I start spinning in the air and, when I look down, I see my body standing completely still with my eyes wide open. It is me. My body is still there by my mind some t is somehow in this other body. I look at my feet and legs and see that I was becoming almost translucent–so fine and transparent that points of light could pass through me.

Effortlessly, I lift into the air and fly high into the sky. There is no ceiling in the room as I soar higher and higher. I keep flying into the sky and when I look back, I see something that I never expected. I can see San Sun below me…it sits stoically above the Earth, nestled on what looks like a bed of clouds but is really The Oze.

I blink my eye and open to see San Sun, floating above a thriving metropolis with thousands of people on the ground, in the open. Trees, ponds, and parks filled with birds and dogs running after them. I blink again and it is all gone. I see only clouds.

There is a deep, rhythmic pounding–a humming or vibration, some-where–distant, yet strong. I continue to feel each pulse of the lightning energy that appeared to me as it dances through my body. I soar higher into a blue-grey haze of ethereal atoms and spiraling lights.

I surprisingly feel relaxed. I have never experienced this type of peace, this oneness with the universe, this calmness. I feel totally free and possess a strange awareness that is like quicksilver. It's deep and penetrating. I feel as though I have been implanted with the wisdom of every Percenter before me. I feel no fear. I have reached The Numinous.

Chapter 17

It is nighttime. Shapes and footsteps materialize from the dark alleys. The moon overhead looks red and wounded. A blitz of orange lightning bursts like fireworks in the sky.

"Where am I?" I say to anyone who will listen.

I sink back and try to disappear into the wall of what was once an apartment building. Everywhere I looked fires were exploding throughout the city.

I close my eyes as images rush into my mind. Fires. Soldiers patrolling the streets. Riots everywhere. Explosions of fire on every corner. Gunshots. Children screaming. Adults screaming. People robbing and shooting their own neighbors. Buildings imploding. Burning. The glass windows shattered into smithereens.

I shut my eyes shut even harder and squeeze my head in between both hands, trying to get the images out of my mind. There is death and destruction on every street. I have to find my family. They're hiding somewhere, I feel it.

I grab a gun laying only a few feet from me, having no idea how to operate one. I take it and lift it in line with my right eye, closing my left, ready to shoot if I have to. My arms tremble as I try to hold the gun steady.

All around me, the air is pierced with screeching sirens. A drone passes overhead, sweeping lights on the ground to track everyone. I press back even further into the outer wall of the building.

Everyone is screaming and crying. A group of people run down the street not far from me. They are quickly followed by a few guys, dressed liked soldiers, lumbering after them. I stay hidden and within seconds, I can hear multiple gunshots.

My heart drops. The world has gone mad. I slowly realize that I've phased into the original city below San Sun but in the past, the time when the Great Ozone Event, or The Oze as we call it now, catastrophe took place. What I'm experiencing now is just the beginning. It will get much worse before it gets better.

This is when the secret Percenter society revealed themselves in order to save the human race...and take control as the superior, evolved human species. It is when war broke out between those wanting to be saved and those wanting to keep power. Most people, Percenter and human alike, fought for survival and afterwards, the new civilization of Percenters, Middlers and Barrens were born.

It is when the Sky Cities were built for those with powers and the Barren Bubbles to rescue the humans. It was only a matter of time before the surviving humans realized they were also enslaved. It only took the Percenters a few generations to complete forget how terrible it was to live on The Ground.

I start running aimlessly, looking for Alexander, Avelino and anyone else familiar. I can't find anyone. I keep my gun in my hand and begin to run in long strides from shadow to shadow to make sure I'm not spotted. Two steps, three steps. Almost past one block. I'll make it, I tell myself, even though I don't have any specific destination except safety.

I trip on a stone block at the corner of a building and stumble, falling down on the sidewalk and dropping my gun. As I quickly grapple for the dropped weapon, a foot stomps on my hand. I scream, not seeing who it is as a massive hand wraps completely around the back of my neck, lifting me up to where my toes barely touch the ground. I feel someone's hot breath on my neck.

"Not so fast," the man says with a deep, raspy voice.

I shove my elbow back into the man's stomach, but he just laughs.

"Don't move," he says, "or I'll end you here and now."

"Let me go!" I say assertively. I am more scared than I'm letting on.

"I don't think so. There are some very important people that want to meet you, *Jena*." He emphasizes Jena with the most disdain I have ever heard in anyone's voice.

"Please, I can get you whatever you want. My family has influence," I try to plead and bargain with the man. But he just continues to laugh at me.

"Hmmmm...If you're nice to me, maybe I'll let you go," he says. "But it will come at a price." I try, but I can't turn to see his face. He has me pinned in front of him. But his voice sounds familiar...so familiar.

A shot from a gun rings out and the hand around my neck slacks as he lets out a grunt. Out of the corner of my eye I see a young woman standing in the shadows of the alleyway I just came from. She fires a second time but misses. She runs to hide. Momentarily, he lets go of me as he feels where a bullet pierced his shoulder. I drop down and turn around quickly to look at the man that held me hostage.

I can't move. I can't breathe. It can't be! It's Hunter!

"It's you!" I shout. "Why are you here? How are you here?"

"I told you," he sneers, continuing to hold his shoulder where he was just shot, "I will hunt you down, kill you and take your powers. You can't hide from me no matter where, or when, you go. Stupid Jena, you have no idea who you are up against!"

Another drone flies overhead. Footsteps run past us down the street and around the corner. Most likely more people running from soldiers. With my attention turned toward the noise, Hunter takes off in the opposite direction.

"I'm not afraid of you!" I shout at Hunter as I stand up.

"You should be!" he yells back. He flees down the road, disappearing into the melee.

The woman who shot Hunter runs up to me. I can't believe it. I have to look twice to make sure what I'm seeing is correct. It's my mother!

"C'mon, we have to get out of here," she says, her gun at her side. She extends her arms around me for a brief embrace.

"Mom?" I ask. "What are you doing here?"

"I came for you, Jena," Mom says.

133

"But...how...I don't understand! Where is Alex, AV, the others?"

"I'll explain later. There's not much time," Mom says. "I'm afraid you're in real danger, Jena. Not just here, but at the exam."

"What's happening!? Is Dad here?" I ask.

"I'll explain later. We need to move, now!"

Mom leads the way and we run as fast as our legs will go through the narrow alleyways. The smoke fills my lungs, and I cough. This toxic air is alien to me. The Oze is just days away from being completely life threatening.

From somewhere far away, I hear Za's voice. "Jena, remember, my power is your power."

Mom leads me through a doorway and suddenly stops, shutting the door behind us.

"Now Jena! Go! You have to get back to Alexander NOW! Think hard about the simulation room. Good luck, darling..."

I don't hesitate. I have no fear.

"I love you, Mom!" I say with more calmness in my voice than I have had in days as I reach to hug her one last time.

My mom fades away and there is nothing more than a glimmer in the air where she was standing no less than a second ago.

I close my eyes and think about the exam room. I picture myself next to Alexander before all this happened. My back touching his. My hands locked with Avelino on one side and Sven on the other. I think about the white light just as my teammates begin to appear to me, and I am back in the room. I open my eyes and release a huge smile.

"Wow! That was intense!" I say as I look at them, expecting them to have a similar reaction. But I was wrong.

With shock in their eyes, they all stare at me as if they've seen a ghost. "What's wrong? Why do you all look like your grandma just died?"

"Jena," says Avelino, taking my hand, "that...that...guy who's after you...he came into all of our simulations."

"What?" I ask. "All of you...all of you saw Hunter?"

"Yes," says Alexander. He's shaking visibly. Something I have never seen Alexander do before. "I don't know what you did to piss him off, but that guy is after your powers in a bad way. Who is he anyway?"

"What exactly did he say? What were his exact words?" I ask, barely able to breathe I am so nervous he might have said something about my mission.

"He warned us that if we help you, he is going to kill us all. He said it's either you, or all of us," says Sven.

"Anything else?" I ask

"One thing," Avelino adds, as he lowers his head before picking it back up and looking me straight in the face. "He said that if we helped you that we'd all end up like Jessica." Pausing for a brief second, but continuing in his calm and steady voice that I have come to rely on, "Jena, do you know what happened to Jessica?"

Chapter 18

I am trembling. More like shaking. So hard that my body is rocking. Avelino holds my hand firmly in his, trying to steady me, hoping this will comfort me.

Alexander is silent. His brows are furrowed together like Father's are when he worries about something. And Sven looks like she's going to cry.

The proctor opens the door into our simulation room and walks right to where we are standing without saying a word. I'm trying to comprehend the danger that we've just encountered and afraid of what we may still encounter before the day is over.

"Very interesting results so far on your exams," the Proctor says, an eyebrow lifted.

"Is it over?" Alexander asks. A bead of sweat pops onto his forehead. He is nervous, I know, because it's a rare emotion to see him express. He's guarded. He's direct.

"Oh no, The Numinous is next and quite strenuous, I'm afraid," she says with a little smile of delight.

"Wait, The Numinous? I thought we…" I stop myself and look at Alexander. He's looking blankly back at me waiting for what I'm going to say next. I look to Sven and Avelino to see if they get where I was going but they also have a blank look on their faces. I guess the lightning power and traveling to the time of the Great Ozone Event was a precursor to The Numinous. "…I thought we were done."

The proctor and everyone else looks at me but stays quiet, as if I just said the stupidest thing you could ever say.

"Let me warn you," the proctor continues without acknowledging what I just said, "There are risks to this test. But the potential rewards are endless and far outweigh the risks." I think she's actually enjoying our panicked expressions.

"What do you mean? What risks?" asks Alexander.

"While it's rare, on occasion, some candidates don't come back right in the head, or back at all," says the Proctor very cavalierly. "However, you can choose not to take this part of the exam, it is not mandatory. If that is your choice, you may have powers that are never activated. Reaching The Numinous is your one chance to activate all of your powers."

"But..." she adds, "it is your choice."

We all look at each other. For a moment, I ponder the situation, not sure if I should take this part of the exam. But I remember what Za told me and know I have no choice. I must activate all of my powers of I'll be useless to the Saviors.

"So, the downside is either we go crazy or get trapped in an alternate reality forever?" asks Alexander.

The Proctor simply nods her head up and down slowly one time while smiling at all of us. Alexander, without pausing or looking at the rest of us, confidently exclaims "I'm in!"

"What do you mean by right in the head exactly? Do you really mean crazy like Alex said?" asks Avelino. He glances quickly at me with a worried look on his face and squeezes my hand tighter.

"Going into The Numinous requires advanced Percenter skills," continues the Proctor. "We have no way of knowing when or where a candidate will go. Unfortunately, some candidates can't handle the extraordinary powers needed to reach The Numinous and return home, so they become trapped in a false reality, constantly being tortured in their minds trying to find a way out. I like to think of it as being trapped in a maze, but the maze can't be solved."

"I thought that someone will come and rescue us if we're in trouble," says Sven. "At least, that's what you said in the first part of the exam today."

"Yes, that was possible in the first Part, my dear. Just like how we rescued

Jacob and Jessica." The Proctor nods her head and adjusts her eyeglasses that have slipped down on the bridge of her nose. For the first time I notice her name, Vicky, embroidered onto her lapel. "But in this part, you're going to go deeper than we can. Because of this, we can't always find you and it makes it too risky for us to go looking. The Numinous has the power, we don't."

A chill runs up my back, and my hair stands on end. All of this sounds horrifying. I cannot imagine being trapped inside one's own body that way. None of these potential outcomes sound good. And yet, I know I have no choice. I have to do it.

"I-I-I'm not sure, but I think I want to do it, too," says Jessica, appearing out of nowhere.

"Um…where did you just come from?" Asks Alexander

"Jessica, oh my God! Are you OK?" I ask Jessica with some urgency, especially after what Avelino told me Hunter said to them. I reach to hug her, but she folds her arms instead.

"Oh, yea, thanks for leaving me everyone. Remember. Suppose to be a T.E.A.M!" Jessica responds in her normal irritating tone.

"Okay, fine," I say withdrawing my arms but still keeping an eye on Jessica.

"Like I said, I'm in," Jessica affirms.

This surprises me, but I know that she is trying hard to prove herself. Jessica is worried that she won't pass the exams at all, and will be sent to the Ground, anyway. That is more embarrassing for her and her family than being trapped in a timeline. And if she can pass this part of the exam, it really will boost her chances of getting into a good Prep School.

"So do I," agrees Alexander. "I'm not afraid, bring it on!"

"Me, too." Avelino nods his head. "What about you, Jena?"

"Alright, I'm in." I am not half as brave as I sounded. Sven agree as well. No one wants to miss out on the chance to activate more powers. I think our greed gets the best of us. 'Surpass all others before you', after all. It's the Percenter way.

Vicky smiles. "That is wonderful! Trust me, candidates, if you pass this, you will be marked to be one of our great leaders of tomorrow. I'm sure of it. Follow me to the chamber for this part."

"Wait! Where is Jacob? I thought you said you rescued him, too?" I ask Vicky.

"We did, with Alexander's help. But Jacob has decided not to seek out The Numinous."

We follow her down a hallway and enter a different expansive room with chamber-like cubicles. They remind me of the cubicles I sat in on the first day. We step inside and each one of us settles into our assigned cubicle.

Vicky hooks us up to video monitors, then injects the tracing antigen that will archive our results in the exams. Thankfully, I know mine won't be.

Vicky asks me, "Are you comfortable, Miss de Fenace'?"

"Yes, ma'am, I'm fine," I tell her.

She smiles mysteriously at me.

"Can you give me an idea of what to expect?" I ask her.

"Let me just say this. If you thought the exams have been intense so far, and if you thought the force beyond," using her fingers to create air quotes for the word beyond, "was powerful, then be assured, this will be tenfold!" She laughs as she turns away from us.

I'm not sure why she's saying these things to me. Maybe she's just trying to scare me. I realize that is a silly thought. Proctors generally want the best for us. She is probably just trying to frighten us—me—to make us use the best of our skills and activate all of our powers.

"Good luck! And may you surpass all others before you!" says Vicky as she leaves us.

Chapter 19

The blades of two swords, long and gleaming, made of a shining white metal that is definitely not from the Sovereign Sky Cities, slash down at me inches from where I stand. The odorous scent of evil leaps up like a geyser, spurting down over me, announcing that Death is here.

I look around and have no idea where, or when for that matter, I am. I don't have time to think as the swords slash at me again, this time they pierce my forearm as I block my face. I am so scared my legs tremble and my teeth chatter together. I fall to the ground, barely able to move. I see other Percenter candidates all around me. They are screaming and running away from demonic looking creatures.

I notice that these demons are not like the hooded ones I have been seeing in my peripheral since the exams started, but much larger and scarier looking. They look like men, but their flesh appears to be continuously melting, like they are walking through fire, minus the fire.

"Run, Jenavieve, run! They're after you!" shouts Avelino. I look at him as I stand to my feet.

I look around for Jessica and Alex, but I don't see them anywhere. I see Sven running away, too far for me to catch her now. AV tries to get the demon's attention by yelling at them, but they seem to be laser focused on me. He jumps on the back of one closest to him, punching it in the head.

I whirl away from the demon slashing his swords at me and run as fast as my legs can carry me through a long hallway. I look back to see AV running in the same direction as Sven. I turn towards what looks like an old library.

I don't recognize it but I feel like it has to be one of the Prep Schools.

I hear the demons behind me. Questions overwhelm my thoughts. Where have they come from? What are they? Why are they after us...after me? I take a deep gulp of air and say to myself under my breath, "What the Hell is going on?"

Two giant figures carrying the long swords are shrouded in black cloaks and hoods. Their faces have disappeared into the darkness provided by the hoods. They are at least ten feet tall, with nothing visible but the fiery red eyes of hell, burning holes out from under their hoods. Without a shadow of a doubt, though, they are trying to kill me. They continue chasing after me, not at all distracted by the other kids running and screaming.

Heavy footsteps are close behind me, getting closer every second. My heart thuds in my chest as I charge further into the maze of books lining the massive library. Sweat is streaming down my forehead.

When I reach the furthest wall of books in the library, I turn around and look back. It is the scariest site I have ever seen in my life. Candidates screaming uncontrollably, some with blood shooting from their bodies where limbs used to be.

Others, crawling across the floor. Some not moving at all, dead. The demons are much closer than I thought, only some thirty feet back and they are coming straight at me, slashing their gleaming swords at everyone in their way. I hear a low, intense roar and then bellowing, bloodcurdling sounds.

I find a door. I quickly pull down the handle and open it. Shutting it behind me just as fast as I opened it. The very second I turn to and enter the room, I make eye contact with a peculiar man hiding in the corner. The room is barely lit but he can still see the panic in my eyes and in turn, I can see the growing fear in his. I recognize him, at least I think I do.

I walk closer and realize it's Mr. Hampton, our neighbor in San Sun. I don't really know him, outside of the occasional "hello, good morning" type conversation. He was a long-time bachelor, never married and no kids. My parents never really talked to him much either, so he has always been that familiar stranger to us.

"Help me, they're coming for me," I scream. I slam the heavy oak door behind me, leaning against it with all my weight.

Mr. Hampton runs to me and turns the massive bronze key, locking it. "Get in the tunnels, Jenavieve! They won't be able to follow you," Mr. Hampton shouts. His voice is strong, commanding. He knows who I am, too, but why is he helping me.

The demons ram against the door with so much force that it throws me forwards, and almost knocks the door off its hinges.

Mr. Hampton helps me up and pushes me aside. He opens a secret passageway from behind another wall of books by simply taking one off the shelf. I noticed the title of the book he grabbed he was titled "America's democracy is dead."

"Run!" Mr. Hampton shouts. "I'll try to hold them back as long as I can!"

"Who are they?" I cry. "Why are you helping me?"

"There's no time to explain," he yells. "You must get out of here and quickly! You'll know your way through the tunnels, just trust me. Get out of here–get to the water and you'll be safe."

"The water?" I am not sure where that is, or why it's important, but I have no reason to question it.

"Za will be waiting for you," Mr. Hampton continues.

"But if I leave, they'll kill you!"

"Do not let my age or looks deceive you, Jenavieve," says Mr. Hampton. "Go! Our paths will cross again!"

"OK" I nod, flinging my long hair back off my shoulders and not wasting another second as the demons break through the door being braced by Mr. Hampton. He flies through the air clear across the room. There is no time to think. I slip behind the open bookshelf and inside a dimly lit tunnel just before the demons enter the room.

On my tiptoes, I peek through a pin-size hole in the secret bookcase door.

I am astonished to see Mr. Hampton move easily with unbelievable speed across the room to attack–and to a point just outside my line of sight–all without the use of his silver cane. I remember him as an old, arthritic man who can barely walk. But I guess we are all full of surprises.

What comes next is even more shocking as I hear the terrifying sounds of the otherworldly demons roaring as they engage in a violent battle with Mr. Hampton. As fast as lightning, one of the hooded monsters flies some forty feet high through the air and slams into one of the bookcases on the other side of the room.

"Holy shit!" I say. "Go, Mr. Hampton!"

All of a sudden, I see Mr. Hampton's body hurl backwards, slamming over tables and chairs in his path. His lifeless body sprawled across the floor.

"They killed him! Oh my God, they killed him!" I whisper in total panic.

The hooded demons lurch in front of me with their backs turned to the secret bookcase door. One of them whispers in a deep and sinister voice. I hear them clearly, but I cannot understand a word they are saying. They speak in a strange language that I cannot decipher.

One of the demons sniffs around the room and slowly turns to where I stand behind the secret door. He is about twenty feet away. Long sharp talons curl around the gleaming white metal sword that he holds in one hand. With his other hand, he pushes his hood back off his face and turns his nose upwards to catch a better scent of his prey–ME! My heart skips a couple beats.

He is half-man, half-beast. He has razor sharp teeth like a vicious, mangy-looking dog, and long dark hair that looks like gnarly barbed wire and pasty white skin. He utterly terrifies me.

The unhooded demon looks directly at the pinhole in the secret door where my eye is staring back. A slow, sinister smile spreads across his melting face as he moves towards my secret location. He can smell me.

I suck in my breath and quickly take two steps backwards. I realize I have wasted too much time. I grab the torch along the wall and race down the stairs of the secret passageway.

As I bolt through the tunnel with the torch lighting the path in front of me, I hear the crashing sound of the secret door being broken down behind me. They are coming after me! This could be it. I might never see my family, or Avelino, again.

I continue head down the passageway, letting my free hand guide me along the narrow walls. The tunnels are too small for the demons to follow but I can hear them behind me as their voices echo through the chamber.

I go further into the darkness and disappear into the safety of the underground labyrinth as the destructive sounds of the old library being destroyed fade behind me. There is only one way to go now.

I start wondering about Mr. Hampton. I have this nagging feeling Mr. Hampton is much more than just my neighbor in San Sun. There was just something about him that was… familiar. It's just too strange that he would be here, in the exams. He has no reason to be. He especially has no reason to help me.

The tunnel starts to get wider, and I no longer need to feel the walls to guide me. Chairs and old tapestry line the tunnel, getting in my way. I am running so fast, I trip over something and tumble forward, sprawling uncontrollably on the floor. The torch flies out of my hand and hits the wall with a thud. The flame blows out, and I am suddenly in pitch darkness.

I roll onto my back and huddle to the side. All I can see is darkness. I sit there, catching my breath in panic, hoping that nothing has followed me when I start to notice a sound coming from where I just ran. Out of the darkness I see the same pair of burning-fiery red eyes that have been haunting me this entire exam. They are coming towards me. And then I hear him. His mischievous laugh. Hunter comes out of hiding, rushing toward me in the darkness of the tunnel.

He grabs me, pulling me close to its face. He's grinding his sharp and pointy piranha teeth. The sound is screeching, like metal against metal. He smells of garbage and feces, just like the demons. I begin gagging uncontrollably as I lay lifeless in his grip.

He laughs again as he drops me to the floor. With both hands, he raises his sword as it ignites into a silver flame, as if connecting to some ancient energy.

"I told you. You can't escape me, Jenavieve de Fenace,'" he shouts.

For what seems like the hundredth time during the exams, I know I am going to die. Just then, a voice calls out to me. "Remember who you are,

Jenavieve! Remember your powers!" It is Za's voice.

I focus with all my strength. I envision Hunter stabbing himself with his own sword, but nothing happens. I try to produce the same orbs of energy I used to turn the soldiers into ash but again, nothing happens. My powers aren't working.

Beneath the light of his glowing sword, Hunter morphs into a hulking beast unlike anything I could have imagined. Massive, with basketball sized biceps and his head nearly touching the ceiling. He starts laughing again, almost making a growling sound.

"Why are you trying to kill me? What have I ever done to you?" I scream at him.

"I already told you Jena, your powers," Hunter says cavalierly.

What comes next shocks me.

It all happened so quickly but played out as if in slow motion. Hunter swung his sword at me with what looked like every bit of strength he had. I raised my arms in a futile attempt to stop his razor-sharp blade from slicing me in half. His grunt of power as he began to lower the blade didn't frighten me, but woke something up instead.

Just as his sword was about to strike less than an inch from my face, my body released an outward explosion of blue force 360 degrees from my body. I stay conscious only long enough to see Hunter blasted down the length of the tunnel quickly followed by the ceiling collapsing on top of him, and me.

Chapter 20

"Where am I?" I barely mutter out of my lips as I rub my throbbing head.

I'm kneeling in the dark tunnel, as if it hadn't just collapsed on me. Except now, I have Hunter's sword firmly in my hand. I blink my eyes rapidly, trying to clear my foggy mind.

"What is happening?" I say as I push from the ground to stand upright. I'm so confused. I can't help but think what just happened wasn't really supposed to be part of the exam simulation. If it wasn't for Hunter's sword, I'd think it was all just a bad dream, but I'm living this bad dream instead. I just don't understand how Hunter can always find me when nobody else is around. It's like he is watching me at all times and waits to strike.

"Za," I plead inwardly with a weak and broken voice, "get me out of here. I give up. I can't do this anymore. Please, just do this for me."

I close my eyes and try to phase out of here, back to the simulation room, but nothing happens. I focus every bit of my energy on my power. Still, nothing happens. I don't understand. I haven't been able to call on any of my powers. I look around. All is quiet. Too quiet.

I start to see a shimmer, more like a green light cracking through thin air a couple feet from where I'm standing. It's where Hunter stood before he attacked me. And just as I realized the coincidence, an image materializes out of the light break. Hunter's ghostly face lurches in front of me with a smirk on his face from ear to ear.

"Looks like kitty is finding her claws!" The mirage of Hunter sarcastically addresses me.

I stare back at him given no recognition of what he just said with a look on my face clearly saying "I'm not even remotely entertained!"

"So… it looks like it's just you and me, Jenavieve de Fenace'. Just you, and me." He licks his lips in exaggerated movements, waiting for its prey. His tongue is split at the tip and pointed like a serpent. "I bet you thought you finally got rid of me with that little trick of yours. Tell me Jena, what do you call it? That force."

"Enough. What do you want from me?" I ask him, keeping the sword poised to strike if he attempts anything beyond talking.

"Come now, Jena, it must have a name. Hmmm…" He rubs his little chin, toying with me. "I got it! Let's call it the Supersonic Warhead!"

"Shut up!" I command with the sword raised above my head and it starts to glow.

"Easy, Jena. Fine, Supersonic it is. Jeez…who knew you were so sensitive," Hunter continues with the smirk on his face I am quickly starting to detest. "Now, I'm going to need my sword back. So why don't you just hand that back, now, Jena."

"Go fuck yourself!" I take a swing at Hunter only to slice through thin air. The sword channeled my force as it sliced through the air releasing a blue laser and cutting into the tunnel walls as I swung.

Hunter's image disappears only briefly and reappears out of the light as he laughs uncontrollably.

"Well look at that Jena, you can control the Destiny Sword! Good for you."

I don't react to him naming the sword but I do recognize the name. I remember childhood stories about a Destiny Sword that once helped kings rule their lands. The steel was somehow enhanced by the power of a Founding Chancellor, Spencer Tilbury. He was lustful for power when he created it and passed it down from generation to generation, making whoever held it unbeatable. Some stories say the most power Percenter of the times. The stories also say it was lost at sea centuries ago and has never been found. I always thought it was just Percenter folklore.

"Let's move along, shall we?" Hunter asks rhetorically. "It's rather simple. And if you do as I say, I'll leave you alone, Jena. All I want you to do is stop what you're planning, go to the prep school of your choice, and stay out of things that are of no concern to you."

"Right! Like I'm supposed to just take your word. How dumb do you think I am?" I respond.

"Come now, Jenavieve. Do you think you can trust me?" Hunter pauses for effect and reintroduces his annoyingly large grin. "Be a good little girl now. Don't make me ask you twice." He smiles slyly at me. Wickedly. Knowingly.

"And if I don't?" My heart races.

"You see, over the years many Percenters have shared their powers with me. Well, in all honesty, since you and I can be honest with one another, right Jena?! Once I kill them, I take their powers. You see, I can't be stopped so when I finally catch you, you'll wish I would have killed you already. But before I kill you, I'll get your smart-ass twin brother. And then your handsome but unavailable boyfriend, Avelino. And let's not forget about precious mommy and daddy!"

"I will never surrender to you Hunter so bring everything you think you have," I scream at him and swing the sword back and forth at his head only to evaporate the mirage briefly before he reappears.

He laughs. That wild, high-pitched hyena laugh that I remember from the first day.

"Then, goodbye, Jenavieve de Fenace'. Oh, I forgot to tell you. Enjoy your new life stuck here forever. No one is coming for you now. And you think the Ground is scary…just wait!" He laughs ominously. "You are going to live in these tunnels where you will have to fight demons and monsters every day for the rest of your life. Cold. Alone. Frightened. You will never see the light of day again. And in the end, I will get all your powers anyway. I'll just wait until you wither and die."

"You can't. You can't do that. The simulations are controlled through the exams in San Sun, there is no way you could…" I stop, realizing that it had to be one of my teammates to invite him. The only way Hunter could hack our exams is if someone on my team, in the simulation with me, reached The Numinous and invited him. Someone has betrayed me.

"Who? Tell me who helped you? Was it Jessica?"

"Wouldn't you like to know, Jena." He pauses, but only briefly. "OK, fine, Jena. I'll tell you. Phineas Riley the third, Chairman of the Chancellors, of course! He thinks you are dangerous to the Percenter way of life. I have to agree with him, Jena," Hunter says, laughing.

"You mean the leader of the Cleansing Coalition. That's where his real loyalties lie. Who else? Who helped you on this side?" I say with strength and conviction. Feeling confident in my mission now more than I have ever before.

"Oh, so you have heard of him?" Hunter looks at me slyly with his beady red eyes and continues to laugh, ignoring my request to identify the trader. "Yes, the one and only. So, you see, my pretty little Jenavieve, you don't stand a chance against me—against us. You may as well surrender your powers right now. If you surrender them to me, then I'll—we'll—make sure you get into a prep school and you can continue living your life of luxury. Without any real powers, of course."

He snickers.

"We'll leave you just enough powers to be a Percenter, but you will be weak and your future children and their children will be even weaker. But if you don't want to play ball, you'll live out the rest of your life stranded—imprisoned—in this hell-hole. It's your choice, Jena. I don't really care. Actually, I do kinda want to be a Supersonic Warhead now. Ooops... Sorry, Supersonic!"

"I'm not giving you anything," I say defiantly. I am trying my best to sound fierce, but inside, I am cowering into myself.

"Have it your way." He is flippant, mocking.

With that, Hunter disappears into nothingness, evaporating. And all that is left of him is the haunting laughter echoing throughout the tunnels, chilling me to the bone.

I am not ashamed to admit this. After all, I, too, have my limits. I break down into sobs and fall to the floor.

Chapter 21

The tunnels are hot. They smell of everything putrid and rotten. I feel nauseous. Fear blankets me, making me feel as though I am already dead.

I do not know how long it is that I cry. I cry until there are no tears left. My eyes feel puffy and swollen so much so that they are just slits, barely open. Snot runs down my nose. I wipe it off with my sleeve. I am a mess.

I try to get up but I slump down on the cold, dark tunnel floor. Stiff and sore, my body aching desperately for a hot bath. Slowly, I stumble around and make my way through numerous dark passageways, carrying the sword with me. I have to find an exit, but I cannot find a way out. I wonder if Hunter was right and he's trapped me here forever.

I call into the darkness for my teammates, one after the other.

"Sven? Avelino? Alexander? Jessica?" I cry out time and again until the nagging feeling left from my conversation with Hunter begins to haunt my restless mind.

"Who?" I say as if continuing my conversation with Hunter. "I said who? Tell me which one of them betrayed me! I need to know. I bet it was Jessica. It wasn't Alex. My brother would never do anything to hurt me. Was it Sven? Hunter, tell me. Was it Avelino who let you in?"

The thought of Avelino helping Hunter made me sick. Maybe Avelino was only flirting with me so I'd let my guard down. I remember the Proctor told us not to trust anyone but yourself. I pause, my mind blank for just a few moments while I linger on that thought. But also waiting for Hunter to respond to my lingering question. Not surprisingly, there he didn't because he wasn't there, and I was talking to myself.

"Fuck! Hunter!" I scream until my voice fades away. "Is anyone there? Za? Mr. Hampton? Mom? Anyone?"

My stomach caves, and I am filled with terror. I sob some more. Long, heartbreaking sobs that echo far out into the tunnels, reverberating eerie sounds off the walls.

"OK. I'm not going to go crazy. I am going to figure this out," I say to myself in an attempt to keep my mind sharp.

"Who did I think I was? I am a Ms. Nobody! My parents were wrong about me. I am nothing special. I'm no Savior with special powers. Why did my parents think I could help them? My powers don't even work. I can't even escape whatever this is and get back home. I am nothing more than an insignificant speck of dust in time. I am going to die here and nobody will ever know."

I think I hear something in the distance and stop walking. I stand there quietly for what feels like five minutes but was only about thirty seconds. I continue my diatribe, "I'll probably die of thirst. Or I'll be killed by the demons Hunter controls. Neither is really a way that I want to die."

I try to fight the panic that's building in my chest, sending my heart into an erratic rhythm. I continue to wander aimlessly through the passageways, stumbling against the sides of the walls. Rats and mice skitter in the corners. They scare me more than they should. I feel like a rat in a maze myself. The tunnels are twisting, labyrinthine spaces.

Finally, after hours, I give up wandering through the tunnels. I can't stand up anymore. I thud heavily to my knees and crumple up in a corner where there is nothing but darkness and despair. I run my fingers through my long hair. It feels like it's matted into a thousand knots. My eyes ache from crying so much. I wish Avelino was here.

I wish he could put his arms around me and comfort me. I think about him kissing me, lying next to me in my bed, back in San Sun. It's finally starting to set in that I may never see anyone I love again, or find my way back.

I drift off into a nightmarish sleep where monsters and demons haunt me.

My night terror screams wake me to reality. I'm not ready to die.

Chapter 22

"Not yet," I say out loud to myself in nothing more than a mutter. "Come on Jena! You are better than this. Remember those stories Mom and Dad used to read? The ones where the princess is always rescued by the prince? In the end, good always beats evil! Right!" I tell myself in an attempt to regain my optimism.

I try to pull myself together. I try to calm my mind and erase the fear. I try to focus on feeling light as a feather. I think of my toes, then my feet. I imagine them weightless before I imagine them disappearing. Then I move on from my feet to my legs, and then my waist and shoulders until, finally, the tips of my fingers.

"Za, I surrender myself. I surrender myself to you, to...to...to save others who cannot save themselves," I say, my voice not much more than a croak. "I don't know what to do next. I need help. How do I find my way back? How? How do I? Za, I need your help."

I listen for any answer, but hear nothing. I sit in silence, completely numb for minutes turned into hours. Instead of falling asleep, my mind jolts my body awake. Preventing me from getting much needed rest. My breathing becomes more labored, and I begin feeling my body's weight again. A hysterical feeling begins to build in my chest as I hyperventilate. I try to force myself to sit, wait and listen longer. But I can't stay focused.

I can feel myself becoming more and more paranoid. My mind starts to wander away from itself and spiral with fear. My eyes open with a burst of energy. My mouth starts speaking faster than normally.

"Where is Za? Why won't he listen to me? Why isn't he helping me? Where is everyone? Why did they leave me? Who set me up? I bet the Proctors are part of the Cleansing Coalition. I bet they did this to me. I'm sure of it. I bet they are all working with Hunter to destroy me. To keep me locked away in this...this place. Forever!"

I begin to remember what the Proctor told us about this part of the exam, specifically The Numinous. She had said, "You're going to go deeper than ever before. Because of this, we can't always find you. We can't always get you out. It's just not always possible."

She also said something about how The Numinous is entirely different from anything we experience in ordinary life. It evokes a reaction of silence. It provokes terror. It is an omnipresent power. But The Numinous is also merciful and gracious. A gift of the Elixir. To venture into these worlds beyond takes great power. One must be a high Percenter to achieve this level of mastery.

"Where is this merciful and gracious Numinous I wonder?" I say to the Proctor who isn't there.

"Yeah, where the hell is it!"

All of a sudden, I remember the amber pendant that Za gave me. The talisman he said would always help. I reach inside my bodysuit and pull it out. Then, I lift the necklace over my head and hold the amber in my hand. I can barely see it in the faint light of the tunnels. I begin to hum a melody that reminds me of the chant that Za sang when he gave this to me. As I hold the pendant and hum the tune, a subtle yet noticeable buzzing begins to fill the tunnel and a sphere of bright light begins to glow from within the pendant.

For the first time in a long time, I hear Za speak to me. "Jena, listen to me carefully."

"Za, is that you?" I whisper, my voice coarse. I wipe the tears from my eyes with the back of my hand. "Is that really you?"

"Yes, Jena. I have been with you this entire time," Za says. "But your fear has kept me hidden from you."

"I thought you abandoned me like everyone else. I don't know what to do! Hunter trapped me here. Please, tell me what to do next!" I plead with Za.

"Yes, Jena, you have succumbed to the illusions of this underworld," Za says. "You let your fears trap you. Hunter can only defeat you if he stops you from activating all your powers. He knows that only your fear will stop you, nothing else. You must reach The Numinous to survive."

"But Hunter is the reason I'm imprisoned here!" I cry. "This is not my doing. It's Hunter's. He told me so!"

"No, Jenavieve," Za explains. "The illusion of this underworld is that it makes you think you have no powers, no strength, no support. A world that has convinced you that you will remain trapped here in loneliness and despair for eternity, no matter what you try to do. It uses your own doubt against you. The fear of what Hunter will do the next time he finds you, and the fear of being abandoned by those that you love."

"How do I stop it? I've tried. How do I overcome it?" I ask.

"Do not forget who you are, Jenavieve de Fenace'" Za says. "The energy of that amber stone in your hand is more powerful than either you or I can imagine. It connects all of us; every one of your ancestors trailing all the way back to me. It enables our powers to bind to yours, enhancing each of your Percenter powers. But first, you must let go of your fears. Let go of your control. Let go of the power you have. You must be willing to let all of your energy flow out of you and find its way to The Numinous. Only then can you reach a harmonious balance within yourself, allowing more life force from us to flow into your body through the amber. And then, only then, will all of your powers be truly activated."

"And remember, I am always with you. It is only when you forget who you are and you start letting fear rule your mind, then I cannot reach you. Your fear will ensnare you with a deep, evil prison like this underworld and if you are not careful, you'll forget who you are and be trapped alone, forever. Good luck, Jena! I believe in you." Za's voice disappears, and I am left alone, once again.

I start humming Za's melody the way I did before. I caress the amber in my hand, feeling the round smoothness. I close my eyes and once again calm my mind and begin to meditate on blank, black space, where my body feels weightless and invisible.

Within seconds, a white light shoots out from the amber resting in my open palm. The light is brilliant. Streams continue to shoot from the pendant as light bounces on the tunnel walls. The light rays begin to form a prism of multicolored lights as if a rainbow had been captured and liquified. An extremely loud ringing sound echoes from the prism and fills the tunnel before a thunderous crash, followed by silence.

Sven and Jessica appear before me. Their clothes are torn and dirty, their faces scratched with what look like bloody claw marks. I notice that Alexander and Avelino are not with them. I remember to slip the amber pendant underneath my bodysuit as fast as I can, not wanting either of them to see it. I immediately feel its warmth, its radiating vibrations next to my skin. There is a prickling on my chest as if electrical currents are emanating from the amber stone itself. I feel a warmth throughout my body. I can sense that my powers have been activated.

I can't really make out where they are but before I have more time to think about it, Sven reaches out her hand to me.

"Jena! Take my hand," Sven shouts. "There's no time. C'mon, Jena, we've got to leave now!"

I pause for less than a second, wondering if I can trust them. I look Sven directly in her eyes. She has panic in them, like she's authentically concerned for my safety and not trying to trick me. No fear, I remind myself. I need to get out of here and they are my only option.

With a smile growing across my face, I slowly reach my hand out to join Sven's. I'm still a little confused by what is exactly happening, but I feel this undeserving sense of confidence rush over me.

"Where are Alex and AV?" I ask without getting a response.

"Hurry!" yells Jessica. "We can't hide from Hunter much longer!"

I lock my fingers with Sven's hand as she urgently pulls me into the portal of light.

Chapter 23

I land on my feet briefly before collapsing on to both Sven and Jessica. I couldn't be more relieved to see them. I ask what happened, but they don't know, exactly. Within just minutes of the big battle, everyone except me, were brought back to the simulation room. They never had the chance to find The Numinous.

"Within minutes?" I ask both of them.

"Yes, Jena. That's what we said," Jessica snaps.

Sven looks at Jessica, scolding her without saying any words. "Within minutes of you running into the Library. Do you remember running into the Library?" Sven continues.

I thinks back and realize it was only a couple minutes after entering the Library that I ran into Mr. Hampton. He opened the bookshelf to the hidden tunnels and told me to go into them.

"Mr. Hampton!" I say with an unusual amount of excitement. "Mr. Hampton, my neighbor in San Sun, he was inside the library and opened a doorway to these hidden tunnels. But he saved me from... from those demons!"

"Mr. Hampton for the win!" says Sven.

"You know Mr. Hampton?" I ask.

"Of course, I'm the reason he found you. Mr. Hampton has this unique ability to hack simulations within the exam. All he needed was for me to bring this library card with me so he could track us. He jokingly calls it his Librarianism!" Sven smiles as she pulls her library card out of her pocket.

"If you brought Mr. Hampton in, who brought Hunter?" I say quickly.

Jessica and Sven exchange indiscernible looks.

"We aren't really sure. One idea is that he somehow attached himself to Mr. Hampton. I read about this ancient power where you can literally become someone else's shadow. We think Hunter hitched a ride on Mr. Hampton, so to speak. Sounds totally weird, but apparently possible," Sven added.

"Hunter told me that he has the ability to steal other Percenter powers. Maybe that's exactly what he did," I interject.

"Anything is possible. What happened to you next Jena?" Sven asks while Jessica sits there, looking skeptical of me.

"I'm not really sure how to explain it. I was trapped in these underground tunnels and felt complete despair. I felt lost and alone."

"That's it? That's all you remember over the last two months?" Jessica says to me, even more skeptical of me than I thought.

"Easy Jessica. Easy!" Sven calming both of us before tensions rise.

"What do you mean two months? You mean two days, right? I can believe I was there for two days. But not two months," I tell Jessica.

"No, Jena. It's been two months since we completed the exams. The proctors said you had been lost to The Numinous, just like they warned." Sven pauses, giving me a few moments to digest what she's telling me.

"I know it doesn't feel like two months to you, but here, it has been two months. You have been lost to all of us and you would still be if you hadn't been able to truly harness your powers! How did you do it?" Sven asks with some excitement.

"The Numinous!" I slip from my lips. "I reached The Numinous."

"Of course, you did. That means you were the only candidate to do it. No one else in the entire exam," Jessica added.

"None of you reached it? Not even Alex? AV? No one?" I ask with complete surprise.

"Here, give me your hands and I'll show you." Sven grabs my hands and softly holds them in her palms. She closes her eyes, so I do the same.

"Jena, I know it's tough, and you have no reason to, yet, but you must trust me." Sven pauses. "Just like the Saviors do," Sven adds.

No one has mentioned the Saviors to me except for my parents the night before the exams. My eyes jolt open quickly out of surprise from what she just said. I want to ask Sven what she knows but before I have the chance, my thoughts bolt through a web of connected lights and when my eyes see clearly again I am in the simulation room. I look down at my hands, turning my palms up and down. I examine them closely not recognizing them as my own.

"Sven? Are you OK?" Alexander asks me, putting his hand on my shoulder before he repeats himself.

"Sven? Sven? Did you see what happened to Jena?" Alexander asks with so much concern and panic in his voice.

I realize that I'm not actually there but I am in Sven's mind, reliving her memory of when they returned from The Numinous simulation.

"No…" I, or rather Sven, says, "I mean, Yes I'm fine but no, I don't know what happened…"

"Welcome back, candidates!" interrupts Michelle, the Proctor. She is carrying a clipboard and her eyeglasses have slipped down onto the bridge of her nose. "That was some test, huh?"

We all look at her like she's crazy. We can't remember much…at first. My head hurts. It feels foggy and blurry. This must be how Sven felt. Everyone's clothes are torn and charred. Flashes of the battle rush through my mind. Sven squints her eyes as if trying to clear her thoughts while simultaneously shaking off a headache.

"Be quiet and listen" Sven says intending for only me to hear but audible for everyone else.

"Excuse me?" Michelle says to Sven.

"What…what happened?" Sven asks. Pretending as if she didn't say anything else.

Alexander and Avelino stand with Sven. They look just as confused as Sven felt.

"You did well, Sven," Michelle says. "All of you did. You were just excellent. I admit, it was touch and go there for a while, but you managed to escape the challenge." She motions to the Alexander and Avelino standing beside me. "And just in time, I might add."

"What about Jena? Where is Jessica" Avelino asks as he looks at between Alexander and Sven before back to Michelle. I can see a look of sadness in his eyes as he makes contacts with Sven's.

I look over to Alexander and see panic, anxiously waiting for Michelle to answer.

"We had to rescue Jessica, unfortunately," Michelle explains. "I'm afraid she didn't pass this part of the exam. And poor Jena. Poor, poor Jena." Michelle sighs and lowers her eyes for effect. She pauses for no more than three seconds, and with a quick change of her tone, Michelle adds, "Well, at least we got one de Fenace' back, huh, Alexander! Now, on to next business."

"No. Wait. Where is my sister?" Alexander adds in a heated voice as he reaches out to grab the proctors arm. Fortunately for him, Sven reaches his hand first and holds it in hers, as she did to mine just moments ago. Alexander looks directly into her eyes, my eyes, for just a brief moment before the anger left his eyes for what looked like a moment of clarity, of understanding. As if he has all of the answers he needs.

I can't help but be impressed by Sven and whatever powers she appears to have.

"She is gone Alexander. She has been lost to The Numinous. It will be best for you if you accept this and move on." Michelle says curtly, raising her left eyebrow as she turns and walks away.

Avelino just stands next to Alexander, putting his arm around his shoulder to provide comfort. While it looks like Avelino is sad I didn't return, he also doesn't look surprised.

"Like I said, tonight, all of you will learn how you did on your exams. Now, go on back to the dorms and get cleaned up for the Grand Reveal Celebration."

"Thank you," Sven, Alexander, and Avelino all mumble before heading out of the simulation room.

As soon as they got outside, Sven asks them, "Guys, what really just happened in there? Do you remember anything?"

"All I remember is fighting some soldiers, no demons, I mean, soldiers I guess," Alexander says.

"I remember the last time I saw Jena she ran into the Library," Avelino says.

"I heard Jessica screaming for help," says Alexander, "but I couldn't find her. I tried looking, but there was so much…destruction."

"I couldn't get to her either," says Avelino. "She's going to be so pissed about failing the exams! I can't believe Jena is gone. I'm…I'm so sorry, Alex. I don't know what happened to her."

Alexander was about to say something but I found myself back in my own body, looking at Sven as she releases my hands.

"Don't worry. Your brother, while still mourning you, is doing fine at Freelinn Prep. Avelino is at Stillstone," Sven says to me.

"And I am here with you two! Totally not fair!" Jessica says as she stands up, clearly frustrated, and walks away.

"Ignore her. You know how the Saviors engineered that blocking serum so proctors couldn't track your powers being activated? Well, Jessica blames us for her Horti power…you know, when her tears made the plants grow, and she rescued us in the exam? Anyway, she blames us for the low score on her exams. Apparently, the blocking serum affected her differently. She hasn't been able to shed a tear since the exam to keep a simple houseplant alive let alone access her Horti power. When she couldn't produce her power on Reveal Day, she failed.

The rumors say that she's even tried cutting herself all over her forearms to make herself cry. It didn't work and now she only wears long sleeve shirts. So, it seems she isn't much of a Percenter after all! But don't tell her that!" Sven giggles in a way that school girls do.

"So, no one stepped forward to save Jessica from the Ground? No one offered to Middle her? No one?" I ask cautiously, not really understanding the dynamics of their relationship.

Sven shook her head sideways.

"Supposedly that's why she cut herself. She was completely distraught to have her entire family turn their backs on her, even though she knew she had powers. We all saw them, remember? Poor thing."

We both sigh thinking how terrible Jessica must have felt at that moment before changing the topic.

"I don't think anyone else except for me, Jessica and the Saviors know you are still alive. And before you even ask, yes, I have been working with the Saviors this whole time. We recruited Jessica when she was exiled to the Ground."

I take in the information realizing that Sven is the closest thing I have to an ally. I'm not convinced Jessica is helping because she's an ally or because she has something to gain or maybe it's that she has nothing left to lose. All I know is that she's here now, Sven trusts her, and I at least need her to think I share that trust.

"OK. Where are we and what's next?" I ask them, taking a deep breath.

Chapter 24

My body is a pile of legs and arms. I groggily prop myself up onto an elbow and then lie back down on my back. I twist and turn, trying to get comfortable. I want a pillow. I want a blanket. I want to cuddle with my cat, Sebastian. I want to be back in my comfy room so badly. I'm so uncomfortable that there is no way I am going to get any sleep.

I sit up and hug my legs.

The sun in below the horizon and the temperature is dropping quickly. I must have dozed off at some point. My body is so exhausted from walking all day in the heat. I'm just not built for this rugged way of life. I look around for Sven and Jessica but they are nowhere to be found. They are probably out searching for more food or water. It's been days and we still haven't found any. Sven's supplies were only meant for one person, not three. So they are running low rapidly. I make sure not to call out their names. You never know what could be watching in the darkness.

I hear a crunching sound a couple of feet to my left. My ears prick up. I turn my head to look. I tense, my eyes desperately searching the darkness.

I hear the crunching sound again. Like feet slowly stepping on dried twigs. Or maybe an animal walking.

Suddenly, a flash of bright lightning brightens up the sky in the distance and offers brief illumination around me. I wonder if it is going to start raining. It only lightly rains in San Sun, if you can call it rain. Little showers that sprinkle daintily over the lawns to keep the trees and shrubs brilliantly green. All controlled automatically by the San Sun Water & Irrigation department. I've never felt real rain from clouds before, almost no Percenter alive today has.

I look again towards the lightning as it zigzags in fireworks spewing down towards the ground. Thunder cracks the sky open and sounds like a thousand buildings are crashing together. A crunching sound much louder than I had heard previously. It is an eerie sound that chills me to the bone. There is no lightning or thunder in San Sun City, but I have seen it in movies.

I sit up straighter, afraid of the storm that's approaching. I peer into the darkness. Something is moving in the distance. Whoever it is, they are trying to hide their steps in the roar of the thunder. Out of the darkness of the night I can see someone start charging towards me at full speed.

I look around for a place to hide. All I can see in the flashes of lightning are tiny dried shrubbery and vast spans of empty Earth. The person is still running towards me, close enough for me to hear them.

"Move!" a male's voice shouts at me. "Get up! You need to run now!"

I am confused. I don't recognize his voice and it's too dark out for me to see his face. All I can make out is that he's tall, at least six foot and wearing torn up ragged clothes that look like they'd stink.

I quickly slither backwards on my hands, trying to get my feet under me. A bright cloud funnel twirls in the sky. Darkness returns just as a heavy weight pushes me down. The back of my head strikes the hard dirt. A hand grips the edge of my shit and pulls it up to hit the bottom of my jaw.

"Hurry! Don't make me an idiot for rescuing you. Or we'll both be dead."

"Get your hands off me. No one is rescuing me from anything. Who are you?" I scream back.

The lightning strikes again. Too close this time, only meters away. But it gave me a good chance to see this guy's face more clearly. In front of me is one of the most handsome faces I have ever seen. And this shocks me. I thought Grounders would be hideous looking. I thought, given that they spent their lives living in a toxic environment from The Oze, they would have deformities. Or at the very least look mentally slow and inbred. But this young man is anything but hideous. With large dark, animalistic eyes and wild brown hair that reminds me of Alexander, this young man is sort of beautiful.

I'm puzzled by his good looks for too long. My mind, fearful of the unknown, wonders. Maybe he's not a Ground and that's why he's so handsome. Maybe he's a Percenter, working with the Cleansing Coalition. Or Maybe he failed the exams as was exiled to the Ground. I couldn't stop thinking about who this guy is and why he's here.

He definitely doesn't dress like a Percenter. Even in the dark, he's close enough now that I can see his outfit is some kind of animal fur and skin. His shirt is opened in the front, leaving him bare-chested, exposing his chiseled abs. This guy is extremely fit.

"Follow me. Closely! Got it?" he shouts at me.

His voice is strange, the inflection of his words sounding odd. He speaks very differently than I do. Everyone in the Sky Cities sounds the same, no accents. This guy is definitely not from the Sky Cities.

He yanks me up by the arm and quickly lets me go. I almost lose my balance but manage to stay standing.

"This will protect you." He throws some type of spandex running suit. Similar to what we wore during the exams, but thicker, and with a hood.

"From what?" Jena asks.

"You are about to find out one way or the other. I recommend my way!" he says jokingly.

Jena quickly puts it on.

"Move, Percenter, move!" he yells. Under his breath, he turns his head and swears to himself, "Goddammit, I don't know why I'm doing this."

The air picks up in swirls and blows dust into my eyes. Lightning and thunder crash again in the sky. The light so bright it blinds me for an instant. The storm is getting bigger, closer. I look him in the eyes.

"Who are you?"

"I'm with Sven and Jessica. Let's go, follow me now!"

Fear explodes through me. I'm not sure if I should be more afraid of the storm or this guy. I guess I'm going to have to trust his fear of the storm; otherwise he could have just left me to die.

I grab my small pack. I stay as close to him as I can but he's running much faster. My legs aren't yet awake and the rest of my body is exhausted. I'm somewhat surprised that I am running at all. The guy runs back me and, without warning, he body-checks me behind a nearby boulder. He throws himself over me.

"What are you doing?" I scream as I try to move under the weight of his body. I can feel how solid he is as I wiggle beneath him. I quickly realize it's pointless to try and move him, he has me out-powered.

There is another loud crash in the sky followed by several smaller ones. Lightning is zigzagging into streaks on the ground all around us. The Ground lights up like an electrical grid.

"Don't move," he says. "If we're lucky, it will bypass us. If it hits us, we're dead."

I nod. I stay pinned under his body. He's trying to protect me, again. But the lightning moves closer.

"We're going to have to make a run for it but you have to step where and when I do," he says. "It's too dangerous here. Can you do this?" He looks into my eyes, only inches from my face. I've seen these eyes before. I recognize them.

"Xavier?" I respond.

He only smiles at me before getting up to run, holding my left hand in his right. I do not know how long we run but the storm seemed to chase us for hours. As we move farther away from the lightning, the rain begins.

"Hurry, pull your hood up. You aren't going to like the rain!" Xavier says to me. I feel the first few drops hit my sleeves, not my skin. One raindrop finally makes contact with my face. It feels like a tiny bullet greeting my skin or like the edge of a lit match. Followed by a quick rush of cooling as the same raindrop explodes.

"Ouch!" I say in surprise.

"Get up Jenavieve!" he shouts at me. "You'll die in this storm if you don't get up!"

My energy is gone. My legs feel like noodles and my arms are useless. I try but I can barely walk let alone run. Half-carrying me, Xavier and I run as fast as we can on the edge of the rainfall.

The rain soaks me through and through, and I begin to shiver uncontrollably. My body is in complete shock from the tiny bursts of pain each raindrop delivers to my skin before it breaks open. I feel like I cannot go any further and each step is a miracle.

We run in silence until the rain stops. When we stop, I realize we are no longer in the desert. There are low hills and tall grasses blowing in the wind. I see very little below the light of the stars in the freshly clean sky but there is something calming about the night air in this place. I collapse, my body limp on the Ground.

I'm in an out of consciousness but I feel Xavier's arms around my waist as he hoists me up from the ground and over his shoulder. I lift my head barely enough to see that we're approaching a dark opening in the side of a grass covered hill. Xavier carries me like I'm a sack of potatoes until we are fully inside the cave. He puts me down, gently, making sure my head rests slowly to the cave floor.

"I'll be back, I promise. Jenavieve, you are safe here," he says confidently in his calming voice. He then leaves me and disappears deeper into the cave. To where, I do not know. But my eyes close just as fast as he is gone.

Chapter 25

I struggle, and with all my might, I finally stand up. I'm soaking wet and still shivering from the cold. I have no idea where I am. I look into the darkness of the cave and stare for a few moments to see if I hear anything. Nothing.

Hobbling to the opening of the cave on my semi-asleep legs, I peek out. All I can see is rain slanting down in sheets towards the ground. The storm must have reached us while I was passed out. I can hear the rain. It sounds hard, pelting, rock-like even as it hits the tall grass. It is definitely a different type of rain than I was running in with Xavier.

I use the wall of the cave for balance and walk back to where I was sleeping. I sit back down, hugging my knees closer for warmth. I put my head between my knees and fall asleep thinking about if Sven and Jessica are OK, and how Xavier found me and when they will come back for me.

The smell of smoke wakes me. I feel a warmth through my body that wasn't there when I fell asleep. I open my eyes and lift my head to see a fire a few feet in front of me and an animal fur wrapped over me. I examine the dark granite walls of the cave and see nothing but stone. I look to the opening of the cave and see the black outline of Xavier's standing against the wall, backlit by the sunlight.

"Xavier! You are back," I say with excitement in my voice.

He turns to me, still back lit from the light outside the cave.

"Oh, good, you are awake. You must be starvin'!"

He walks closer to me, extending his hands in a way I anticipate he would to help me up. As soon as he gets close enough, I can tell it's not Xavier.

"Wait! You're not Xavier. What...what happened? Where is my brother?" I ask. "How did I...how...I mean, I thought you were—,"

"Xavier? Naw, I'm not Xavier. But I've met him a couple times before. Good guy," he says. Continuing to offer his hand to help me up.

"Where did he go? He was her last night. He helped me into this cave," I say, confusedly.

"Sorry, Jenavieve. That was me. All me. You called me Xavier and seemed to be comfortable by the idea that I was him, so I went with it. We had to get goin' out of that storm you know. So..."

"Oh, my God!" I say, rubbing both my eyes and shaking my head from side to side. "But you said you knew Sven and Jessica?" I say in a heated tone.

"I do," he responds.

"Then who are you? How do you know them? Me? Where..." I say, still a little heated although I'm calming down.

"Look," he says, interrupting me, "I get it. You're not the first Percenter I've had to rescue when they arrived on the Ground."

"I'm not?" I ask.

"No, you're not."

"But it's only once a year that Percenter's are exiled during the exams," I explain. "If they don't pass, that is."

"Huh. Once a year?" He looks at me as if I'm delusional. "It happens all the time. You are just like all the others. Where have you been hiding?"

"All the time?" I ask in surprise.

"Of course," he says. "From what I can tell, any time one of yous causes problems, they're dumped out on the Ground. You Percenters can't survive down here. Um...didn't you know that? Or maybe you got the idea from the storm last night? It's a death sentence, usually."

"I guess there's a lot I don't know a lot about Percenter Society," I say, hating the reminder about how clueless I really am.

"Oh...right..." he says. "I imagine many of you don't know what's going on. I mean, you only live there. Why would you know?" I pick up on his harmless sarcasm.

169

"Funny," I say. "That was pretty funny, and I get what you mean," I respond, letting him know that I may be naive to what happens to some Percenters, I'm not stupid.

"You still haven't told me your name. Or who you are?" I say pointedly.

I get no response from him. He walks over to the fire he created and turns a stick with some dead animal on it, cooking over the flames.

"How long was I out?" I ask, keeping the conversation going.

"Not long," he says, glancing sideways at me. "A few hours, maybe."

The fire crackles and pops as he tends to it.

"What is that?" I ask.

"Rat. While you were resting, I caught us a rat deep in tunnels of this cave. We'll eat fine tonight."

"A rat? You can't be serious?"

"Yes. Why wouldn't I be? It's great protein and it's fresh. Did you miss the part that I just killed it?"

"OK," I say, not wanting to sound too ungrateful for the food. After all, I haven't eaten anything substantial in days. "It smells good."

"It's almost ready."

"Thank you," I tell him.

"It wouldn't be very wise of me to let you starve after I went through all the effort to save you."

"Why did you save me? Why won't you tell me who you are? Are you a-a...Barren?"

The young man laughs a contagious and honest laugh.

"What's so funny?" I'm not sure if I should join in the joke or not, but it's hard to keep a straight face.

"You called me a Barren." His boisterous tone quickly changed to condescension. "All the Percenters think that if we are born on the Ground, we are automatically an uneducated, poor human slave who exists solely to serve you."

"I'm sorry," I say ashamed for not knowing.

I look at his face again, he is so handsome. His face perfectly symmetrical, his skin, although covered in filth, is flawless. His lips are deep red, and plump, surrounded by the scruff of his beard. His eyes, dark and mysterious.

"You're all just wrong," he says simply. He inhales deeply, as if he has explained this a million times. "We are not all slaves. We do not all live in the Bubbles. And we are not all stupid and inbred. And guess what, we can live on the Ground!"

"Then, what are you? How do you survive? Where do you live?" I am truly intrigued to learn more about him. Maybe it's because I'm attracted to him, but mostly I am hungry to understand what life is like outside of the sky.

"I'm not a Barren, as you call those human slaves—those people in the Bubbles. People outside, like me, prefer to call ourselves an Indie."

"Why Indie?"

"It means an independent human. Born free on the Ground. We have no governments or ruling societal structures that encumber our ability to make free, independent, choices. Of course."

"Oh. I never heard that term before," I say honestly.

He turns the rat on the spit. It's turning a golden brown. My stomach clenches. I realize I am starving.

"Of course, you haven't. All that fancy studying up there doesn't help any when the books you read are written with lies and taught with mistruths."

"But I can't blame you for that," he adds.

Not exactly sure how to respond to him, I change the subject completely. "How did you know I was a Percenter?"

"Well, I was specifically looking for you Jenavieve. Haven't you figured that much out yet? Sven sent me to find you. She shared a memory of you so I knew exactly what you looked like. But, yes, all y'all look the same to me. You Percenters. The same clothes, the same pale skin tone. The same shocking look on your faces and fear in your eyes. You, not so much, but the others I've rescued sure do."

"Why do you rescue Percenters and if Sven sent you, where is she?" I ask now that I have him talking more.

"You can call me Sam," he responds, as if I never asked my questions.

"OK, Sam. My name is Jenavieve, but everyone calls me Jena."

He just nods at me and simply says, "Got it."

"What do you want from me?" I ask him.

"Nothing," he says. "Not a thing."

Sam takes the rat off the spit and puts it in a makeshift rock bowl for me. "Please put the bones in the boiling water," he orders. "We can have a stew later." He motions to the pot of water that's boiling on the edge of the fire.

"Thank you," I tell him. "For helping me. For this…"

While nervous for my first bite, I have to admit, the rat tasted like the most delicious thing I've ever tasted. For the first time in what seems like weeks or even months, I start to relax for some reason. I continue eating, licking my fingers, until there is no meat left on the bone. I didn't realize I was so starved. Both Sam and I throw the leftover bones into the pot.

"We will sleep here tonight," Sam says. "It will probably rain all night. I'll bring you to Sven tomorrow."

I say nothing. I just smile with the comfort in the knowledge that Sam volunteered the plan. For some reasons I trust him. I trust his candidness and brutal honesty.

"Hey Sam?" I ask.

"Why did the rain burn so much but then the pain went away?"

"Well, I'm no scientist now, am I. I'm just a simple Indie doing his thing. But if I were to wager a guess, I'd tend to think that there are toxic chemicals remaining from the Great Ozone Event in the upper atmosphere, where clouds form. You see, the Ground is livable in some areas, not all.

But when it rains, when big storm systems move from one area to the next, they bring those chemicals with them and the chemicals grab on to the rain droplets and fall from the sky with them until they land. You see, I would wager The Oze is more like a virus that feeds off of Oxygen. That's why it killed most life forms on the Ground unless they were protected by one of those Barren Bubbles.

But once everything on the Ground died and no more fresh Oxygen was being produced, the virus itself began to die. But there are still areas, most areas in fact, that The Oze lingers. The virus still lives in those areas. I would guess that those areas are concentrated near the Barren Pods. You see, some might thing Percenters were forcing The Oze near the Pod, deceiving the

Barrens into a false dependency, and forcing them to live in fear of The Oze. Some might even call it slavery.

But I digress. Yes, the rain carries the virus from the atmosphere but once the raindrop breaks, it washes away the limited concentration of the virus making it too diluted. The only difference is that when you are in a storm, the heavy rain means more virus and the winds mean the virus can travel on its own.

My mind goes in one direction and one direction only.

"Water! Oh, my God, it's Water. Mr. Hampton you genius Librarian!" I exclaim with what I believe is a major realization.

"That must be it. Mr. Hampton told me to find the water right, well...what if he meant the rain. What if he meant for me to find this rain? You know how you just told me that once the raindrop bursts open and splashes on the skin that the initial burning from the chemicals or virus or whatever, the sensation stops!?"

"Yes," Sam responds

"Don't you get it? The rainwater must somehow counteract the chemicals of The Oze in the air you are talking about."

"Rain isn't the answer. Believe me. I've seen people die in rain storms Jena and it's something you wouldn't wish upon anyone you loved, or even hated for that matter."

"Wait, not the rain itself, as it's falling. Yes, it's a carrier of the virus, but it also stops the virus. Don't think of it as a single drop. But as it collects. Like a puddle. But a very large puddle. Like a lake. No. An ocean! Are there any oceans around here?" I ask Sam.

"Goodnight, Jena," Sam says to me.

I'm not sure if he's annoyed with my sudden exuberance or if he feels I didn't listen to him the way he had hoped. Regardless of his reaction, I know that I'm on to something, and I better not push my luck with Sam. While he seems nice enough, I don't really know him.

We hunker down around the fire. I can't help but imagine this strange world of Indies and Barrens that has existed below me my entire life. I feel so far from home. Far from anyone I know or love. But I'm starting to realize there is so much more that I am fighting for that I can even begin to understand.

I fall asleep feeling comforted by the fact that I haven't died…yet.

Chapter 26

"So, you know your way? Your way to Sven?" I ask first thing as I wake.

Sam looks over to me and shows me a half smile.

"Good morning to you to sunshine and sort of," he says.

"How far do you think it is?" I ask.

"It's not too far," Sam says. "About eighty, ninety miles or so."

"That far?" I am surprised and disturbed by him not thinking eighty miles is far. "Tell me again, Sam, why are you helping me?" I ask. "How do you know Sven, exactly?" I woke up with in a determined mood that Sam is just going to have to put up with.

"I already told you, I don't want nothin' from you. Like I said, I've met a lot of you Percenters arriving here on the Ground for the first time. I'm just helping you find where you need to be, to survive. Don't think anything more about it, ya hear!" Sam says in a firm tone.

I don't say anything back to Sam. Taking his word as final. Last night I started to feel that I could trust him but for some reason I woke up this morning feeling like I might have been too quick to trust. And I still have to wonder why he's so willing to help me. I know there must be something he wants in return. I don't know anyone that would risk their own life for a completely stranger like he did, rescuing me from that storm.

I use my fingers like a comb and try to smooth my hair back from my face the best I can. I feel like a mess, yes Sam looks just as good as I remember. It must be his muscles peeking out of his barely clothed body that has captured my attention. I catch myself staring and before he notices, I turn my head to check my small pack to make sure everything is still there. It's not much but it's all Sven and Jessica could give me before they left in search of food and water. I reach out to check how wet my shoes are before putting them on. They're mostly dry from sitting on the edge of the campfire all night.

"You ready?" Sam asks me. "We really do need to get movin'." He jerks his head towards the opening of the cave.

"I'm ready," I say.

"Look, I'm going to give you a knife to protect yourself with," Sam says. "Do you know how to use a knife?"

"Of course," I say. I don't want him to think I'm helpless. I don't tell him that I've never needed to know how to use a knife for anything other than cutting my food.

"Will I need a knife?" I ask, hesitating slightly.

"There's lots of things that could attack us out there," says Sam. "So, yes, you might need a knife."

I take it from him and put it in my pack.

"Let's get goin'," he says. I follow him out into the open sky.

We begin hiking through the hilly fields covered in a variety of tall grasses. We walk in silence for what seems like hours before Sam finally broke it.

"I've heard all about the exams," he says.

"Oh yeah!? like what?" I say, happy that he's broken the silence.

"And the revealing of powers. I've also heard that they're rigged, those tests you take. I mean, they must be because they send plenty of people to the Ground who pass those exams. I know, I've met them."

"How do you know all of this?" I ask suspiciously but also utterly curious.

"As I told you before, I've met many of you types. I've helped many of you survive. I pro'ly know more about what's really going on in those Sky Cities than you do."

I must have had an immediate look of defeat on my face. It's clear that he at least knows a few things that I don't and probably should.

"No offense," he says quickly. "It's just that most of you Percenters, as you call yourselves, are kept in the dark. You live in a false reality. One that was created for you by your leaders."

"None taken. I'm starting to see what you are talking about," I say. I want to keep probing to find out what else he knows, but I refrain. It seems I learn the most from Sam when I let him volunteer conversation on his own so I wait for him to speak again.

The bright blue sky allows the sun to shine down on the golden grasses blowing back and forth in the light breeze. I find myself taking deep breaths of air, surprised at how easy it is to breathe on the Ground. The grass fields turn into random trees before we reach an area where the density of trees is thicker than the visible sky. We tread through thickets of foliage, gnarly bushes and trees. I have never seen so much greenery in all my life.

As we push further into the forest, the trees grow to be monstrous in size, often large enough for ten people to stand around with their hands held around the circumference. They were truly majestic and beautiful. But as we ventured further, there were fewer and fewer trees still standing. And of those still standing have branches sparse with leaves hanging on for the little bit of life they have. More trees appear to have fallen to the Ground than remain standing. They look burnt, covered in grey and black soot, and dry as can be.

"Jena, time to put our fancy rain suits back on." Sam throws me the suit I was wearing in the rain. This time I don't hesitate to put it on as soon as he gives it to me. I may not trust Sam completely, but I do know he was right about the suit before.

A loud roar sounds through the forest.

"What was that?" I ask, frantically looking around the fallen trees. Looking for a place to hide just in case I need to.

"Pro'ly just a wolf," Sam says. "Or maybe a cougar. Something hungry, I'm sure," he says jokingly followed by his cute laugh.

"Haha…not funny, Sam," I scold him before changing the subject. I feel like he might have opened the door to talking again.

"Can I ask you something, Sam?"

"What?" he responds in a friendly tone, just like yesterday. I take advantage of it and go for it.

"Did you have any schooling? Your English is very good."

"Yes, Jena."

"Yes, you had schooling? Or what?"

"As I told you yesterday, we're not all savages here on the Ground. Some of us go to school and learn things. Maybe not in fancy places like you have in the Sky Cities. But we are educated. Pro'ly smarter than most Percenters."

There's a fire in his eyes I haven't seen before. I clearly struck a nerve. He shakes his head like he thinks I'm an ignorant moron.

"Oh. I see. I'm sorry. I didn't mean to assume that you, or anyone on the Ground aren't smart. Only the opposite. You sound very intelligent. Like when you were telling me about the rain pain yesterday. I would have never thought of that. I am just curious how you know so much and what school was like for you." I feel so stupid for asking such a dumb question.

Sam continually looks around as if he's looking for someone but never falters on his pace. It's a determined pace on a mission, and I'm struggling to keep up.

I have to admit. I am becoming more and more intrigued by the Ground. This mysterious place where we are not supposed to be able to survive. Where we're not supposed to be able to breathe. And just as I get lost in this freedom, I collapse to the ground and gasp to breathe in air. My eyes water immediately, and I feel a burning sensation in my chest. My lungs feel like they are on fire.

Sam notices and sprints back to me. He grabs some type of mask out of his pack and pulls it over my face and head until it syncs with the rain suit, creating a complete vacuum seal. He slaps something on my back and within seconds I'm able to breathe normally again.

"Just breathe normally, Jena, you'll be fine," Sam says in the gentle tone you would only expect to hear from your father.

"What happened? What did you put on my back?" I ask.

"It's a micro air purifier. It's designed to work with your suit so you can be in The Oze and survive. Well, as long as you keep an airtight seal," Sam says.

"Oh, and the purifier only works for a few hours, so there's that," Sam adds.

He reaches into his sack and pulls his mask and purifier out to put on. He's clearly not as sensitive to the quality of air as I am. He must be acclimated to it from living on the Ground his entire life. Even though I am breathing fine now, my lungs still burn with each breath.

I can't help but wonder where Sam got this air purifying equipment and rain suits. They are such a stark contrast from the rest of his animal skin attire. I guess it doesn't really matter and the last thing I want to do is offend him again by asking.

"It's time you experience the real Oze," Sam says jokingly, but also with a hint of warning.

I look out the clear face mask to see dense, brown clouds growing across the sky directly in front of us. These are definitely not normal looking clouds. They are growing into a solid wall extending hundreds of feet into the air from the Ground level. Streaks of with weird red and orange lightning zigzags within the clouds, exploding every time they hit the Ground.

"Is it going to rain again?" I ask Sam.

"And then some!" he says excitedly after the crash of another lightning bolt strikes near us. "If it's not too bad, we'll keep walking but we only have a few hours of good air in the suits so we might not have many options," Sam warns.

"We have a lot of land to cover, let's keep moving!" Sam finishes in a loud voice as the winds pick up.

Chapter 27

We keep walking directly into the head winds as the storm engulfs us. Sam grabs my hand so we don't get separated and pulls me behind him. The fog is so thick our visibility is no more than five feet. My legs feel like they are being weighed down with concrete. Each step grows harder and harder, for both of us.

Sam finds a hollowed-out tree trunk and guides me into it. I sit down inside the deepest part of the tree's bowels.

"I'll see if I can find out where we are," Sam says. "Don't go anywhere. Just sit tight."

"Don't worry about me. I'm not moving any time soon," I tell him.

We've only been walking for about forty or fifty minutes, but the storm is so fierce and the landscape so tough to navigate that it feels like we have been hiking for days.

Sam jumps around the collapsed tree and within a blink of the eye, he's gone. I pull my knees close to my chest, wrapping my arms around my ankles. I rest my forehead down as I exhale. In the moments that I pause my breathing, I hear what sounds like a male voice. It's so hard to hear anything clearly with the intense noise of the storm. I lift my head up to see if I can hear better.

I definitely hear voices, maybe two or three. I stay a still as possible hoping that Sam returns soon. My body breaks out in goose bumps from head to toe. I have this feeling that these guys are not going to be as friendly as Sam.

I hear someone moaning. No, crying. It sounds more like a woman's voice. They must be just outside of the hollowed-out log I am hiding in.

"Shut it, I said." One of the guys mumbles in a thick accent, almost like his tongue is swollen.

I look out the holes of the tree bark hoping to see who it is. I can't see anyone yet so I maneuver to another hole to change my line of sight. I crawl slowly but the old shell of a tree creaks with every inch I move. I hope the storm covers my noise but as soon as I get to the new hole, one of the guys snaps his head in my direction. He looks over my tree trunk expecting to see someone standing in front of them.

"Did you hear something?" he asks his buddies.

I can see all of them now. Three guys standing just inches from the bark of my tree with a girl slumped over on the Ground in between their feet.

"Not sure," another responds. "Maybe princess here has some friends. Do you, huh? Do you have any friends, princess?" He laughs a sinister laugh as he nudges her with his foot.

I look closer at each of the guys and realize they are not much older than I am. They have on similar rain suits and masks so I can't see anything defining on any of them.

"Who's there? Here, kitty, kitty, kitty?" The guy who's back is facing me shouts out to the trees. He pulls a long knife, twice the size of the one Sam left me with, from the sheath strapped to his massive leg.

"Help! Help me!" the girl screams, lifting up her face. "Please, someone! Help me!"

My jaw drops and my heart misses a couple beats as I see her face for the first time. It's unmistakable. It's Jessica. I don't know what I was expecting but it was definitely not Jessica.

"There's no one here you idiot. It's just the storm," says the guy who kicked Jessica.

I watch as he reaches down and grabs Jessica under the armpit.

"Stand up, princess!" he tells her.

She makes her body go limp, refusing to stand on her own legs. "Fuck you, asshole!" Jessica replies. "You want to go. You are gonna have to carry me!"

"Or maybe I'll just take your mask off and see how well your Percenter powers help you!" he retorts, reaching for her mask.

"Fine. Fine," Jessica says, defeated. "I'll go."

She slowly climbs to her feet, one foot at a time while he hoists her up. She has her hands tied behind her back. For a brief moment I make contact with her eyes. I saw anger in her eyes, not fear. She stared forward, directly at me, with a very determined look. She must have seen me, but there was no recognition in her eyes. I watched her more closely. I was expecting to see tears, or at least red puffy eyes from crying, but I didn't. She looked defeated, but not done.

"Jessica! Jessica! Look at me!" I whisper to myself hoping she sees me hiding in the tree. She doesn't.

"This one has some fight in her. Think of the price we'll get this time!" says the guy closest to me.

All three of them whoop and holler like they just won the lottery. With Jessica in the grips of two of them, they start walking along the tree trunk until they are out of sight. I quickly crawl to the opening of the trunk, trying to gain the courage and strength to stop them. I grab the knife Sam left me in my right hand. If only I still had the Destiny Sword I took from Hunter. Without it, I question whether or not I could be of any help against three captors.

Without warning, the third guy reaches down from the top of the tree trunk he was standing over me. He grabs me by the throat and lifts me out before I can stop him.

"Looks like we've got ourselves another one of those high-falutin' Sky people!" he screams to get the attention of the other two.

"Wahoo!" shouts from the depths of the fog beyond my eyesight. Within seconds, the two guys emerge back into sight as they pull Jessica along with them.

Jessica realizes it's me instantly but doesn't say anything.

I try to struggle free from his grip, but he is now standing behind me with his knife to my throat.

"Agh! Agh! Agh! Pretty, pretty princess!" he joyfully says to me as he moves my neck further into the bend of his arm, squeezing me with his massive bicep until I can barely breathe.

"You don't want me to accidentally pierce this suit of yours or it's bye-bye, Percenter!" he adds.

I freeze, remembering what Sam told me about the suit. Using my eyes only, I look to my right and see one of the guys holding Jessica grinning and licking his lips like he sees the most delicious meal he's seen in days. His teeth are dirty with decay and sharpened to points.

"This one's just as purty as the other one," adds one of the other guys. "We might have some fun wit' her before selling her off."

Jessica and I make eye contact. She looks at the knife in my hand that the guys haven't yet seen. She stares at the knife and then back to my eyes, trying to tell me something that I finally decipher on the third try.

"Looks like we have a two-fer!" says the guy standing alone. "Maybe we should keep this one?" The guys seem distracted, chatting amongst themselves.

Jessica mouths the words "One. Two. Now!" to me and on the count of 'now' Jessica elbows her captor in the gut, causing him to lung forward in pain.

"Run!" screams Jessica "Run!" And she darts off into the thickness of the fog.

Before the guys realize what's happening, I take the knife in my hand and slice the forearm around my neck. I hear a gush of air release from the suit as I push free from his arm. I turn to look directly into his face. I take note of the scar across his right cheek. It's almost from his ear to the corner of his lips. I push him, and he falls back into the tree trunk he grabbed me from. I notice him struggling to put pressure on the hole in his suit before his buddy runs over to help.

"Ouch! You bitch. You are gonna pay for that!" he yells excitedly, looking back up at me.

"Try me!" I say as I turn to run as fast as I can after Jessica.

"They throw you out of a Crawler like your friend? Huh? No powers I bet!" he yells after me.

"We are coming for you, pretty, pretty princess! You think you can outrun us?" One of the other guys yells into the fog.

Just as I am about to run beyond the sound of their voices, I hear Sam.

"Let 'er go!"

I slow my pace and eventually stop. I squat next to some trees for shelter.

"Jena!" I hear a loud whisper, Jessica's whisper.

"Jena! Shhhh! Here!" Jessica says as she reaches out and grabs my foot. She's lying beneath a bunch of twigs and branches that have been pulled over her for cover. I would have never seen her in this fog if she didn't grab me.

"Oh my God Jessica! Are you OK?" I ask in a panic, momentarily forgetting about Sam.

"I'm fine. Can you fight?" Jessica asks quickly.

"Fight? Yes. I can fight," I respond, holding the knife in my hand.

The lightning and thunder get louder as they start striking the ground all around us. Dead, old trees ignite into flames as they get struck. Fog mixes with smoke and the air becomes even thicker, making sight nearly impossible. We can feel the heat of the fires growing all around us.

"Forget it. We have to run!" Jessica says.

"Run where?" I say back to her. "I have no idea where to go! Do you?"

Jessica's air purifier begins to beep. She takes a pause, realizing what the mysterious beep represents. We both know what it means.

"Anywhere is better than here," Jessica adds.

"I think I heard Sam," I tell her. "Right before I stopped running. Somebody yelled at those guys. He was supposed to come back for me."

"Sam can protect himself," Jessica adds coldly. "We need to get out of here now."

I look her in the eyes. I see the same anger and pain that I first saw. Jessica is in self-preservation mode, and I can't leave Sam to fight off our problems.

"Jessica. Sam saved me. For all I know, he's helped you, too," I plead with her, yelling now as I can barely hear myself.

Jessica stands ups, wiping herself clean of the debris.

"Fine. But I get the knife," Jessica says as she reaches her palm out for me to place the knife into.

I don't even think twice as I place it in her hand. We turn to run back in the direction that we came from.

A whirring sound blazes through the burning trees. We jump through flames and dodge lightning landing all around us. When we get back to where we left Jessica's captors, we find one of the guys strewn over some rocks. His head is cracked open and he's obviously dead. We scan the immediate area but can't see anyone else. We hear nothing except the sound of the storm.

We keep running further while calling out for Sam. I'm positive nobody can hear us because I can barely hear Jessica and she's right next to me. I reach out to grab her hand, like Sam did for me. I can't lose her again.

We reach a clearing where there are no trees to catch on fire. The air is still thick but we hear someone nearby.

"Well, son of a—" It's one the other guys, slumped over himself on the Ground. There is a pool of blood all around him. I notice on knife sticking out of his throat and another several feet from him. I pick the loose one up. Jessica walks up to him and stands over him. She stares down at him, waiting for him to look up at her. He doesn't. The next thing I notice, Jessica lifts her foot to his shoulder and pushes him over. His eyes make contact with hers.

"Looks like I have the power now, doesn't it?" Jessica says with little emotion in her voice.

He gags a little of his own blood before spitting it out on his shattered mask. It's tough to tell if his face is bloody from the spit up, or from being exposed to the air. In either case, I don't have enough time to find out.

Behind Jessica the third guy stumbles forward with his weight falling on his sword like a crutch. But not just any sword. The Destiny Sword. My sword. He's clearly wounded and struggling to stand upright. Jessica turns to him and with immediate recognition, grabs the sword from his hand. He falls to the Ground.

"Please! Please!" he says to Jessica as he lay at her feet.

"Please what?" she responds. "Please help you? OK, if you insist."

Jessica raises the sword above her head. But unlike when I had the Destiny

Sword in the tunnels, the sword doesn't glow blue. Maybe because it didn't' have time before she plunged it into his chest.

"Jessica!" I exclaim. Frozen with shock. I am stunned with how cold and callous Jessica has become in such a short period of time. But at the same time, I'm thankful he can't hurt us anymore.

Jessica stands over the body, removing the sword slowly from his chest before plunging it in a second time.

"Are you OK?" Stunned, I walk up to her and gently place my arm on her shoulder. "You…you…you killed him!"

"I had to. I saved your life," Jessica states plainly.

"I-I… Are you sure they would have killed us? That was the only way?" I ask.

"These guys are…" Jessica pauses, obviously thinking about whatever it was that they had done to her before she continues. "They weren't going to get out of here alive. I wasn't going to let them. Let them sell me."

Jessica looks deep into my eyes and with a force I have not seen before, she tells me. "Jena. This is real. This is not some stupid simulation. They. Will. Kill. Us. If. We. Don't. Kill them first!"

"OK," I say calmly. "OK."

Whatever it was that these guys did to Jessica, they were going to do to me. Whatever they had planned for Jessica, they had planned for me. If it was enough to turn her into an efficient killer, I have to consider myself lucky. I decide not to ask any more questions and instead, I gently reach my hand down Jessica's stiff arm to her hand holding the sword.

She lets me take it from her without any reluctance. I use my free arm to embrace her in a hug that isn't reciprocated. Jessica merely rests her head on my shoulder in exhaustion.

"Love Fest over! Let's go girls!" We hear a much-welcomed voice from the dense fog before Sam walks close enough for us to see him.

"Did they hurt you?" He starts examining Jessica's arms and legs before looking at mine. "Any tares in the suit?"

"No, we are both fine. Thanks for coming back," I say to him, smiling through the pain.

"Umm hmm... OK. Good!" Sam responded to while inspecting Jessica once again.

"Well, it looks like you know how to protect yourself after all Miss de Fenace'!" Sam says with a chuckle as he looks down at the dead bodies, then at Jessica, then at me.

I give him a smirk back. When we make eye contact it's clear that he has a twinkle that wasn't there before. He knows Jessica was the victor here today, not me. He knows Jessica.

"Sam, it's good to see you again!" Jessica chimes in. "We weren't sure you were gonna make it this time."

"Ha!" Sam replies with a cocky smile directed at Jessica. "I make it to you every time, right!"

He winks.

Both Sam and Jessica smile from ear to ear at each other. Jessica leaves my side and reaches out to embrace Sam. I am completely caught off guard by this display of emotion from both Jessica and Sam. It seems so foreign from how I know them.

"Okay. Wait a minute!" I say. "How is it that the two of you know each other?"

I get no response from either of them as they engage in their own secret conversation. Their whispers are too low for me to hear in the deafening wind from the storm we are still surrounded by.

"Hello!" I say louder and slightly annoyed.

"We'd better hurry," Sam finally says. "More of 'em could come at any moment."

Sam walks over to double check my air purifier and then Jessica's.

"Let's go, now. Jessica's purifier is almost empty and we don't have much left either," Sam says, completely ignoring my question about how they know each other.

"Wait? Where's Sven? Where are we going?" I ask, again to no response.

"This way," Sam says as he takes the lead with Jessica's fingers locked between his, leaving me to catch up on my own. It seems I've become the third wheel. It's a surprisingly welcomed feeling that I'm not used to.

Jessica turns to me with the same big smile from moments ago still on her face.

"Sam found me. After I was…" Jessica searches for the right word.

"Exiled," Jessica says, before turning her attention fondly back to Sam.

"Alright then!" I add with a sound of surprise in my voice. I am taken aback by the transparent affection Jessica and Sam share. I am also a little jealous that Sam choose Jessica over me. But, ultimately, I am just happy to follow them and get out of here safely!

Chapter 28

We finally reach the end of the storm just as Jessica's purifier stopped working. We take our masks off but leave the rain suits, on just in case.

"This way. We are almost there" Sam says encouragingly, still holding Jessica's hand.

Exhausted, we push forward knowing the wind could change at any minute and put all of our lives at risk. We come to a rock wall that's covered with vines and shrubbery. Sam hurries over to the wall and begins pulling the foliage to one side.

Jessica and I stand there watching. I have no idea of what to expect. Jessica seems to know exactly what's going on. Two months on the Ground has definitely changed her. Hopefully for the better.

Sam motions for us to follow him into what looks like another cave. It looks different from the small enclosed cave Sam and I spent last night in. This one is manmade. As I walk under the opening, I notice the letters "ATTERY" are engraved overhead. I repeat "Attery" in my head several times. I feel like I have seen them someplace before.

I pull the foliage back further to reveal the entire engraving: 1938 BATTERY DAVIS. I'm positive I have either seen this before, dreamt about it, heard about it or read about it someplace. I just can't place it.

I catch up to Sam and Jessica further inside. The structure looks like a shelter made of super thick concrete. I scan the walls and see faded graffiti everywhere. Most of it is illegible. I wonder how long its been here. I quietly walk deeper into the structure not knowing what could be hiding in the darkness. Sam confidently walks over to a corner directly in front of Jessica and pulls out a bag from beneath a pile of sand. He shakes it a bit and then wipes off the remaining sand before opening it by placing his fingerprint on the handle.

"Just as promised. Sven left this for us." He reaches inside and pulls out some fresh water and food. He takes a sip of the water before handing it to Jessica. He hands me the food, and I quickly open it from the package, shoving it in my mouth without even reading the label to find out what it is. I take a second huge bite before exchanging it with Jessica for the water. It's been so long since we've had anything to drink or eat. I feel a sudden surge of energy course through my body, like watering a dying flower and seeing it bloom again

I look over at Sam who is still rummaging through the bag. I'm a little curious about what else is in there but figure he'll let me know on a need to know basis. Just like everything else with this guy.

"Is this place safe?" I ask in between gulps of water.

"Not entirely," Sam says. "But mostly. Indies have kept this hidden for the most part. We'd be dead without this network of caves." He closes-up the duffle bag and throw is over his shoulder.

"This way!" Sam says to both Jessica and I. "Let's keep moving!"

"Hey?" I start asking right before I take another swig of water and begin jogging to catch up to Sam. "Who were those guys?" I ask as casually as I can before taking another bite of food.

I don't get an answer so I probe further. "You know. The ones trying to take us prisoner? Come on. The ones you both killed?" I say with a raised tone compared to my normal speech.

I notice Jessica and Sam smile at each other before they bust out laughing at me.

"Funny? What could possibly be so funny?" I ask annoyed that I'm the butt of their inside joke.

"They hunt Percenters who have been exiled, like me. The ones that don't die are sold, like slaves, to the Cleansing Coalition," Jessica says as a matter of fact.

"Which is virtually a death sentence in itself," Sam adds. "The Cleaners, we call them, are technically Indies, from the Ground, but they work with the Coalition and are compensated heavily. They will sell anyone they can hunt, not just Percenters. The Coalition has been kidnapping Barrens and conducting tests on my people for longer than my father's father can remember."

Sam pauses, and then says, "They took my sister when I was too young to stop them."

He shows more contempt for the Cleansing Coalition in that moment than I am yet to feel. I finally begin to understand why he's been helping me. We are in this together, fighting the same enemy.

"I'm, I'm so sorry Sam." Is all I can think of to say. Both Jessica and Sam spoke to me directly and honestly. Regardless of our differences, in that moment I felt respected enough that they both told me the truth. I also felt tremendous sorrow for Sam.

"I can't even begin to imagine," I add.

"You don't need to, Jena. You might find out one day," Jessica says before we all continue walking in silence.

I think about what Jessica said over and over. I couldn't make out her tone. Perhaps she was warning me or maybe it was more of a threat. But then I realize, she wouldn't be helping me now just to turn me over to the Coalition later. That wouldn't make any sense. I have to start trusting Jessica. I know I can trust Sam so I convince myself that if both Sam and Sven trust Jessica then I should be able to as well.

"Hey, Sam!" I shout out in front of me. "Where does this go?" I ask him, pointing down at some type of door in the floor. It looked the like lock of a bank vault, but instead of being on a wall, it was on the floor. Sam and Jessica come running back to me.

Sam has the flashlight he found in the duffle bag in his hand and shines the light on the half-covered door. He wipes the sand and grime off of the rest of the door to inspect it for anything that would help identify the door.

"It's probably nothing," Sam says. "This was built as a military defense station before The Oze. It probably led to a storage room or something."

Sam tries to twist the lock but has no success.

"Here, let me help!" Jessica volunteers. She kneels down next to Sam across from the circular handle and they both try to twist the door open. It creaks a little, but doesn't even budget and inch.

"It doesn't matter really," Sam confirms as he leans back off the door and stands up. "We need to keep going this way. Sven said we'd know it when we see it," he adds.

Both Jessica and Sam start walking further into the tunnel, leaving me behind in the fading light.

"Hey, can I get a flashlight if you two are going to keep leaving me?" I say to what appears to be an empty cave.

I throw my hands up in frustration before starting to walk after them, staying completely on the back edge of the flashlight's glow. I think about what Sam said. He told me that Sven thought we'd know it when we see it.

"What could that mean?" I mumble. "How would we recognize it?" I haven't recognized anything since I got to the Ground. Everything is foreign to me. Then I hear a screeching sound. It was distant, faint, but it was definitely a new sound. I hear it again.

"Did you hear that?" I yell to Sam and Jessica.

"Hear what?" They both ask at the same time. Followed by a look of adoration shared between the two of them.

"Listen!" I say and within seconds I heard the screech again, followed by three more.

"Run Jena! Hurry up!" Sam calls to me. "This way!"

"No, I say. I know those screeches. Jessica, you remember them, right?" "How would I know random screeches in a cave system Jena, Honestly!" She screams back at me.

"Trust me. You guys have to follow me back to that door. Remember Jessica, in the simulation, when we were all running, and I fell down a hole. I wanted to go further but Jacob told me not to. Remember?"

"No, Jena. I don't, sorry. Let's go Sam's way. Hurry!"

The screeching is definitely getting louder. It sounds like several different sources, not just one or two.

"Jacob said that he recognized the cave and that the hole I fell into wasn't the way out. What if it is this time? Sven told you Sam that we would recognize it when we see it right? Well, it didn't have a door on it in the simulation, but everything else feels like it's where we need to go," I plead with them. My gut is telling me so strongly that the door is the right way to go. I remember the Amber pendant beneath my suit, and I turn and run in the direction of the screeching back to the door.

"It's not going to matter, Jena. We can't even open it!" Sam yells to me. I keep running anyway.

I hear Sam tell Jessica to "Come on" and I can hear their footsteps behind me as I reach the door. As soon as I get their I take off my pendant and hold the amber in my hand over the door. Within seconds Sam shines his light on the door. The amber does nothing.

"What are you doing?" Jessica asks me. The screeching so loud that we can now hear claws on the cave floor and walls. If it's the same gremlin like creatures from the simulation than we need to get out of their way quickly.

I close my eye. I think more intently about Za and my ancestors. "Please!" I whisper under my breath. I open my eyes again and with the amber pendant still in the palm of my right hand, I place both hands on the door handle and without much effort, it opens. Both Jessica and Sam look at me utterly surprised but neither one of them wanting to ask me how. Sam simply leans the opening and shines his flight light down to illuminate a ladder that fades away with the darkness beyond the light.

"Well, let's go!" I say with a sudden sense of confidence.

"You first!" Sam says to me as he hands me the flashlight. I don't hesitate. I immediately begin climbing into the passageway and down the ladder. Jessica follows me before Sam pulls another flashlight out of his duffle bag and crawls into the passageway, closing the doorway behind. He manually secures the lock and after breaking off the top rung of the latter, jams it into the lock to prevent anything from following us.

"So, you did have another one, after all," I say to Sam only to receive a smile back.

"Is this like what you remember?" Jessica asks.

"No, not exactly. In the simulation it was more like a hole, you know with dirt walls." I'm surprised Jessica doesn't remember me falling in the hole from the simulation.

I would think the memory of when she activated her Horti powers would be fresh in her mind. It was, after all, only minutes after I fell into the hole that the gremlins chased us and Jessica saved us all. I almost bring it up to see if it helps trigger her memory but before I do, I remember what Sven said about Jessica not being able to access her powers and decide not to.

All of the sudden the door above us starts making sounds like something jumping up and down on it. The gremlins must have arrived. The heavy tunnel down muffles their screeches. They are clawing at the door, without any success.

"But it feels right to me. It feels like this is the right way!" I add, kind of joking but kind of relieved. I continue down the ladder as fast as I can. I finally have enough distance between myself and Jessica and Sam so I put the amber pendant back on and tuck it under my suit again before they see me.

We reach the bottom of the ladder and have only one direction to go. I see a red light further down the tunnel and mention it to Sam before he reaches the bottom. He jumps off the ladder, skipping the final rungs and reaches back into his bag and grabs our masks.

"Put these on, quickly!" Sam shouts.

"Red means the air is dangerous. It's a warning system we created years ago," Sam says to both of us before adding, "Green, air is fine."

We do as he says. I immediately feel the vacuum seal of the suit once I get my mask on. The air purifier starts providing fresh oxygen.

As soon as Jessica's suit makes the seal her purifier beeps twice.

"OK. Jessica has less than fifteen minutes of purified air and we aren't too far behind her. Let's move!" he says as he starts running down the tunnel faster than he has run yet. We follow him, matching his pace.

Chapter 29

Within minutes the red lights of the tunnel mostly disappear as they become covered in fog. I have my flashlight, but it doesn't do much against the density of the fog. The wind slams against my body just as the tunnel opens to the outside. I can't see anything.

I turn around and around looking for Sam and Jessica, they are gone again. I roll my eyes and continue walking. I hear a new crunch with every step. I look down to see what I'm actually walking on. The fog is so thick that I can't even see my feet, let alone the Ground.

I bend down to feel with my hands and pick up a dried crab claw in one and tiny fish bones in the other. Everywhere I grab, the Ground is covered in fragments of bones. Many pieces no larger than grains of sand. I hear a loud crash followed by a thunderous roll. I can barely make it out with the noise of the wind blowing so forcefully. I stand still, listening to the repeated rhythm of the crash and roll.

"It can't be!" I whisper to myself. "It can't be!"

I yell for Sam and Jessica again and again with no response. Every step I take I crush more pieces of fragile bones. Old remnants of birds, shellfish and other small animals that used to live along the coast before The Oze killed them all. As I get closer to the crashing sound, the pieces of bones turn into sand beneath my feet.

I want to take off my mask and smell the air. As a child in San Sun, we were told that the Great Oceans of Earth smelt like salt. But as tempted as I am, I can't risk the air quality. I run in the direction of the crash and roll before my feet reach the water breaking on the beach.

"Mr. Hampton, you devil!" I say to myself before yelling out to Sam and Jessica. "The Ocean...this must be what he meant!"

Not surprisingly, neither responds.

"Hello? Where are you guys?" I ask, playfully wanting to share the Ocean with them. I continue to enjoy the sound of the waves crashing when Jessica sneaks up behind me, smacks me on my back and yells.

"Boo!"

"Seriously? Did you think that would work?" I respond.

"Honestly. Yes," Jessica answers, with her hands on her hips, less than a foot from me.

"Where have you been? I've been calling for you. Didn't you hear me?" I say, a little frustrated but still feeling relaxed next to repetitive sound of the waves rushing up the coastline.

"Yeah, we heard you but you were up wind so there was no point in yelling back, you wouldn't have heard us," Jessica responds, not really paying attention to my obvious hurt feelings for being left alone and ignored. But I get over it quickly. They clearly want some privacy, and I want to give it to them.

"Sam found it! Come on, let's go!" She says exuberantly.

"Jessica, the Ocean! Can you believe it!" I scream with childlike excitement. She just looks at me, smiles and nods her head. I can see by her expression that this isn't her first time on a beach or near an ocean. I can only imagine everything that she has seen, or lived through, these past two months and hope that, one day, she'll tell me.

Jessica takes my hand in hers. We start skipping down the shoreline, giggling like little school girls. This might be the most fun I've had since the exams started. I've never really had a close girlfriend and as much as Jessica and I get under each other's skin, we have a connection that I don't really understand.

We keep skipping all the way until we reach Sam, his air purifier beeps twice and so does mine.

"Just in time!" he says to me

"Why didn't you tell me we were coming to the water like I thought we should?" I smack Sam on the shoulder playfully. "I told you Mr. Hampton..."

"And I didn't want to spoil the surprise for you," Sam adds. "Now, if you are done playing around, we have to find our way in. And I don't think I need to remind you, but I will. We have less than fifteen minutes and since it took us ten to get her, Jessica has less than five." Sam makes eye contact with both of us to make sure we understand the situation.

"Got it," I say.

"Me too," Jessica adds.

"OK, so you see this." Sam places his hand on a solid wall of cement, covered in graffiti just like the Battery. I join my flashlight with his, showing a wall painted with layers of reds, yellows, whites, and purples. All faded from their former brightness. Sam walks along the wall until he reaches a corner.

"We need to find a way in. It's not going to be obvious so look for the smallest details," Sam tells us.

We each have our flashlights in hand and our faces just inches from the structure as we scour for anything that's a clue. Jessica goes in the opposite direction of Sam, turning around another corner out of my few. The cement can't be more than ten feet wide on the side facing the ocean. I'm not sure how deep it goes but the cliffs of the tunnel we came out of are only feet from where we stand now. I shine my light upwards to see that the wall isn't that tall.

"Hey, Sam! Help me up." Sam quickly comes back around his corner and cups his hands for my foot. I step into it and put both of my hands on his shoulder after putting the flashlight in my mouth. My head and neck are enough that I can see a flat roof and nothing more.

"What do you see?" Sam asks in a hurried voice.

"Not much. Help me high, I think I can stand here." He easily lifts me higher, allowing me to pull my body up the rest of the way.

"Anything?" he asks.

"Not yet."

"Ok, hurry!" Sam adds just as Jessica comes back to where he's standing.

"Nothing on my side. It's just a flat wall, covered in paint until it ends at the cliff.

"Same, same," Sam says to her.

"Hold on!" I say. "There's some railing here, it looks like it's a square, only a couple feet wide."

"What's inside? What do you see?" Sam asks.

Jessica's air purifier starts to beep. But this time, it doesn't stop.

"Oh shite!" Sam exclaims. "Jena, you have to find it. Look for something familiar. Anything."

"Ok, I'm going to climb into the fenced area." I step on the first bar. It seems sturdy enough to hold my weight.

I quickly step up three more rungs of the fence before lunging my other leg over the top and landing inside the small square. There is barely enough room for me to stand and turn so I take my pack off and set it down on the side of the fence I just stepped from. I shine the light down at my feet, I don't see anything significant. Just more random graffiti spray painted on cement.

"I don't see anything! I'm looking! I don't see anything" I shout down.

Just as I do, Jessica collapses.

"Jessica!" Sam exclaims. "Jessica, stay with us!'

Jessica starts coughing, struggling to get air. The beeping on her air purifier finally stops.

"What's happening?" I yell down to both Sam and Jessica.

"Jessica!" Sam yells, shaking her body to get her to wake up.

"Find it, now Jena!" Sam yells at me in complete panic

"Jessica! Jessica. Come on," Sam keeps repeating.

I drop to my knees, using my hands to feel the surface of the cement for anything that stands out. Nothing.

"I don't get it. It has to be here. It has to be here!" I say to myself.

Jessica's body begins to seize. She's running out of air.

"Jessica's almost out of air," Sam reports to me.

"Okay. Okay!" Sam whispers to himself before taking a deep breath of fresh air. He grabs his air purifier and without even thinking, he swaps it out with Jessica's. Jessica stops seizing and gulps air in. She wakes up just in time to see Sam's face, smiling back at hers. He mouths to her, "I Love You!"

Jessica hugs Sam tighter than she ever has before. Relieved that she has air again and before she notices her air purifier lying next to her on the Ground. Sam faints, collapsing in her arms.

"Sam! No, Sam!" I hear Jessica. "Why did you do it, Sam?" she screams as she shakes Sam.

"Jena! Hurry. Sam's unconscious!" Jessica yells with complete fear in her voice.

I frantically study the graffiti. There is no other reason for this area to be fenced in. I'm confident that the way in is where I am kneeling. Amongst the paintings I notice a lion wearing a crown. It's hard to make out, but it looks like the lion is holding something into the air with rays of light shining from it.

"The Destiny Sword! It's the Destiny Sword. That's why Hunter didn't want me to have it."

I reach through the railings and into my pack. I pull out the Destiny Sword.

"Now what?" I ask the sword, as if expecting an answer.

Sam's body is completely limp now in Jessica's. She is holding him, rocking him back and forth slowly. Muttering the words, "Please. Please don't leave me. I love you," inches from Sam's face. Jessica's mask pushed against his.

I stand up, right above the graffiti of a lion, and raise the sword straight above my head like I had done when Hunter attacked me. The sword began to glow the same brilliant blue it had done in the tunnels. Jessica looks up at me to see what's happening. I look down and we make eye contact.

I can see her heartbreaking before me, yet she still has no tears in her eyes. I look at Sam's lifeless body in her arms and close my eyes, squeezing the sword's handle as tight as I can. I feel the intensity of the light coming from the sword increasing. The cement structure below my feet begins to shake violently. It's moving.

The entire area below my feet starts to drop lower than the rest of the structure. Everything inside the railings is going down.

"Jessica! It's opening! It's opening." I lower the Destiny Sword and jump over the railing. I walk to the edge.

"Hurry, lift Sam up to me and I'll come back for you!" I say in a rush.

Jessica struggles to her feet. She tries to lift Sam up to me but he is too heavy for her.

"I can't! I can't," Jessica cries out.

"Yes, you can, Jessica. I know you can do this!" I say to her calming her down.

I watch as Jessica lifts Sam up to her shoulders high enough for me to grab under his armpits and hoist him up the rest of the way. I pull his massive body over to the railing and try to lower him inside without dropping him. I'm not successful. His body tumbles over the edge, falling about three feet before hitting the bottom what looks like a platform.

He doesn't make a single sound. The platform, or probably better called an elevator, continues to go deeper at a snail's pace. I paused for a second, wondering if I have enough time to get Jessica too. I shake my head as I suddenly catch myself even debating and reach back down to grab Jessica's hands, who is still waiting very anxiously.

I kneel over the edge once again and reach both hands down to clasp hers. In no time at all, she jumps up the wall and scales it to the top. We both run over to the elevator to see that it is now about eight to ten feet below the surface.

I look at Jessica and yell, "Now!" We climb over the opening and drop ourselves down towards Sam.

Luckily, we fell against each other as we hit the bottom, both of us taking extra care not to step on Sam. We squeezed together, half vertical, barely able to fit in the tight space. Just as we secure our footing, the sky above us disappears as the elevator closes above us.

We barely made it.

Chapter 30

As soon as the elevator closes above us, we are overwhelmed with intense air being blown into our tiny coffin of a space. Just as fast as the air blows in, it is suck out the other side. The air pressure normalizes just as we begin being sprayed from head to toe with a fine mist. In seconds the wet spray is over and we are air blown dry again. The elevator continues to lower when suddenly we have an abrupt stop that makes us all collapse. A few seconds later, a section of the wall opens like a door and a bunch of people, dressed in similar rain suits but without masks, rush in and grab Sam's lifeless body from our feet.

I look over at Jessica in silence, watching her facial expression as they lift Sam to a gurney and take him down a long hallway before he disappears out of site. Jessica has no reaction at all. She has a disturbingly flat effect on her face that is a bit haunting. I reach down and grab her hand in mine, using my free hand to rub her arm as I try to console her. We are too exhausted to even protest. We stand there in disbelief. In silence.

People are talking to us but there is so much happening, I can't focus enough to understand what anyone one person is saying. Both Jessica and I eventually step out of the elevator to a solid concrete floor and within two steps we both collapse. Clinging to each other's arms, the people who were talking to use rush to our sides and begin lifting us off the ground.

Right before I lose consciousness, I notice the face of one of the many people running over to us. The face looks familiar, but the dark hair and smile are throwing me a curveball. I wonder for only a moment longer before he bends down to my face, and I can see him clearly.

"Jenavieve! Everything is going to be OK," he says in a very familiar voice.

"Ben?" I say before closing my eyes completely and joining Jessica in a much-needed deep sleep.

I wake up and stretch my neck, arms, and shoulders. I'm lying in the most comfortable bed since the morning I woke at home the first day of the exams. I sit up with my back against a super soft headboard covered in a floral fabric. I close my eyes, take both of my hands, and rub the base of my neck while I release a subtle moan of awakenment. When I open my eyes fully, I can see a window beyond the foot of my bed.

I pull the covers off, noticing I'm wearing mismatched pajamas. My pants are plush, with a red and black square pattern reminding me of the Checkers board game we used to play as children. My shirt, while also comfy, is a solid navy blue, with a long V-neck and three-quarter cut-off sleeves.

I step off the bed and into grey slippers, thin and worn. They are heelless and easy for me to put on. I walk over to the window where curtains are blowing in fresh salty air. I stumble a little on my weak legs when I first start walking but quickly regain my footing. I stand in the window and take deep breaths of the freshest air I have ever inhaled.

I watch the waves of the ocean crash on to the sandy shore just meters from me. I see a group of kids, no more than ten years old, chasing each other around on the beach. All of them are shoeless and some of the kids are even shirtless. I notice them kicking a ball between each other as they run up and down the shoreline.

I look into the sky to see a warm, shining sun like I used to see in San Sun. Only this time I'm on the Ground. Birds with white and grey feathers chirp as they fly by my window. A rare species I have never seen before. A few of them land on the red tiled roof of the house next to me. It's a blue cottage like house, with white shutters and a wraparound porch. I can see similar white drapes blowing in the wind.

"Good morning!" says a familiar voice from behind me.

I turn quickly to see my cousin, Ben, standing in the doorway. His smiling face is shadowed by a tight beard and his beautiful dark hair. I only remember him clean shaven, even his head, like all Middlers. I haven't seen him with air since before his exam's. He's holding a tray with a yellow rose standing in a crystal vase in the corner. I notice a white bowl, filled with deep red strawberries. Next to it, a tall crystal glass filled with what looks like my favorite morning shake.

"I thought it was a dream!" I say as I muster the strength and run over to Ben, losing both slippers before wrapping my arms around his neck and hugging him. I squeeze him so quickly that I almost make him drop the tray before he manages to set it down on a desk nearby. Ben hugs me back, laughing like I remember he did when we were kids.

"Oh my gosh, I'm happy to see you too!" Ben says with a true happiness in his voice.

"Ben! Oh, my God! You have no idea how happy I am to see you! Where are we? What is this amazing place?" I say as I push him back and give him a head to toe examination. "Gone is the grey!" I add, swinging both of his hands in mine as I look back into his eyes.

"Yup. At least for a few more days," Sam says as he squeezes my hand right before letting go and directing me to the chair in front of the tray of food.

"I have to head back to San Sun now that you have arrived safely. I'm sure you have tons of questions so why don't you eat first. You must be starving. Then you can freshen up in the bathroom," Ben points over to a set of French doors on the other side of the room, "and I'll be waiting for you downstairs to fill you in."

I smile back at him and shake my head from side to side as I lower it. I reach out and grab his waist, pulling his body next to mine, and hug him again.

"Aw…" I say. "It is so good to see you Ben and yes, I'm starving and would love to clean up a bit!" I look at my pajamas and back to Ben. Before I can say anything, as if he were reading my mind, Ben says: "The closet doesn't have too many clothes like you are used to, but I'm sure you'll find something that will work!" Ben lets out a little laugh as he points to a hallway, "The closet is that way."

"Thank you!" I say, feeling a sense of contentment to be around a familiar face and someone who truly knows me.

Ben starts to walk out of the room. He reaches the doorway and with his left hand, grabs the doorknob.

"Hey, wait!" I exclaim before he opens the door.

"Jessica? What happened to Jessica? And Sam?" I say softly, masking an immediate rush of anxiety and fear.

In a calm and reassuring voice, Ben says, "Jessica is in the room down the hall," he uses his head to nod back and to the left. She's still sleeping. We have her being monitored."

"What about Sam? Is he…?" I start saying, but Ben interrupts me before I can finish.

"Sam is still alive, but just barely. His is in great hands with the doctors over in the medical building." Again, using his head to signal a direction, nods forward, looking right past my head.

"Eat. Freshen up. And I'll see you downstairs and fill you in with everything I know," Ben adds with his beautiful smile.

I notice how handsome my cousin has become in such a short period of time. He wears a confidence that I have never seen from him before, not even before he failed his exams.

I look down at the tray of food in front of me and begin devouring each strawberry, one by one until they are gone, leaving only a pile of stems. I chug the protein shake, licking my lips when I finish. I rush into the shower as quickly as I can. I set the water to the warmest temperature my body can handle before jumping in.

I stand in the shower for so long that I forget about everything else going on in my life. I allow my mind to escape to the vision of the beach I just saw moments ago out of my window. Not a simulation like the ones Buzz would display on our walls in San Sun. A real beach with real sand and surf. I zone out and loose complete track of time.

Chapter 31

"I see you took full advantage of the closet," Ben says to me as I walk down the staircase and into a cozy living room.

I do a quick little twirl as my soft, linen dress lifts off the ground. "I think beach life suits me!" I say with a giggle.

"I think it does!" Ben says back to me. I run over to him and give him a kiss on the cheek.

"OK, I want to know everything! Starting with how are you!" I say to him as I jump down into the softest sofa chair, full of pillows. I land so my legs are able to cross over the edge of one arm of the chair while the other props me up.

"OK, OK!" Ben exclaims. "Where should I start?" He taps his chin as if he's pondering where to begin, torturing me with the delay.

I throw one of the pillows I'm half laying on at him. He barely dodges it before the pillow flies out the open window behind him. We both laugh like school children.

"So, you know you were trapped in The Numinous, and that it all happened over two months ago, right?" Ben asks to find out exactly how much I know about my own life.

"Yes. Until that portal opened to Sven and Jessica and I've been on the Ground since. With Sam," I answered.

"Where's Sven?" I add. "Is she here, too?"

"OK. Gotcha. So yes, Sven is here. Let me go back a bit to catch you up. I'd say get comfortable but…" Ben looks at me, smiling with his eyes as he watches me pull a throw blanket around my shoulders and snuggle into the chair further.

I notice him watching me and gently laugh at him. "Do you know what it's like out there, on the Ground?" I say like a spoiled little princess. "It's rough, man! Rough!"

"Mmmhmmm," Ben says before continuing, "When you got lost in The Numinous, nobody really understood what was happening. Not the proctors. Not your parents. No one. The plan was for you to arrive on the Ground and meet Sam, near the place you first came to with Sven and Jessica, within moments of you talking to Mr. Hampton. We quickly found out you were trapped because we learned that Hunter hacked your simulation. But there was no way to find you. So, all that was happening right, and we were all worried for you Jena!" Ben adds with some delight. "But, meanwhile, back in San Sun..." he continues like he's catching me up on the latest soap opera, "Alex completed the exams. But, as number two! You'll never guess who beat him?" Ben adds with mischievous excitement.

"Who?" I say, not having any idea. "Trevor? What's his last name?"

"Wrong! Fitch, by the way. It was Raquel Hawthorn!" Ben says with the biggest smile on his face.

"Of course, she did!" I laugh.

"Anyway, so Alex is doing great at Freelinn. He's completely devastated about you being lost to The Numinous and still being kept in the dark. Your parents think it's the best way to keep him safe and to stop him from searching for you. Of which he's always threatening to do, and if you ask me, he is in his free time. But speaking of your parents, your mom will be here soon. She left San Sun this morning. Your father can't leave Freelinn just yet, it would look to suspicious."

"My mother is coming!?" I say, both questioning Ben and showing excitement for the news. "Oh, thank God. I have no idea what I am supposed to do!" I laugh so uncontrollably that it ends kind of awkward, as if reality set in that I actually have no idea what I am supposed to be doing to help myself, let alone an entire human race.

"You have done everything that you needed to do, Jena!" Ben assures me. "I know it doesn't feel that way but, believe me, you have." He pauses for effect with his hand on my knee, just like pre-exam Ben used to do. "So, yeah, your mom will be here soon."

"And?" I say, hoping for more updates.

"And?" Ben responds longingly.

"That's it? I've been trapped in some other dimension or whatever for months! I barely survived the Ground before I show up at this lovely beach house with my Middler cousin in a delightful mood, serving me fresh strawberries?"

"Oh, right!" Ben laughs as if he completely lost his track of thought. His tone refocuses to be more serious, "So, your parents weren't sure what happened to you but they somehow knew you were still alive. They preemptively sent Sven to the Ground to meet Sam, so when you arrived, they'd be ready. Sam was, is, our main contact on the Ground with the Indies."

"How long have you known about what's going on?" I ask Ben.

"Shortly after I became a Middler, I overheard your parents talking one night. I didn't mean to eavesdrop, but when I heard about what was happening on the Ground, to the Barrens and other humans, which basically I am as a Percenter born without powers, I couldn't help but feel indebted to your parents for saving my life." Ben lowers his head as he turns his back to me, showing a little of the insecure Ben I remember from recently. I don't say anything and just continue to listen.

"The next time I heard them discussing the Savior's plans to put an end to all the lies and expose the Phineas Riley and the Cleansing Coalition, I confessed I had been listening and wanted to help. I have been working with them ever since. It's really given me a purpose," Ben adds before turning back to face me.

"And what about Avelino? What happened to him?" I ask.

"Avelino?" Ben responds, acting as if he doesn't have any idea who I'm talking about.

"Yes. You know, Avelino Riley! Phineas' son?" I say with a little too much inflection that my cheeks go a little red.

"I didn't know Phineas had a son!" Ben says as he's obviously playing with my emotions. "Just kidding! Of course, I know who Avelino is, Jena!

Everyone with a pulse knows who he is. He's *fine*." Ben coughs a little at his own emphasis on the word fine. "I mean, he's doing well. He passed the exam and went to a Prep school of course, not sure which one. Counting Jessica, only three students failed the exams this year. Jessica was the only one sent to the Ground. The other two, I forget their names, were Middled."

"I gathered that much. What I'm wondering is if Avelino is…" I pause, not sure exactly how to ask the question. "Is he one of us?"

"Oh, no. I don't think he knows about the Saviors, or if he does, he doesn't know that you are one. The real question is, does he know what Daddy has been up to lately?" Ben answers, pausing before moving on.

"OK, so now you are here. This beautiful place is called Farallon Island. Your parents sent me here as soon as you got lost to The Numinous. They knew you would find your way here, and we have all been preparing," Ben adds.

"Preparing? Preparing for what?" I ask.

"Jena, it's almost time! The S9, you know Xavier and the other Secret children, are ready. You see, they have been training for years. Years! They started when you and I were still eating cereal for breakfast. But they were never going to be ready without you, their leader."

"What? What are you talking about their *leader*? I'm not their leader. I've never even met them," I say excitedly.

"You will, in fact, let's go track down Sven and the S9 now!" Ben adds.

"Wait. Hold on. What do you mean I am their leader and what do you mean they are ready? Ready for what?" I ask.

"Jena, you ARE their leader. You are the only one who can wield the Destiny Sword. I know this sounds clichéd, but it is your destiny, just as your parents told you. Everything they have planned for you is happening. It's happening now! The Cleansing Coalition knows the Saviors have been preparing to attack and we have to strike first. Now that you are here, you will lead the S9 to take down Phineas and the Coalition. It's time!" Ben says with a half-surprised, half-excited look on his face.

"OK, just slow down a moment. Maybe I should just talk to my mother when she arrives. I'm not leading a secret army. I don't think that's what they had in mind."

Ben just looks at me smiling, like he's waiting for a light bulb to go off in my head, but it doesn't. "Let's go find Sven. And Xavier!" Ben adds.

"Xavier? He's here? Now?" I ask.

"Yes. He's training with the other S9." Ben moves towards the door and invites me along with him. "Come on, let's go!"

I get up, throwing the blanket off my shoulders and follow Ben out the door. As we walk along the sidewalk, I notice that the community looks like every single movie I watched as a child with a beach. Everyone is laughing and smiling as if they don't have a care in the world. People are holding hands as they walk side by side eating ice cream cones. The houses are all tiny, but with well-maintained yards.

"You said Farallon Island. I've never heard of this place before. Why here?" I ask.

"Almost no one has, Jena. I certainly didn't until two months ago. This is where your parents and the other Saviors have been raising the S9. Helping them activate their powers and learn how to control them. This is like the Saviors hideout!" Ben adds, completely enjoying the storytelling.

"It's in the middle of the Pacific Ocean. Most Percenters, including the Cleansing Coalition, believe that the entire Ocean is covered by The Oze, and while that's true for some parts, not all, as you can see."

"But who are all of these other people? Are they Percenters?" I ask.

"Oh no, Jena!" Ben kind of laughs at me. "All of these people are direct descendants of pre-Oze humans. When The Oze hit, the people living here were isolated from the rest of the world. They had no idea about Percenters, Barrens, or..." Ben pauses to take a breath, "or Middlers. We introduced all of that to them when the Saviors discovered Farallon. They have been helping us prepare for this day by raising the S9 as their own. Most of the S9 were born here. This is where Xavier was born. This has been his home his entire life."

"Wow, OK. That's a lot. A lot of, new, information. So, all of these people, they don't have any special powers. But they aren't Barrens, or Indies, like Sam?" I ask.

"No. They don't and they aren't," Ben says.

We continue walking along the beach promenade. I look around and take it all in. I see fountains on the street corners with kids running up to them for a drink. People riding bicycles in single file line. More birds flying above, chirping as they go by. There are shops along the streets with people going in empty handed and coming out with bags and smiles.

"So, this is what it was like! Before The Oze, I mean," I say, not necessarily asking a question but open to anything Ben might add. He doesn't.

"What's he like?" I ask Ben. "Xavier. What's he like?"

Ben looks at me as he has many times before, with calming eyes and a sense that everything is going to be OK. I know family is a tough subject for him so I wasn't sure if bringing up mine was a good idea or not.

"You are going to like him Jena! Surprisingly, he's a lot like you and Alex. Except not as, as…as cocky as Alex!" Ben replies, with a little chuckle as he makes a joke at Alexander's expense since he can't defend himself.

"Oh, that's good! I don't think I could handle another brother with an inflated ego!" I say back, laughing along with him.

Just as we are about to walk into the main entrance of a red brick building, Sven opens the door and runs right into me.

"Jena! You are up!" Sven says with excitement and grabs me in a big bear hug.

"Good to see you too!" I say back

"You are not an easy lady to find," I tell her. "You know, I've been on the Ground and hunted by crazy Indies looking for you. What happened? Why didn't you come back?" I put my hands on my hips, showing Sven my disappointment.

"Sorry about that. You were passed out. Jessica and I couldn't carry you any further. We knew we had to get you help. Jessica took your sword for protection and we went off in different directions. I managed to find shelter when a storm came. Luckily Sam and Xavier found me. Xavier helped me back here so Sam could find you and Jessica."

"It's been crazy, right!" I add

"You'll get used to it, soon!" Sven adds.

Just then, from within the bright light filled gymnasium behind Sven, steps out Xavier. I recognize him immediately, even though I have never met him in person. I can tell by looking into his eyes. Xavier is just as I had pictured him. He's slightly taller than Alexander but almost identical.

Without moving his lips or saying a word, I hear "Sister! Welcome!" he says inside my head as he extends his arms wide open.

"Xavier! It's finally you!" I say back to him telepathically as we did during the exam.

I push past Sven and dive my head straight into his chest. I put my arms around his body as he does mine. I hug him the way that I would hug Alexander, with all my might. Xavier walks me into the gymnasium and introduces me to the other S9.

"OK, everybody, listen up! This is only happening once," Xavier says so loudly everyone in the gymnasium could hear him.

"My little sister, your leader, Jenavieve de Fenace', has finally arrived!"

All S9 cheer in excitement and start making their way over to greet me. The first to arrive and say hello was Corey Robins, also the fastest person I have ever met. He didn't run over to me as much as he looked at me and was suddenly standing right in front of me within milliseconds. Then I met Erinn Partnoy, who disappeared as fast as she re-appeared.

Everyone is so friendly and gracious, everyone so excited to see me and shake my hand. For a short moment, I felt like when Alexander and I were in our Bullet on the way to the Grand Reception of the exams when everyone was cheering us along. It was an exciting and welcoming moment that was happening for me all over again.

"Jena, meet my brother, Daniel Krouse." Sven jumps in with excitement.

"Hi, Daniel. I had no idea!" I say as I look back and forth from Sven to Daniel. "Sven? Why didn't you tell me sooner?"

"When have we had the chance, right!" Sven says to me as she jumps on her brother's back, playing around.

I met the other S9's, Shree Broberg, Kyle Kelley, and Erica Belling. Xavier told me that Peter Perris and Vanessa Parkin we out on a training exercise and would be back shortly. After quick introductions and basic conversation, everyone, including Xavier, went back to doing whatever it was they were doing before I walked into the building.

"I'll find you later!" Xavier says inside my head as I walk outside with Sven and Ben to the beautiful blue sky and fresh sea air. I look back and wave goodbye to my new brother for the first time.

Chapter 32

Sven stops to look into the sky, covering her eyes with the shade of her hands. Ben and I continue walking, more like skipping, as we leave the gymnasium.

"What's that? Sven whispers just loud enough for us to hear her.

"What did you say Sven?" I ask her as we continue skipping down the street.

"What. Is. That?" Sven says again, this time louder and very concise.

Ben and I turn to look at Sven in somewhat confusion.

"What is what?" I ask.

"Look, out there." Sven points into the sky, on the horizon where The Oze meets the surface of the ocean.

Both Ben and I raise our hands to shade our eyes from the sun and look in the direction Sven is pointing. At first, I don't see anything, Then, once my eyes began to gain focus in the light, I could see a plane of some sort off in the distance. I began to notice that it didn't have any wings. Not that it never had, but that they were torn off. What was left the wings were burning.

The plane drops elevation rapidly and gets closer to the island every second. Other people nearby begin noticing the plane as well. Some scream and shout and run off in the opposite direction while others simply stand and watch in awe. For a moment, I found myself in the later camp until Sven grabs my arm, and we start jogging in the direction towards the plan.

As we get closer, the plane becomes unmistakable, it's a Bullet just like the one my parent's own. I notice it's even the same color.

"It's going to crash over there, close to the shore!" Sven points to the edge of some cliff that meets the sand and surf.

All three of us begin to run as fast as we can in the direction of the Bullet and just before it crashes into the sea, someone ejects. Their parachute is released and they are slowly floating to the water. More people start running in the direction of the parachuter to see what happens. I feel a sudden rush of air go past me as Daniel, Sven's brother, runs past us to the water. By the time he reaches the water's edge he has every piece of clothing except his underwear removed before jumping into the water.

"Watch this!" Sven says with utter excitement. "Check out my super awesome bro!"

Both Ben and I watch in wonder, as do dozens of other people, as Daniel disappears into the water only to reappear in the waves several hundred meters from the shoreline. I stood there and watched Daniel catch the parachuter with complete ease, barely moving in the water. After he cut the parachute loose, he carried the parachuter in both arms above the rise and fall of the waves until he reached the shore. We all run over to Daniel and the mysterious parachuter as soon as he gets out of the water.

As we get closer, I immediately see that the parachuter is my mother, unconscious.

"Mom!" I scream out. "Mom! Wake up, Mom!"

Xavier and the other S9 are with us at this point. Someone bends down to perform
CPR but notices she is already breathing.

"I know where to take her." Corey says as he picks her up and cradles her in his arms and disappears in a flash.

"Where did he take her?" I scream out? "Where did he take my mom?" I scream at Ben and Sven.

"Probably to our medical ward. Come on. It's not too far," Xavier says to me. Together, Sven, Ben, Xavier, and I start running away from the beach and down a main street.

Within ten minutes we had arrived at an all-white cottage style house. It definitely didn't look like any hospital I have seen in the Sky Cities. I open the front door as fast as I can, and I am greeted by a friendly woman dressed in scrubs from head to toe, revealing only her face with skin as dark as night.

"Hold on a minute young lady! Just hold on. We are going to need a few more minutes to help your mother out. You feel me?" She says looking at me with a sideways wink.

I try to push by her but she holds her ground and doesn't even move an inch. Her body is as solid as a rock. Xavier and everyone behind me start giggling.

"What? What's so funny?" I yell back at them, still trying to get passed the wall of a woman in front of the doorway. "Let me see my mother!" I continue screaming at her.

"Jena! It's OK," Xavier says to me as he reaches out and grabs my elbow, pulling me back. "Meet Kona. She's the head doctor around here."

"Doctor?" I say in surprise. "You look more like a nurse to me," I add

"Is that a fact now!" Kona replies. "Your momma is gonna be just fine. Why don't you all come back in about ten to fifteen minutes. OK. Buh-bye now."

"Seriously?" I say to Xavier. "That's our mom in there?" I hit him on the shoulder with my fist closed. He barely notices.

"If Kona says she is going to be fine, believe me, she is going to be fine. Kona is a Percenter. I've seen her heal people that have come to her missing a leg in a shark attack and they are out there surfing again the next day...with both legs!" Xavier says, looking back down the street to the distant ocean.

"She's a healer. She'll heal Mom," he says calmly.

"Come here, I want to show you something!" Xavier reaches out his hand for me to follow him.

"What? Where are you taking me?" I respond, somewhat annoyed, yet somewhat relieved. If Xavier trusts Kona so much, I need to be able to as well.

"Just follow me," he adds.

I take his hand and let him lead me down another street. I look back at Sven and Ben with confusion only to see them both waving goodbye. Xavier and I walk in silence. My eyes are big as I take in the local community. It continues to be everything I have ever seen in movies about ground life. We reach a storefront that says, "Donuts," in bright pink neon letters. Xavier opens the door, and I can immediately smell the sweetness of the dough and sugar.

"Donuts? Our mother is probably dying in that house you call a hospital and you bring me to get Donuts?" I say half laughing and half amazed.

He continues to walk me up to the counter filled with donuts behind a plastic display. As he carefully examines his options, he releases my hand for the first time and points at a round donut, covered with dark chocolate icing.

"When I was growing up, here, on this island, I didn't get to see Mom and Dad every day like you did. I had to trust that they would visit me again soon. And every time they visited, Mom would insist on taking me here. And every time we came here, I would get one of these. Have you ever had a chocolate glazed donut filled with custard, Jenavieve? Have you?" he asks me innocently.

"No, I have never had a donut. You dummy, of course I have. It's not like they don't allow them in San Sun, or any sky city," I tell him.

"OK. Fair enough," Xavier responds with a smile. "Let me rephrase. Have you ever tried this kind of donut?"

"No. I'm more of an apple fritter kind of girl," I say back to my brother, matching his tone.

"Well then, Sis, you haven't lived!" He winks at me before he orders two of the same donuts.

"I'm sorry you didn't get to grow up with us and see Mom and Dad more," I say apologetically. Realizing how selfish I can be sometimes.

"You know, all those years, I never had a donut except for when they visited. This donut," he holds the fresh donut up to our faces, "began to represent my happiness and every time I would see Mom and Dad, my reward. I was always so afraid that one day they would stop visiting so I would wait every day, in between their visits, for my next donut. And you know what, I always get my donut!"

I stand there, in a loss for words, admiring my long-lost brother. I barely know him, and I already admire him.

We sit at a table for another couple of minutes, eating the most delicious donut I have ever tasted, before returning to Mom. Xavier told me about life growing up on the island. He told me how each of the S9 share an unbreakable bond, and that they are ready to die for each other and for what they believe in. His stories of love and courage remind me why we are all here.

Chapter 33

When we get back to the medical building, Sven and Ben are already inside. Kona points me in the direction of my mother's room, but I can hear Sven and Ben talking down a different hallway. Xavier heads to our mother's room immediately but I tiptoe towards the room that Sven and Ben are talking in. I peek inside only long enough to see Sam, laying on a bed and laughing with the other two.

"Well if it isn't Jenavieve de Fenace'" Sam says, as he notices me hiding behind the door.

"I've been so worried about you Sam!" I say as I walk over to give him a kiss on the cheek. "I can't believe you risked your own life to save Jessica!"

"Well, you know. I don't like to be made a liar, and I promised Jessica I wouldn't let her die. So, you know, there's that," he says, a little embarrassed and turning red in the cheeks.

"Okay, I have to go see my mom. I'll check in on you later!" I say to Sam.

I wave to all three of them and walk out of his room with a smile on my face. I can't believe Sam's luck. Or any of ours for that matter. I'm learning how tough this world can be, but how great it can be when there are others looking out for you.

"Hi, Mom!" I open the door and expect to see my mom sitting up like I did when I opened the door to Sam's room. But instead I find Xavier sitting next to the bed, holding mom's hand. She's sleeping, calmly, with several machines connected to her body.

"Mom?" I say again, a little softer this time.

"She's fine. She's just sleeping. Kona said she's recovered nicely and will

218

be ready to go by tomorrow, but she has to spend the night," Xavier tells me.

She's bandaged up with bruises and cuts all over her face. I try not to touch her too much as I sit down on the other side of the bed from Xavier, snuggling next to my mother. I reach down and caress her arm closest to me.

"Mom! I'm here," I say to her gently. "I'm here."

We sit there for another hour before Xavier leaves. "I have something to take care of so I'll catch you later. Find me, you know, if Mom wakes up. Huh?" he asks, but it really isn't a question.

"How will I find you?" But before he can answer, I realize I don't need to find him. "Of course. I'll just say 'hey' in your head! OK, see you later," I smile and say to Xavier.

He puts his hand on top of mine and kisses me on the forward before he walks out the door. I continue to lie next to my mother until I fall asleep.

I wake up a couple hours later. My mother is still asleep. I decide to get up and go for a walk down to Sam's room and check on him. When I arrive to his room, he isn't there and the room has been cleaned up for a new patient. I ask the new front desk receptionist about him, and she told me that Sam received a clean bill of health and left not too long ago. Unfortunately, she didn't have any idea of where he went but joked with me that it's an island so he couldn't have gone far.

I start walking back to my mother's room and notice a light shining under her doorway.

"Mom?" I ask under my breath as I start running to the door.

"Mom? Are you awake?" I open the door and the light is on. My mother is out of bed and standing in front of the wardrobe, getting dressed.

"Hi, sweetie!" she says to me like it was any other day. "I'm so glad you made it!" My mother stands straight up and opens her arms to invite me over for a hug.

I run to her and give her the biggest bear hug I can manage without hurting her. A small tear starts coming down my right eye. I let it fall down my check without wiping it off. I am too unwilling to let go of my mother just yet.

"Mom! What are you doing? Get back in bed. You were just in a major accident," I say excitedly.

"I know sweetie, I know!" she says. "That's why we have to get going. Where is your brother, Xavier?" She asks me very point blank as she unhinges herself from my grip and continues to get dressed.

"Ummm…he was here a few hours ago and then had to go do something. He said he'd be back later. I'm really concerned you might have a concussion or something. Let me get the doctor for you," I insist.

"Jena. I'm good. I spoke to Kona earlier. I just needed a few extra hours of good sleep, so I had her put me under for a bit. I'm awake now and ready to go!" My mother says to me as she heads out of the bedroom without waiting for me, but expecting me to follow.

"Good night, Flow! Thanks again!" My mother says to the front desk receptionist.

I'm in complete shock, it's like my mother has been living this double life.

"Listen carefully Jena. They, and by 'they' I mean the Cleansing Coalition, knows about Farallon. I'm not sure how, but someone must have tipped them off about me and my plan to arrive here. Shortly after I left San Sun, I noticed that someone was following me." My mother looks back at me as she pauses.

"Hurry up, Jena, stay with me!" my mother interjects as she motions for me to keep her pace before she continues.

"I tried to lead them in a different direction, away from the island, but they started to attack. I lost them in The Oze just before I crashed. But it's only a matter of time. They know I couldn't have made it too much further. Oh, by the way, Xavier is warning your father and brother."

"You what? When? Why didn't you tell me?" I ask, getting upset with her.

"Jena, listen to me. I don't know if the Coalition suspects just me or your father too, but we can't take any chances. Especially since they are starting to suspect that your disappearance during the exams might not have been a terrible accident after all! The S9 are going to need you here. The battle is coming to us," my mother states affirmatively before turning her fast walk into a subtle jog.

I say nothing. I run following my mother until we arrive at a large colonial house behind the gymnasium. Jessica, appearing rested, is sitting next to Sam on the leather sofa. Across the room I see Sven and the other S9 I met earlier today. Everyone greets my mother like they are soldiers, and she is their general, standing at attention.

"I'm assuming Xavier has updated all of you by now," my mother says, commanding attention as she looks around the room and makes direct eye contact with everyone to see if there is a look of confusion on anyone's face.

"Okay. He should be back soon so we need to be ready. I know Phineas and if there is one thing we can be sure of, he's going to act and act fast. The Coalition knows Farallon is out here, but they don't know exactly where...yet!" My mother pauses for impact.

"We can use The Oze to our advantage, but we don't have much time. This is what we have been preparing for so let's get moving!"

Everyone jumps into action, including Jessica and Sven, but I have absolutely no idea what is going on. How can I be the leader when I have no idea what is happening?

"Wait!" I scream so everyone can hear me. "Wait a second. What is going on? Can someone please explain what the plan is to me? In case you forgot, I just got here."

I look at people's faces and catch some half smiles before seeing everyone's back as they rush out of the house. My mother, Sven, and Ben stay.

"Jena, I'm going to catch you up in a few minutes," my mother says to me in an impatient tone, like she was talking to a young child.

"Ben, you need to get back to the house in San Sun immediately. If anyone comes to the house, do not let them in. Make sure everyone else has left the house, we need to ensure all of the staff are safe. Chef Rose, Dan, everyone!" My mother directs.

"Yes, ma'am. Going now," Ben says back to my mother. He bows his head to me and looks up with a wink before exiting the house like everyone else.

"Sven, take Jena back to the orphanage and get everything ready to leave. Make sure the anti-serums are safely stored and ready for transportation," my mother says to Sven, almost as if I weren't even in the room.

"Absolutely!' Sven responds without even hesitating. "Let's go, Jena!"

"No. Mom, tell me what's going on. What am I supposed to do?" I yell back at her in frustration.

My mother walks over to me, placing one hand on each of my elbows. Calmly looking into my eyes, my mother tells me "Sweetie, I need you to understand that a lot is happening right now, and that I need you to go with Sven. She'll keep you safe, and we'll meet at the orphanage."

"No. You said you'd tell me what is going on," I retort.

"Honey, go with Sven," she repeats calmly before adding a much more encouraging "Now!"

She leans in and gives me a kiss on the forehead. "Trust me. I'll see you in the orphanage and I'll be able to catch you up on everything then."

My mother all but pushes me to Sven, who leads me out of the house. As soon as we reach the curb, we begin running down a new street. As we are running, I notice that there is no one on the streets. Just a few moments earlier, before they arrived to the house, dozens of locals were out on the streets living their lives as they would any other day. Now it's a ghost town.

"Sven, where did everyone go?" I ask, with every bit of breath I have left.

"To the Grotto," she replied

"What's a Grotto?" I replied.

"You know how Xavier can speak to you...you know... in your head?" Sven asks

"How did you know?" surprised, I ask Sven.

"He can do that with everyone, he's telepathic," she added. "The Saviors have prepared all of the locals for emergencies like this. Xavier is the warning system. He speaks into everyone's mind, and everyone can hear him. It's like a silent alarm."

"That is so cool" I say juvenilely. "I thought that only he and I could talk to each other that way."

"Oh, we can't communicate back to him. He can enter our minds but we can't enter his. Could you imagine how crazy that would be if everyone was telepathic. We'd all be talking into each other's heads all the time."

"By the way, when your mom first crashed, Xavier was able to speak to her unconscious mind. It's another one of his mind tricks. Once he confirmed that her crash wasn't an accident, he began sharing the warning," Sven says.

"I never heard anything?" I says.

"You wouldn't, only if Xavier wanted you too," Sven adds.

"Why wouldn't he want me to hear the warning."

"Probably just because you didn't know what it meant yet."

Not satisfied with the answer, I continue following Sven in silence.

"Hey, Jena, I know this is a lot for you to take in, it was for me, too, when my parents first told me about Daniel. So, I get it. But everything will start to make more sense soon. I promise," Sven adds.

I decide not to sulk. After All, I'm supposed to be the one true Savior. The savior amongst the saviors.

"What's a Grotto?" I ask again, exposing my naiveté.

"It's a hidden cave on the far side of the island. It's where we keep most of our water Bullets. You know, Bullets that swim instead of fly!"

"Like submarines?" I ask

Sven nods her head up and down. "We have enough for everyone on the island to escape at the same time in case of an emergency. I think the Coalition coming to attack pretty much meets the definition of an emergency!" Sven continues.

We arrive at the orphanage just before my legs are about to collapse. As soon as we get inside, Sven tells me to follow her as she begins to run down hallway after hallway until she finds what she's been looking for, a hidden door in the wall.

Chapter 34

Sven opens the secret doorway, and I follow her down the winding staircase. At the bottom of the staircase was another door. To the left of the door at the bottom of the staircase I noticed a square hole. Sven walks up to it, rolls up her sleeve and puts her hand into it, all the way to her elbow. A cherry red laser scans her forearm back and forth until we hear the door unlock. I help Sven open the heavy door and we walk inside another small room. As soon as we get in, Sven shuts the door behind us. It locks automatically.

"Hold your breath!" Sven says to me with a smile.

"Why?" I ask with a look of confusion.

As soon as I said it, the ceiling opens and massive fans suck every bit of air out of our little room. It was so powerful that both Sven and I lifted off the ground a couple of inches. And just as fast as the air was sucked out, fresh air was pumped in from the side walls.

"What the hell!" I exclaim. "Next time, maybe prepare me before we walk into a tiny room that suffocates us." I pause for effect before sarcastically adding, "I don't know, maybe?!"

Sven just laughs at me as we continue to stand there.

"It's a cleaning system. It purifies the air to make sure the next room stays completely sealed."

"Like I said, a little more heads up next time!" I look at her sternly before I scan our tiny little box of a room which now looks like four solid walls, a ceiling, and a floor. No more door. No more fans.

"I got us this far. Now it's your turn Jena. Only members of your family, your bloodline, can open the next door.

"What door?" I say as I re-examine the blank room. "I don't see any holes to stick my arm in like you did."

"That's not how you open the door," Sven adds.

"Is this some sort of Jedi mind trick that I'm supposed to know without knowing I know like everything else that has happened since the exams?" I respond curtly.

Unwilling to entertain my childish tantrum, Sven doesn't respond to me.

"Seriously, though, I don't know what I'm supposed to do," I add

"I don't know either Jena. But if only your family can open the door, we need you to figure it out. There's no going back, only forward. Unless you want to be stuck here…forever. I sure as hell don't."

I turn in circles, examining every wall of the room. I scan the ceiling where the fans were a few moments ago for any sign of an opening. Nothing. Both Sven and I begin pushing on every wall, rubbing our hands across the surfaces to feel something unique that could indicate a door or at the very least, access to a door. Still nothing. We are entombed inside a cube. Every surface feels like perfectly-polished stone, cold and smooth.

"There might be one thing," I say, hesitating.

"Uh-huh," Sven responds, clearly waiting for me to pull up my big girl panties and figure it out.

"When Jessica, Sam, and I were trying to find you, I had something that helped us open a tunnel door that we couldn't physically open on our own."

"OK, why don't you try that?" Sven asks encouragingly.

I look her in the eyes for a few seconds, confirming for myself that I can trust her. I reach inside my suit and pull out the amber pendant that Za gave me. I take it off from around my neck and hold it in my hand. Sven and I both look at my hand holding the pendant, each of us making sure we don't accidentally make awkward eye contact given the mounting tension in the tiny room.

I hold the pendant high above my head like I had done with the Destiny Sword. The amber begins to warm and emit a blue globe of light extending beyond my hand. The light continues to grow until it illuminates the entire room, tracing every inch of every wall that has entomb us. Both Sven and I quickly look around the room to find any clue now that the walls are illuminated.

"There!" I exclaim, as I point behind Sven. She turns to look with me.

"Could that be it?" I ask her, looking at a subtle twinkle, almost like a shimmer, of the blue glow reflecting onto itself a few feet away from Sven in midair.

"Maybe. Try it!"

I walk over to the wall and as I get closer, the amber pulls my hand from overhead to straight in front of me, towards the shimmer. As my hand reaches further, the glow of the amber gets brighter and brighter to a point both Sven and I are forced to squint our eyes, barely keeping them open. I continue walking towards the wall with my hand extended in front of me. I should have reached the wall by now so I keep walking forward, using my free hand to grab one of Sven's.

"I can't see anything! Can you?" I excitedly yell to Sven, now walking forward slowly with my eyes completely closed and my hand guiding our way. Even with my eyes closed I can still see the brightness of the Amber's glow through my eyelids.

"I knew you could do it, Jena!" a deep yet calming voice, a familiar voice, says to me.

I open my eyes and see my father standing less than five feet from me. I'm so surprised to see him that it doesn't register at first. I shake my head a little.

"Dad!?" I say with a shocked and confused expression on my face as I rub my eyes until they can focus again. Once reopened, I notice Xavier approaching. With a huge smile across his face, he stands next to my father, *our* father. This is the first time I've seen them side by side, and I can't stop noticing how similar they look. The way their eyes smile is exactly the same. They even have the same nose. It must be true. Xavier is definitely my father's son. My brother!

"What? When did you guys get here?" I ask as I walk over to each of them to grab them both into a group hug.

They both let out the same low toned laugh as they squeeze me back.

"Just a few minutes ago," my dad says to me as he pulls out of the hug. "But I'm sorry to say we have to hurry. Has your mother filled you in on everything?" he asks.

"No. She kept telling me she would, but you know Mom…" I throw my hands up in frustration and turn to walk around the room and explore the weapons right in front of me.

"Just like this place. Some orphanage. It looks more like a military hideout. Hey, where is Alex?" I ask Xavier. "Mom said you were getting both Dad and Alex."

Xavier looks at me and shakes his head sideways before my dad answers for him.

"That's because it is our hideout, code name the orphanage, and we couldn't find Alex. But…but…" he puts his hands up slightly to make sure I don't interrupt him as he notices the redness rapidly raising in my cheeks. "But we believe he's OK."

"How can you know that if you couldn't find him?" I ask angrily.

"I know," says Xavier.

I catch him exchanging a look with our dad before he continues. I wonder if he is telepathically talking to my father at this very moment.

"Well, what then?" I ask, interrupting an obvious conversation that no one else can hear except my dad and brother. Sven reaches her hand up and places it on my shoulder, signaling for me to calm down. I give her a quick glance of dismissal before returning my attention to Xavier and my father.

Both my father and Xavier let out the same laugh, again. My dad looks at the floor as Xavier turns to me.

"I went to pick him up at his dorm but his roommate, Elliott something I think was his name, said he was at some power Management class. So, I went to his class, and he wasn't there. His professor told me that he hadn't shown up for class today," Xavier says with a hint of a giggle behind his voice, not fear as I was expecting.

"OK. So why didn't you just talk to him in your head? You know, telepathically or whatever," I add, trying to hurry Xavier up to get to the point.

"Well, you see, the Coalition has implemented these telepathic traps so I wasn't trying to track down your brother for fear of them finding out. It's one thing if I know exactly where he is, but if I have to search for him my mind is left open and vulnerable," Xavier added.

"Once Xavier told me Alexander had skipped PM, again, I knew immediately where he was," my father added with a smile. "He's been skipping class to meet up with Raquel Norton. Apparently, it's the only time of the day they can find time to meet. Young love!" Dad looks at Xavier and winks at him the same way he does with Alexander. It is sweet to see the same father-son connection. But annoying in the moment.

"Are you serious? That's it?" I ask them both.

"Yes, absolutely serious," Xavier added. "You see, once Dad told me he was with this Raquel girl, I quickly popped into Alex's head to confirm and let's just say, I never want to do that again! That's five seconds that will leave a lifelong impression."

We all laugh with thoughts of what Xavier encountered when entering Alexander's mind.

"Why didn't you go get him? Isn't he in danger like the rest of us?" I finally ask interrupting everyone's laughter.

"Remember Jena, he doesn't know about Xavier yet. He doesn't even know about the Saviors, and he definitely doesn't know about the Cleansing Coalition or your mission. The safest place for him right now is at Freelinn, with Raquel watching out for him. He doesn't know anything so there is nothing he could tell the Coalition about us," my dad adds.

"With Raquel watching out for him? What, is she some Supergirl now? How can she protect someone if she doesn't know he needs protection?" I ask, before I answer my own question. "Aw, because Raquel knows. How?"

My father simply nods his head in response. "The Coalition doesn't suspect him, or you for that matter. They were suspicious about your disappearance during the exams for a while but, apparently, they have completed their investigation and have concluded you were in fact lost to The Numinous and that there was no foul play. We owe a huge thank you to Michelle for that one. She risked her life to make sure Phineas and the others didn't figure out the truth of what happened in The Numinous."

"Who is Michelle?" I ask, having not heard that name attached to anyone my father has ever spoken of before now.

"Michelle Lohrenz. She was your proctor for much of the exams. She is Phineas Riley's assistant, but she's loyal to our movement. She's our mole inside the Coalition so I'm sure you can appreciate the risks she is taking to keep all of us, but especially you, safe!" my dad answers.

"OK. I didn't know that. But what about you and Mom? They know about you and Mom, don't they? So, doesn't that alone put Alex at risk? I mean, they could use him to get to either of you even if they think I'm dead., I ask.

"I don't think that will happen, Jena," my dad says assuredly. "Alexander is too high profile, as are your mother and I, and I don't think Phineas or any members of the Coalition are ready to be exposed…just yet. Right now, it's a war that most Percenters don't even know is happening," he adds.

"But what if he is? What if they go after Alex? What if?" I pause for a second letting images of Alex being tortured run through my head. "We are all here, and he's alone." I start to unravel with my emotions and tears start to form in my eyes. It must be a twin thing.

"We will protect him, Jena," Sven adds. "Raquel isn't the only one at Freelinn that has their eye on Alexander's safety."

I don't know if it was Sven's words or simply exhaustion, but I decided everyone else knows more than I do so I give up the argument.

"So, what is this place anyway?" I decide to change the subject and just as I do, Mother, the S9 and the island people join us from another side of the room. Apparently, there is more than one way in and out of this Grotto.

My mother grabs my father's hand as she walks up behind him, using her free hand to embrace his forearm as she leans in for a soft yet sensual kiss on the cheek. You can see happiness and comfort in my father's eyes as she does this. Without saying a word to my dad, she has him captivated with just a simple smile and touch of the arm.

"Hi, honey!" she says to Xavier, who smiles back at her.

"Alex is fine," Xavier says, as if he heard her question before she asks it.

Without saying anything else, you can see a sense of understanding on her face as she looks at Xavier. He probably just telepathically told her the same story he told us.

My mom smiles gently before making eye contact with me and motioning to everyone else in the room to come closer.

"OK, I need everyone to listen up." Mother starts talking as we all gather closer together, "The Cleansing Coalition officially knows that I am a Savior and, at the very least, they suspect Abraham as well. We can expect they have already begun the workings of a public smear campaign about me and probably about the entire de Fenace' family. The Cleansing Coalition is already silently hunting everyone they think is associated with the Saviors.

They will be making false claims, creating fake news, and spreading propaganda in an attempt to divide us and make us look like dangerous to the other Percenter's in the Sky Cities." Mother takes a silent but long breath.

"Believe me when I tell you, Phineas' number one strategy is to first divide us. If he succeeds at this, his second goal will be to conquer us. The Coalition will build an army of believers amongst the Percenters that share their belief in a purist sky society. They will leave no stone unturned until they find each and every one of us. They will stop at nothing, no lives matter to them, except their own. They will make sure we never have the chance to share the truth about the receding Oze or the mistreatment of the Barrens. They will never stop believing they are better than every Middler and human that walks the surface of this planet." My mother pauses for effect and to drive the point home that the Cleansing Coalition will never stop unless we stop them.

"I have asked the other Saviors to stay hidden, for now. We can't risk anyone else being detected. Too many lives are at stake. So, that being said. We are on our own for this fight. It's time people!" My mother finishes before turning her back to the group and looking at some paperwork with my father, assumingly done speaking.

We all look at each other. A little scared, a little confused. My heart beat heavy two times and on the third beat my mother briefly looks over her should at the audience and lands her eyes on mine. We join each other in a simple blink of the eye that was no more than a millisecond, yet felt like we had just finished a long conversation about the state of the world.

"You know," I say just loud enough that everyone can hear me before I clear my throat, "we know now, more than we did before The Oze, that we are all connected. We can all trace our ancestors back to the Great Ozone Event...when the few who lived started families of their own. We are all descendants of those survivors. We all share that same blood running through our veins. Generation after generation. And now we know that all of us, every single one of you, whether Percenter, Indie, Barren, or anyone else out there, we know that that blood makes you family. And in our world, family means everything. Love trumps fear every day and, today, we are going to show them how much that means to us!" Everyone cheers and yells in excitement for the fight to come! "Tonight, we fight for the first time, as a truly united family!"

My mother gestures a congratulatory clap in my direction with a smile across her face that would tell anyone how proud she was of me at that moment.

"Alright! Let's get moving everyone. You all know what to do," Xavier directs the room as everyone runs off in a different direction, assumingly with purpose.

I, on the other hand, appear to be the only one in the room standing still, with no idea of what I am supposed to do next. But at least I gave a kick ass speech.

Chapter 35

Truly lost, I walk up to my new big brother, Xavier, and with the same sad puppy face that I use on Alexander, I ask him:

"Xavier, can you tell me what to do? I don't seem to have," I paused, looking around at everyone doing something that looks important, "have anything to do to help." I find the strength in my voice and continue, "I mean, I want to help. What can I do to help?" I say more assertively.

Xavier simply smiles at me and immediately understood that I was feeling out of place and alone. He grabs my hand and without saying a word, walked me over to a room filled with more weapons than I could ever imagined.

"Time for a quick brother sister pre-fight pep talk. I'm assuming you have never used any of these?"

I simply shake my head from side to side making sure to close my gaping mouth before I do.

"Have you ever even seen any of these?" Xavier asks with some humor in his voice, as he raises his hands and bows his head graciously at the same time, already knowing my answer was going to be another 'No.'

"Well! What did you expect? That our afternoon play dates involved weapons training in San Sun? Please. Far from it. Did you know that we are highly discouraged from engaging in any physical activities beyond jogging and swimming? That it is considered grotesque to be too strong? Why would we need to be strong? We have abilities beyond weapons?" I catch myself defensively rambling and not even knowing why.

"OK, I understand, Jena. Well, from what I've learned about you, I'm confident you are going to master these in no time!" Xavier calmly reaffirms my need to feel comfortable. I'm struck by how gentle and controlled he is in the way he speaks to me, so much like our Father. I drop my shoulders after realizing they have been in a tight locked position ever since I put my hands on my hips, making my defiant and ridiculous stand.

"Most of the Coalition will have an anti-gun. Remember that serum they gave everyone in the exams? The one that was so important you didn't get?" he asks me.

I simply say, "Yes."

"Well, for the rest of the Percenters and the Barrens who received that injection, if shot by the anti-gun, the bullet has some sort of chemical reaction with the antigens in the serum and you completely go paralyzed. Head down!" Xavier represents with his left hand demonstrating the top of his head to the bottom of his feet.

"The worst part is that your mind is completely normal, but because of the paralysis, you can't even blink your eyes. You are trapped in a lifeless body. That way they keep you alive and bring you back for testing, like a rat used in a laboratory. But you don't have to worry about that, thank goodness because what they do back in the lab, well, let's just say it's not very nice!" He smiles and keeps walking, brushing his fingertips along every weapon he passes.

"But once they realize those bullets have no impact on you, they'll probably bring out the Extinguishers." He pulls a massive gun from the wall and turns it on with the fingerprint of his right thumb, just above his trigger finger. "You see, if the laser hits you anywhere on your skin your lungs will stop. You'll slowly start choking to death, your lungs unable to breathe in the right amount of air. Instead, filling with poisonous gases that uncontrollably spread throughout your bloodstream. You'll be kept alive by your body's innate ability to uncontrollably gulp air, but just enough air to keep you alive until you can barely gulp another breath. If they catch you like this, they'll keep you in this tortured state while they…"

"Got it. thanks. Mental note, don't get shot by anything or I'll probably end up tortured as a human lab rat!"

"I like hearing you call yourself human, Sis, it suits you. Now, pick whatever you want. Just remember, in order to kill some evil fucking Percenters, point the end and pull the trigger! Preferably at their face!" And just like that, I saw the calmness in Xavier's eyes switch to determination.

All I can think to do is smile back and begin picking up different weapons, seeing which one feels the best to me. I get distracted when I hear Xavier yell out to some guys approaching us with a youthful exuberance.

"Hey! It's about time P.P.! I'd like for you to finally meet my one and only sister, the Jenavieve! Jenavieve, my good pal Peter Pan."

"Sister? Good! I was hoping you weren't the competition because if you were, I'd lose!" Peter says as he walks by me to give Xavier a hug.

"Competition? I don't... aw, gotcha and Thank You!" I reply as I realize he's attracted to Xavier and complimented me at the same time. I'm pretty sure the flattery is written all over my face. Collecting myself, I continue, "OK, so... your name, is it really Peter Pan, is that what P.P. stands for?" I muster with some slight flirtation back to this guy who I just met but automatically want to be friends with now.

"Yes and no. You see, I'm the guy who can fly, and I'm never going to get older, so the nickname Peter Pan stuck," Peter says, he pats Xavier on the back and continues, "your lovely brother here got lazy and thought it was funnier to shorten my nickname to a new nickname..."

Xavier jumps in "P.P.! You know, it works!"

"I know, funny, right? So, it stuck, unfortunately." Peter winks at Jena while smiling and putting his arm around Xavier.

"My real name is Peter Parker. No I'm just kidding with you. It's Peter Perris." He reaches out his hand in a gesture to formally introduce himself. His charm is contagious, so I have no choice but to reciprocate the behavior.

"He's one of the S9 and my best friend!" Xavier says proudly as he hits Peter on the shoulder with a soft fist.

"Yup, best friends," Peter states. "But you, Ms. Jena, must think of me like... like a brother to!" Peter says, smiling at both Jena and Xavier. "After all, we are all family, am I right?" he asks rhetorically.

"OK, I'm starting to pick up what you are putting down mister Peter, and I'm liking it!" I say back to him. "And Xavier, I think you sir are my competition for a best friend!"

We all laugh long enough to be interrupted by Sven. "Let's go, they are here!"

Chapter 36

Reaching out their hands at the same time to touch my shoulder, in unison as if it were practiced for hours, both Xavier and Peter say, "Stay close to me!"

We all exchange a quick glance before taking a deep breath and nodding in recognition that the fight is here. We are as ready as we are ever going to be because there is no more time. We have to make our stand.

"The Grotto! Did everyone get out?" Xavier asks Peter.

"Almost, I just came back from there and only a few people were left. They should be gone by now, I hope."

I finally choose my weapon. I reach beneath my shirt collar and pull out the amber pendant. I yanked the chain and hold the pendant in my hand. I stare at it for a moment before telling Xavier "This is all I need."

"I was hoping so." Xavier smiles at me as if he couldn't be prouder. He is so much like our father that it catches me off guard. Alexander is going to have his mind blown when he meets Xavier.

We are joined by Corey, Daniel, and Sven, the last few in the orphanage with us.

"What's going on out there, Xavier?" Sven abruptly asks.

Looking at all of us, with almost a blank face, Xavier exclaims "Mom is running to the Grotto. It looks like she's being chased by someone or something, I can't quite tell. But she's scared, really scared.

"We have to help her! Let's go. Where is she?" I ask Xavier who clearly ignores me.

"Kona and Flow escaped with everyone else in the Grotto. They are all safe and on their way as planned." His tone changes to urgency. "Sam and Jessica. They need us. Let's go! Now!"

"What about Mom? We have to help Mom Xavier!" I yell trying to get his attention.

"She'll be fine. She's with Dad," Xavier adds just as the orphanage is hit with something that shakes the entire structure. "Don't worry, they will never be able to get in here. Only our bloodline can open the door."

I look at Sven for confirmation. She blinks her eyes and motions her head up and down to put my worries at ease.

"If this place is so safe, why isn't everyone else here with us?" I ask, not expecting to get an answer. Unlike me, they have all been planning for this attack to happen for years.

"This way!" Corey directs us. "Sam's getting our escape Bullet ready."

"And it looks like they could use some help. The Grotto is under attack." Xavier adds.

We all follow Corey out of the orphanage. I'm in the middle of the group as we sneak outside along the sides of building still standing. I can't help but notice the crushing sounds of houses collapsing and the smell of smoke from buildings burning. This beautiful hidden village, on a pristine island in the middle of the Pacific, buried behind miles of The Oze, is being destroyed by Percenters. It's only been minutes since the attack began and already most of the landscape has changed. There is hardly anything left.

"Damn!" Corey says. "They didn't waste any time! Just like your mom thought!"

"How could they destroy so much so quickly?" I ask naively.

"Hey, try to stay focused. I know this is all new to you, I get that, but let's survive this first and then I'll fill you in on everything once we are able to relax," Sven says to me softly with a smile.

I nod in cooperation. I feel myself trusting Sven more and more.

We continue to run through smoke so thick that I can't see anyone else. Running from one hidden crevasse to the next, we get closer and closer to the sounds of explosions and metal hitting metal.

I'm suddenly reminded that my mom and dad are somewhere amongst all this destruction. I can't help but wonder how they are going to survive. I know they are powerful, but I've never known them as warriors.

"This way," Daniel adds, as he takes the lead from Corey.

"It's this way Daniel!" Corey corrects him. "This is faster." For a split-second, Corey disappears, and then reappears. "Nope, you are right! Follow Daniel!" We all run down a cobblestone street before I start to notice one of the black hooded ghouls from the exam Grand Reception haunting me when the smoke clears.

"Stop!" I yell before continuing in a whisper. "He's here. Hunter's here. Look!" I point into the fresh cloud of smoke where the ghoul was standing just seconds earlier. "Wait for the smoke to clear. Just wait."

"I don't see anything Jena. We don't have time to wait. They need our help," Xavier says to everyone.

"Let's keep going!" Corey adds.

I don't move, confident in what I saw.

"There, I see something!" Sven points in the same direction as I last saw it.

"You saw it?! Thank God. I was beginning to think I was going crazy!" I say hurriedly. For the first time someone else saw the ghouls that have been haunting me since the exams.

"Shhh!" Xavier tells us.

Everyone stops moving and crouches down to minimize their presence.

"What exactly are we looking for Jena?" Xavier says to me, no longer doubting that I saw something. I was impressed by the calmness in his tone. You could tell that he was already strategizing how to protect us all from whatever lies ahead.

"I honestly don't know what the ghouls are, besides these weird floating figures in black cloaks. Ghoul is the best name I could come up with. Pretty much the only thing you can see are their red-beady eyes." I pause, catching my breath. "But all I know for sure is that every time I see them, Hunter isn't too far behind."

Without asking any further questions, Xavier jumped into command. "Everyone surround Jena. Now!"

Within what seemed like a half of second, everyone had their backs to me and their

weapons out in front of them, surveying 360 degrees.

"Is this really necessary Xavier?" I say in protest. "I've handled myself against Hunter in the past."

"It's not Hunter I'm worried about" Xavier says just as a fireball the size of a watermelon flew through the air, landing no more than five feet from us and exploding. We huddle together just in time to minimize the impact.

"Then tell me, Xavier de Fenace', if I don't scare you, what does!" Hunter commands as he stands in the smoke clearing before letting out a villainous laugh as he has done in the past. "Maybe it's my friends you are so afraid of. Could it be? I mean, they sure seem to scare your little… sister!"

Hunter's eyes glow a deep red as every shadow near him becomes alive and turns into a ghoul. Within seconds he has an army of beady-red eyed ghouls standing next to him.

"You wish it was that easy!" Xavier responded back to Hunter.

Hunter continues with his horrid laugh. "Oh, it is!"

We are surrounded by any army of hundreds. There is no way we can escape.

"Oh, I understand, Hunter," I say, emphasizing his name as a child would mock another kid on the schoolyard. "You are the scared one. You are too afraid to face us without all these, shadows. Didn't your mommy ever teach you not to be afraid of shadows, Hunter?" I mockingly smile back at him, masking my fear with anger.

"Ready? On my count," Xavier orders us. "One…two…" But before he could get to three, Hunter interrupts him.

"Foolish little Jena. Once again, you clearly have no idea what is going on here." He motions to one of his ghouls on his side to get him something. "Why don't you go back to the Ground where you belong and let us…*real* Percenters handle all the important stuff."

Just as he finished his sentence, my dad is thrown at Hunters feet by his ghoul. Dad can barely muster enough strength to lift his head. He lifts his right hand up, blocking Hunter directly from his view.

"Please! Stop!" My father exclaims, begging Hunter!

"Dad!" I yelled as I try to break from the circle of protection still surrounding me. "Xavier! He has Dad! We have to do something, now!" I scream at him.

Hunter lifts his hand, holding open his palm. "I warned you Jena!" Hunter says with pleasure in his voice. "I warned you months ago and yet here we are!" Hunter's giggle turns into a full chuckle. His exposed palm starts to rotate. His palm starts to turn red when suddenly a fireball the size of a ping pong ball takes shape. The fireball looks liquid, like lava, constantly rotating and dripping pieces of fire that evaporate on Hunter's palm. He moves his hand slowly over Dad as the fireball begins to grow.

"No! Dad!" I scream again. "Do something!" I yell to anyone listening.

Xavier looks over at Corey, and they make eye contact. Corey nods in agreement. Whatever it is that Xavier is planning, I'm just happy he's planning something.

"OK. Wait?" Xavier pleads with Hunter. "Wait, we give up!" He looks around at our group and motions to drop our weapons.

"Follow my lead," he says to all of us telepathically.

"Look, we are putting our weapons down. You win. Just don't hurt him!" As we all slowly begin to lower our weapons to the ground, Hunter pauses and holds the fireball above our father. "Too late, de Fenaces! Too little, too late. Now you get to watch your father burn to death!"

Before we completely set our weapons down, Corey quickly disappears into a gust of smoke. Before Hunter and his ghouls realize what has happened, Corey grabbed our dad and disappeared.

"Now!" Xavier yelled as he lifted his weapon and began firing at Hunter. We join him and begin shooting in every direction.

Hunter releases his ball of fire on us, followed by dozens more as he dodges one shot after another from our weapons. The ghouls begin flying all around us, unaffected by our weapons.

"Keep shooting!" Xavier telepathically screams. "Jena, Dad's OK, but Mom needs our help. The escape convoy is under attack. Hunter has been distracting us. He's a decoy!"

Without thinking, I close my eyes and call Za. I hold my pendant into the sky and it begins to glow blue without the same struggle as before. I think about brightness, about a blue sky and nature blooming around me.

"Everyone, get behind me, now!" I yell.

Luckily everyone was close enough to quickly huddle below my waist. Everyone's arms wrapped around one another with me standing tall above them with my hand stretched into the air as if I've already become the victor.

The blue glow turns into an explosion emanating from my pendent in a blue light so bright it is almost white. It was so bright that light was everywhere, destroying every shadowy ghoul. I open my eyes to see the smoke cleared, fires down to smolder, the ghouls gone, and Hunter struggling to stand back up.

"Told you!" Sven says to Daniel! "I told you!"

"Told him what?" I say defensively.

"Only that you are one powerful bitch." She steps sideways and snaps her fingers before continuing, "Not to be messed with!" Sven added.

I nod my head to the side as I produce a growing smile. We all look at each other with the same hint of a grin before chasing toward Hunter, who appears to be defenseless without all his ghouls to protect him. We chase him down the streets toward the Grotto, where we are supposed to meet Sam and Jessica on our way to helping my mom. Hunter vanishes without a trace.

Chapter 37

Hunter is out of sight, but I know he can't be far, it's a half-destroyed island after all. We pick up our pace as Xavier loses his mental connection with Mom.

"What happened!?" I exclaim nervously to Xavier.

"I-I can't find her. I don't know why. It's weird. But this happens every once in a while, and you never know, the Coalition may have…" Xavier says before I interrupt him.

"May have what? What? The Coalition may have done what!" I say as my run turns into a sprint, leaving Peter, Sven, and her brother, Daniel, behind, even though they are running too. Only Xavier is able to match me step by step.

"I don't know, Jena," Xavier says in a calm monotone, as if he wasn't sprinting but casually walking. "I was thinking they may have figured out a way to block my connection with Mom. I don't know," he concluded.

"Stop!" I say after what feels like five minutes of complete silence, but in actuality was less than thirty seconds of awkward silence. Xavier stops with me and the others catch up to us, bent over and winded, trying to catch their breath.

"Shh!" I say softly as I start to inch closer to what looks like the outline of people in the distance. It could be Hunter so I motion for everyone to stay behind, yet no one listens to me. As we get closer, I keep noticing that the people aren't moving. They look like they are statues.

Peter picks up a small rock and throws it at the group of people about fifteen feet from us. He misses. But no one moves, ignoring the rock that was just

242

thrown at them.

"I need something bigger!" Peter says as he picks up a slightly larger rock as he winked at me.

He was right. He struck one of the men in the back of the head, dead center. We all quickly hide behind the wall before peeking out to see what's going on. When we look, nothing has changed except for the guy who was hit in the head was no longer standing. He was flat down on the ground, laying in the same position he was standing, but with a sizeable rock stuck in the back of his head.

"They're mannequins! You know, like fake people for displaying clothes and stuff," Daniel says. "Like the one Mom, I mean Molly, has in her boutique," he adds. We come out of hiding and cautiously walk towards the mannequins. "If these are mannequins, how do you explain the blood?" Xavier points down at the blood oozing from beneath the rock attached to the man's head. "And why would boutique mannequins be dressed like soldiers?" he asks, rolling the guy over to his back.

"I know him. I mean, I've seen him before," I say but unable to place him.

"Who are they?" I ask, half expecting an answer but giving enough air space for the chance of a response. Nothing.

We look around at all the frozen people and notice they are in full combat gear with a variety of weapons in their hands and strapped across their backs. They look like they are in an attack formation and the expressions on their faces support it.

"Whoever they are, they aren't with us so that makes them part of the Coalition. They look kinda dead, or at least dying, to me," Peter contributes. "Should we, you know, make sure they, um, die?" he says, wishing he hadn't.

"What? You want to strike them all in the head with stones? Be my guest," I say as I roll my eyes.

"I think he was one of the moderators in the exam" Sven adds with a look of confusion on her face as she stared at the guy on the ground. "No, I'm positive. That guy's name was Russ. Remember Jena, Day 3?"

"I knew it! I knew he looked familiar. That fucking asshole. If he did anything to Mom..." I stop myself when I recognize another moderator's face from the exams. I walk up to within inches of his face. "This is Elliot! He was the head moderator, remember Sven? What the hell! Were all the moderators part of the Coalition?" I added before hitting Elliot in the face with the butt end of my weapon, surprising everyone.

I started jogging in the same direction as before. "Come one," I yell back to everyone. "Hunter is still out there, and so is Mom and Dad!"

I keep running and after another dozen steps I quickly look back over my right shoulder and see everyone closely behind.

"Um, I just realized I have no idea where I'm leading us." I half-smile out of the corner of my mouth. "Anyone want to take the lead?"

"This way, doll," Peter says as he runs past me down a crack in the side of the mountain, hidden by vines that I would have ran past in another few steps had he not opened it first.

The crack turns into a tunnel.

"The Grotto is just through here!" Peter says, proud of himself for finding the secret passage and leading the way.

Just after entering the opening, Peter motions for us to stop and be quiet by squatting down and raising his right fist. I figured this out after I watched Xavier, Sven and Daniel do just that within moments of Peter's fist going into the air.

He turns to face us, and using his palm, tells us to back up. Peter doesn't say a word until we are halfway back to where we entered the tunnel. "They, um, are dead. They are all dead," Peter says in disbelief.

Chapter 38

"Who's dead?" Xavier asks Peter.

"They all are. Everyone... is," Peter musters with barely any air in his lungs and the color gone from his face.

"What? That's not possible Peter." Xavier pushes him aside as he slowly walks forward, examining everything in his path to make sure he moves undetected. "Stay here," he orders us as he goes back to where Peter first stopped us. He disappears out of sight as we wait for him in silence.

"Jena, listen to me," Xavier says in my head. "You have to leave. You and Peter have to go."

"Go? No way. What are you talking about?" I say back to him. "Where's Mom? What's going on? I'm coming to you!" I start moving forward before stopping in my tracks when I hear Xavier.

"No! Do not! They are still here and we are outnumbered ten to one. You have to get out of here."

"What is he saying?" Daniel asks, knowing full well that Xavier is talking to me. "What does he see?"

"He said not to follow him, and that the Coalition is still here, and they severely outnumber us."

I start walking towards Xavier, disobeying his orders. "We aren't leaving you," I say back to Xavier.

Just then, a strong hand grabs my shoulder, halting my next step. It's Sven. "Jena, you can't," she says compassionately. She turns to her brother, still keeping her tight grip on my shoulder, and in the same compassionate tone says, "Daniel, it's time."

Peter and Daniel exchange a look with Sven, and then with me. I can see the sadness in their eyes as Peter walks up to me and trades places with Sven. "It's OK, Jena," Sven says as she and Daniel walk past me in the direction of Xavier. "Peter is going to get you out of here to safety, trust me."

I stand motionless, confused. "What's happening? Where are they going? Peter? Let go of me," I demand. Unlike Sven, Peter is using every bit of strength to hold me back as Sven and Daniel disappear after Xavier.

"Go with Peter," Xavier whispers inside my head. "We'll meet you soon, I promise."

Before I know it, Peter and I are back outside the hidden tunnel to the Grotto.

"Hold on!" Peter tells me as he positions himself for me to climb on to his back. I look back at the vine covered entrance one last time; hoping Xavier, Sven and Daniel will emerge with my mom and everyone else. But they don't. Peter jumps into the air and we launch from the ground. Within seconds we are nearing the top of the mountain that houses the Grotto. The wind is blowing hard on my eyes so I close them. I let my mind drift, afraid to look back at all the devastation on the island, wondering what could have gone wrong.

"Peter," I say softly but just loud enough for him to hear me over the wind. "What did you see?"

He doesn't respond.

Chapter 39

The air is clean and fresh, but cold as ice. We fly in silence. I have no idea where we are going or why we left everyone else on the island. I tried to telepathically reach Xavier but he's not responding. My mind starts to spiral thinking about my last conversation with Mom. How I yelled at her and now I don't even know if she's alive or dead. I don't know if any of them are alive. The sadness overwhelms me, and I lose consciousness, and my grip on Peter. I slide off his back and begin tumbling to the ground. "Jena!" Peter exclaims as he feels me slide off his back. It only takes him a few seconds to catch me in midair but he can't fly easily with me in his arms. "Jena, wake up!" he yells. "Jena! I need you to wake up!" We slowly fall through the sky as Peter fights to keep us in the air.

I wake from my momentary coma in panic as I realize we are falling through the sky.

"Get on my back, hurry!" Peter yells with a bit of panic in his voice.

He lifts me over his shoulder as I climb to his back and wrap my arms around his neck with a death grip.

"Not so tight!" Peter squeezes out as he begins to chuckle.

"Oh, sorry!" I respond, not realizing I was basically strangling him.

"We are almost there," he added.

"Where is there?" I ask sarcastically, to which he doesn't respond.

"Here, put this on." He pulls a breathing mask from his vest and hands it to me. I grab it and fasten it around my head. As soon as secure it, it expands to cover me like a suit. I notice Peter does the same.

Suddenly, he dives from the clean air above and into The Oze below us. I have no idea where we are, but it's definitely far from the island. We are flying faster now with the help of gravity.

"There, do you see it?" Peter exclaims with excitement. He points toward a dark spot floating within The Oze in the near distance.

"I see a dark cloud, that's it!" I respond.

"Then you see it!" he retorts.

We continue to accelerate as he adjusts our direction toward the dark cloud. As we get closer the darkness starts to take form, it begins to look like a Bullet. But not just any car, my family's red Bullet.

"Is that our Bullet?" I ask in disbelief.

"I sure hope so because I'm getting tired!" Peter laughs.

I notice that no matter what the situation is, Peter always seems to find a way to be happy. No wonder Xavier likes him so much.

Within seconds, we land on the top of the hovering Bullet. Peter bends his knees slightly so my feet can reach the roof. I stand, releasing my grip from Peter's neck.

"I don't understand. How is this possible?" I ask Peter and, again, I don't receive a response.

The sunroof opens, and Jessica sticks her head out, followed by Sam. "It's about time you two," Jessica says.

"Jessica? Sam? How did you? I mean, how is this happening right now?" I ask bewildered.

"Hurry up! We can't be in The Oze for much longer. Remember what happened last time?" Sam adds with an all too familiar look of intensity.

Peter helps me over to the sunroof, and I climb in first. As soon as we get inside, we take our breathing masks off and the suits retract. I look around and see Vanessa and Shree, two of the S9 I haven't had a chance to get to talk too much. They look like they barely escaped Hell with bloodied faces, clothes torn and sadness emanating from their weakened bodies.

Erinn, another S9, fades in and out of sight. I can see glimpses of her as she paces back and forth, mumbling to herself as she cradles her own torso. I try to make eye contact with her, but she quickly avoids all glances.

And then I see Sven with Daniel's head laying in her lap, his body severely

248

burnt and lifeless. She looks up at me with her red tearful eyes before returning her focus to Daniel. She strokes his hair gently.

"Sven!" I say happy she's alive but saddened by what I see. "What happened?" I ask as I walk over to sit next to her. Peter sits next to me, also wanting to hear what happened. Sam follows sitting next to him.

Sven tries to speak, but no words come out, only deep breaths holding back what can only be devastating anguish. Jessica sits down across from Sven, and starts speaking for Sven.

"We were in the Grotto." She pauses, searching for the right words. "We thought Kona and Flow had escaped with all the others. That was the plan." Her eyes shift and roll to the side, avoiding Sven and Daniel. She blinks several times before reaching out a hand to rest on Daniel's chest. "We planned for everything!" she exclaims.

Jessica begins biting her lips, her eyes rapidly fill with tears, and she can't figure out how to continue speaking. She looks at Sven, gently shaking her head from side to side before placing both of her hands in front of her face and sobbing uncontrollably. I had no idea Jessica was capable of showing such compassion. So much emotion for something, or someone, other than herself.

The car is still, the only sound you can hear is Jessica crying. Sam switches seats to comfort Jessica. She turns to him and continues to cry into his chest as their arms wrapped around each other.

"We couldn't stop them. I told him to swim from the Grotto, but he wouldn't leave me." Sven's swollen eyes continue to produce silent tears as she wiped her runny nose with her free hand. I watch as one tear drips from her cheek and lands on the ashy forehead of her brother. "He jumped in front of one of Hunter's fireballs. He saved me." Sven leans down to gently kiss Daniel's forehead where her tear had just fallen. She starts rocking back and forth as she places her face next to Daniel's. "He saved me," she repeated in a barely audible whisper.

"I'm so sorry, Sven," I say as I put both arms around her shoulders, holding her tightly as I rest my head in between her shoulder and neck. "I'm so sorry."

I realize as I hold Sven, who's holding her dead brother, that it could have been me if they didn't make me leave with Peter. Daniel sacrificed his life not only for Sven, but for me as well. I close my eyes and try hard not to cry. I desperately want to be strong for Sven. I fail.

"There's more," Sam says.

I opened my eyes and slowly lift my head to look at Sam, my arms refusing to let go of Sven.

Without waiting for him to tell me, I calmly ask with a flat affect, "Where's Xavier? Where's my mom? Where are they, Sam?" I've prepared myself for the worse. My face already showing the exhaustion of losing a loved one. "Are they dead? Just tell me, Sam. Are they dead?" I say more aggressively as Peter tries to reassure me but not clear on what the answer might be.

Just then, Xavier enters from the driver's cabin. He looks at me with soft eyes and sadness on his face. My heart skips a beat. I look up to the roof of the Bolt before I close my eyes and let out a deep sigh of relief. I release Sven from my grip and run to Xavier.

"Hi, Sis," he says before I wrap my arms around his body in a giant bear hug. He returns the hug, holding me tightly against his body. After a few moments of silence, he grabs my arms and pulls me away from him, looking me straight into my eyes.

"There's something I have to tell you. But I need you to sit down first." He motions for me to sit next to Sven who is still pressing her check next to Daniel's.

"Hunter and his Shadows..." He pauses, trying to remember the words he's been rehearsing. "they...they were just a distraction. Phineas and his Coalition killed everyone in the Grotto before we got to them." He exchanges looks with Peter and Sam before continuing. "I couldn't reach Mom because he killed her."

I sit motionless. No change in my expression. I look back at Xavier as if I were looking right through him. As if I didn't hear what he just said.

"Phineas tortured Mom. It was..." He paused, closing his eyes tightly as if trying to erase a memory, "Gruesome. He made an example of her in front of his fellow Coalition members to demonstrate his power and incite fear, loyalty." Finding strength in his words, he continues, "In turn, the Coalition murdered every human from the island. No one was left alive."

Still not showing a bit of emotion, I ask, "And Dad?"

"He's gone, Jena. I'm so sorry."

I take a deep breath before I lunge at Xavier with both fists. My composure is completely gone as I hit Xavier repeatedly on the chest.

"How? How is this possible?" I scream. "How did they beat us on our own turf? I thought you had been planning this for years. I don't understand," I continue screaming.

"I don't know, Jena. Somehow, they knew what we were planning. They knew what we were going to do before we did it."

"I know," says Jessica, emerging from her cry with utter anger, "someone betrayed us. Just like I betrayed Jena."

We all look at Jessica, waiting for her to continue.

Chapter 40

Jessica points to a healed scar on her face, not one of her fresh wounds. She takes a deep breath and continues.

"In the exams, Hunter came to me during The Numinous simulation. He promised to help me reach The Numinous, which was the only thing I could do to raise my score high enough to pass. I was desperate, and he knew it. He took advantage of me, and I let him. I didn't know what he was trying to do to you Jena. I swear I didn't!" Jessica exclaims in an attempt to receive forgiveness.

"As soon as I found out why Hunter was helping me and what he was really trying to do to you, I tried to stop him. He used the destiny sword and sliced my face." Jena uses her ring and middle fingers on her left hand to gently rub the scar on her once perfect jawline before she continues.

"He told me I would never be a true Percenter, and that I would have to live with this scar as a reminder of my betrayal. I passed out after that and the next thing I remember is waking up in the hospital ward. But more than the physical pain of the Destiny Sword wound and the loss of ever becoming a Percenter was my regret for betraying you." Jessica looks me straight in the eyes before continuing, "Not for betraying Hunter."

I look at Jessica with disbelief. I knew something had happened to Jessica but I would have never guessed that it was her that led Hunter to me.

Seeing the hurt and confusion on my face, Jessica continues to say, "I promise to always follow you and protect you, Jena. I promise on my life."

I could tell that she was truly sorry. And I knew how much she fought to save us all on the island. I also knew how conniving Hunter was and that the pressures Jessica felt to pass the exams were tremendous. I will never forget that she betrayed me, but I will also never forget how she saved us. I look around at the nine of us, beaten and exhausted, and realize we are all each other has. My mission is also their mission. "I forgive you, Jessica." Without hesitation, she begins to sob uncontrollably.

Chapter 41

"What do we do now?" Vanessa asks the group.
"We find the first clue," Sven answers.
"First clue to what?" I ask.
"Have you ever heard of the Invisible Percenters?" Sven asks the group before telling us what Daniel told her right before he died.
"Everyone knows who Akshay Riley is, the Founding Chancellor, right?" Sven asks us all. We nod our heads yes.
"You see, he loved his family, especially his brother and sister." She pauses to gain the strength to continue talking. The pain of her brother's death is palpable.
"Well, unlike the other eleven Founding Chancellors, Akshay realized that even just a fraction of the amount of the elixir they all drank could manifest into Percenter powers. But Akshay kept this secret to himself. He pretended to drink his entire portion of the elixir but, really, he split it, drinking only a third and sharing the other thirds with his siblings.
"After their parents died as young adults, they each left their native land for opposite ends of the globe, never to see each other again or return to their homeland. Their shared secret was to protect the powers of the elixir by keeping it alive in a secret bloodline no other Percenter would even be able to trace. We know that all Percenter ancestry is tracked by The Archivist, and each and every Percenter can be traced back to one of the Founding Chancellors, staring with their children. When Percenters from around the World came out of hiding to build the Sky Cities during the Great Oze, the descendants, or as legend has it…the Invisible Percenters remained in

hiding. Away from the corrupt world many of the Percenter society leaders created. Generationally, the Invisible Percenters' powers became stronger. It is said that they possess powers unlike any Percenter known to the Sky Cities. It is with them, with the Invisible Percenters, that we will find a way to defeat Phineas and the Cleansing Coalition," Sven concludes.

"But where are they? How do we find them?" I ask

"No one knows exactly where Akshay's sister and brother settled, but some believe there is a record. A living record. One person from generation to generation that is the protector of the true Riley family tree."

"Before he died, Daniel was convinced that if we find that person, the direct descendent of Akshay Riley who knows that, they will be our only hope." Sven looks directly at me.

"Jena, think about it. You know who I'm talking about. You know who it is. You must believe the legend. Your mom believed the legend and told Daniel he must convince you."

"What do you know mean I know who it is? I don't know anything. If this legend, as you call it, was true, my mom would have just told me. She would have told me Sven! I know she would have told me!" I scream enthusiastically.

"You need to talk to him, Jena. Be honest with him. Tell him who you really are. Only then will we find what you need."

I think about who it could be, and there is only one Riley family member who she could be referring to.

"AV? Don't be dumb. He's not some secret holder of the world's longest and best kept secret. I would know."

Sven laughs. "Jena, you're right, you don't know shit! Your mom didn't tell you because she didn't think you were ready. Well, now you know. So, what are you going to do?"

I think about it while everyone stares at me. I look at each of their destroyed faces waiting for my next words. I look at Xavier, pausing on his face and trying to read his mind. He's no help.

"Well, it looks like we're going to prep school after all!" I say with a smile.

Xavier looks at me for confirmation and heads back to the driver's seat. The rest of us get comfortable and rest up for what's next.

The End

The Coming of Percenters

At the time of The Great Ozone Event, known as The Oze, the average human used very little of their brain's potential. But long before The Oze, a group of young explorers hunting for the infamous Fountain of Youth discovered something far more fantastic.

As the story goes, Akshay Riley, the lead explorer and horticulturist by trade, stumbled upon a mysterious flower believed to be extinct. Akshay called out to rally the others around the unprecedented find. He explained the history of the Parrot's Beak, as it was commonly referred to, highlighting the uniquely vibrant orange petals as being part of the Lotus family. Within the delicate flower's petals pooled a liquid as blue as the Caribbean Sea.

Many cultures believed the Parrot's Beak had unique healing powers. As the group rested next to the flower admiring its beauty, the heart of the flower began to pulsate a gentle glow from within. Subtle teardrops dripped along the curve of each petal as they wilted, one by one. In true horticulturalist style, Akshay quickly scrambled to empty his water bottle and collected samples. Shortly after, the beauty that once was a rare flower was gone. Within a matter of minutes, it had withered until it became a powder before their eyes.

The group soon discovered the liquid's true power, a power beyond even their wildest imaginations, beyond the eternal life they sought. This sap, eventually referred to as the Secret Elixir from one Percenter generation to the next, purified the blood of anyone who drank even just a drop. So powerful was the Elixir that one hundred percent of the brain's cortex was activated by anyone who drank even a thimble worth. The Elixir was shared equally amongst twelve explorers, and those twelve became known as the Founding Chancellors of the Percenters Society.

The Founding Chancellors soon manifested extraordinary powers that defied natural law. Their altered cortex resulted in a rare nucleotide, or genetic code, hosting the magnificent power of the Elixir. Forming a secret Percenters Society, the families of the Founding Chancellors quickly became amongst the world's elite. Their hidden powers provided an innate privilege allowing them to more easily secure wealth, influence, and power over their fellow mankind. Generations later, a new superhuman species had secretly evolved: The Percenters.

It was believed that any time a child was born of both Percenter and a non-Percenter, the Percenter bloodline was weakened and treated as a threat to their elitist society. The purity of the bloodlines became as important as their secrecy. Only those who possessed the perfect percent of Elixir markers in their DNA would be born with Percenter powers. Just like any other genetic code, the extent of someone's power varied and was sometimes unpredictable. The most powerful were the Hundred-Percenters, the purest bloodlines and direct descendants of the Founding Chancellors.

Centuries passed since the discovery of the Secret Elixir and manmade pollutants eventually led to the Great Ozone Event. The Earth was ravaged for years by a toxic ozone layer, extending hundreds of feet from the surface of the Earth. The Oze rapidly made the ground uninhabitable. Scientists compared it to the volatile surface of Jupiter. Airborne poisons meant certain death to anyone, or anything, that required oxygen to live.Even Percenters fell victim to The Oze's plague. All life on the surface of the Earth was dying. Mankind was forced to adapt or die.

Within weeks of The Oze devastating the entire globe, the secret Percenters Society revealed their powers to the humans still alive. Many believed the Percenters were a gift from God. Humanity's last hope.

The Percenters built three major Sky Cities spread across the country formerly known as America. These Sky Cities reigned majestically in the clouds, high on carved out land masses mysteriously tethered to skyscrapers lost to The Oze.

These Sky Cities, San Sun in the West, Crystal Sky in the East and Grand View in the Center are completely toxin free. Only Percenters with powers are allowed to reside in these luxurious Sky Cities. The Percenters created agricultural bubbles, dome-like structures that maintained a somewhat habitable environment for non-Percenters willing to grow and harvest food.

These dome-like structures provided shelter and work for the people without elixir streaming through their blood, the last remaining true humans. In exchange for protection from The Oze and certain death, the humans in the communities were happy to be laborers in exchange for life. They felt lucky to be alive and owed everything to the Percenters for saving them. In turn, Percenters were treated like Gods. The people living in these communities would eventually become known as Barrens. All other humans born without powers were left on the ground to survive the best way they could, if at all.

This was the new world. And almost no one remembered the world before.

About the Author

P. H. Perrine is an award winning entrepreneur and a new breakout author in Dystopian Fiction / Young Adult (YA) Fiction. He started writing *Percenters and the Amber Pendant* shortly after moving to Austin, Tx from California. *Percenters and the Amber Pendant* is the first book in the Percenters series.

You can connect with me on:

◔ https://www.thepercentersbook.com

Made in the USA
San Bernardino, CA
29 January 2020